THE SIGN OF THE SERPENT

Also by Sara Hely

The Legend of the Green Man

The Sign
of the Serpent

Sara Hely

St. Martin's Press
New York

Library of Congress Cataloging in Publication Data

Hely, Sara.
    The sign of the serpent.

    I. Title.
PR6058.E4915S5   1984   823'.914   84-13277
ISBN 0-312-72426-8

First published in Great Britain by André Deutsch Limited

First U.S. Edition

10 9 8 7 6 5 4 3 2

To Jan

One

'GO TO MOUNT SWEENY?' said Caroline Morrisey in a shocked, blank voice. She looked at Mr Rance as though she thought he had suddenly taken leave of his senses. 'Certainly not!'

Mr Rance pursed his thick lips, drawing them in at the corners so that he appeared to be on the verge of smiling. Caroline had never greatly cared for Lord Vale's agent. Her father used to say that he was not to be trusted, and she wondered why he should have come to Dublin seeking her out. She also wondered why he should look at her so smugly, as though he was sure of her acquiescence. Nothing would induce her to go to Mount Sweeny. She shrank from the very idea.

'No, sir,' she said firmly. She stood up, meaning to go. 'I have no wish to leave Mrs O'Mahoney, or to leave Dublin. Besides, you must see that I could not work for Lord Vale. He, of all people! You must find another governess for his little girl.'

'Don't be too rash, I implore you, Miss Morrisey,' said the agent, remaining seated in Mrs O'Mahoney's gloomy, lace-curtained parlour. Somewhere in the distance Caroline could hear the youngest children reciting their two-times table. There was something penetrating about their shrill young voices. She ought to get back to work. But Mr Rance was still seated and seemed unaware that the interview was at an end. He said: 'You should never reject an offer out of hand, Miss Morrisey, not in your position.'

7

Caroline stared down at him. She wondered what he was hinting at. Mr Rance was a large man, red of face and growing bald on top. He was looking up at her with an expression of sly determination which she did not at all like. She said coldly, 'I see nothing in my position, as you call it, that makes it necessary for me to leave my present employment and work for Lord Vale. Why, Lord Vale is the man who ruined my father! He might just as well have killed him. No, Mr Rance; it is quite out of the question.'

She could see that he thought her words exaggerated; yet she did blame the Earl of Vale for her father's untimely death. If Vale had not come into Ireland things would have been different. But he had been at Mount Sweeny, and Colonel Morrisey – another card-playing addict – was five miles away at Whitefield. And between them they had embarked on that terrible duel of cards which had ended with Colonel Morrisey losing Whitefield, his house, his lands and all he possessed. In one night of play, all these things had changed hands. They told Caroline that the Earl had smiled his way to victory, uncaring, heartless. She did blame him, bitterly.

For on the morning after that disastrous bout of gaming, Colonel Morrisey had shot himself through the head, and his pet shooting dog was found dead at his side. The Colonel left no farewell note, no explanation. There had been no need. It was generally agreed that Colonel Morrisey had been unable to face life without Whitefield and without money, and had taken this drastic way out.

There had been no money left for anything. Caroline had been in Dublin when the tragedy took place, and the news had been first brought to her by her distraught and shocked twin brother, Gilbert. Gilbert was in deep trouble on his own account, having killed a man in a tavern brawl; and at the time it seemed that Mr Rance's offer of a passage to Boston was a lifeline. The new world held promise of adventure for an eighteen-year-old youth; promise of employment, too, and of refuge from the consequences of killing the exciseman. It had been an accident, and Gilbert swore that there would be

8

people to vouch for him; but did not relish the prospect of standing his trial.

So thanks to Mr Rance's good offices, Gilbert took ship for America, and despite her distrust of the man, Caroline was grateful. She had Mr Rance to thank, too, for finding her a place at Mrs O'Mahoney's Seminary for the Daughters of Gentlefolk. It was all very well for her father's old friend, Sir Giles Mannering, to talk of writing to Lord Vale on Caroline's account, or for Lady Mannering and her daughter Perdita to throw up their hands in horror at the notion of Caroline's decision to earn her own living as a lady governess. Why in the world should she wish to take such menial employment, they demanded her tearfully, when she might consider the Mannering house her home? Caroline had been unable to make them see why she shrank from accepting their charity – and would have died rather than ask Lord Vale to help her. There were times, too, during the next four years when she regretted her decision – almost – but in her better moments she knew that she had been right.

And now, four years later, Mr Rance was offering her another way of escape. If only it had not been at Mount Sweeny, which she had for so long thought of as the house of her enemy! Whitefield, her old home, was only five miles from Mount Sweeny. It would be so wonderful to see it again, yet in another way it would be unbearable. She told Lord Vale's agent so.

'Mr Rance, you must please believe me! I could not do it!'

'Don't be so sure, Miss Morrisey. You may find, after all, that you can.'

'No, sir.' Caroline moved towards the door, a tall, thin young woman in a drab grey dress with a starched white cap on her head. She turned, one hand on the doorknob, and curtsied slightly. She said with quiet finality, 'I will bid you good day, Mr Rance. I am sorry that you have come all this way for nothing.'

He looked at her out of the corner of his bloodshot eyes, maintaining his calm, yet inwardly resentful of her cool attempt to dismiss him. He needed her. There was so little time: and it had not occurred to him that Caroline Morrisey would be anything but pleased to oblige him.

He licked his lips and smiled. He had never liked the girl. Even when she was a child he remembered feeling ruffled by her cool, clear regard. He supposed he could not truly accuse her of giving herself airs; yet, she had a way of pricking the bubble of his self-esteem, of making him feel less sure of himself. Well, this time she was going to learn a lesson, to do exactly as he wished her to do; and the fact that she did not like it would make his inevitable victory all the sweeter. Yes, he thought, it was going to be a pleasure to humiliate Miss Caroline Morrisey, to bend her to his will. It even gave him an obscure sense of satisfaction to see that four years of working for her living had done nothing for her looks. There was nothing of beauty about her now.

He took his time, battening down his impatience, savouring his triumph. He said, 'I have news for you, Miss Morrisey.'

She did not move away from the door. She looked at him with her grave grey-green eyes, and said: 'Yes, sir? What kind of news?'

'News of your brother Gilbert, ma'am.' He pursed his lips again, and added, 'But I rather doubt that you'll think it good news.'

She flinched, almost as if he had reached across the dismal, lace-curtained room and struck her. Her eyes, which only a second earlier had been faintly disdainful in expression, widened and seemed to darken. 'Gilbert?' she echoed, in a voice which was scarcely more than a whisper. 'Gilbert is in America, sir. Wh . . what are you trying to say?'

He spoke softly, relishing the taste of each word as he uttered it. 'Why, simply that your brother is once more in Ireland. . .'

'Gilbert in Ireland? Oh pray, sir, tell me where I may find him?'

There was no mistaking the glad excitement in her voice,

and her thin face under the severe cap glowed into sudden vivid animation. 'If you know where I may get in touch with him, sir, I implore you to tell me!'

'You may have a chance to visit him in Waterford jail before long, if I'm not much mistaken.'

It was a moment or two before the meaning of the agent's words sank in. Caroline had known such an upsurge of joy at the thought of seeing her twin again, that it took a little time for her to realize what Mr Rance had just said.

At length, gulping because she seemed to have a sudden odd difficulty in breathing, she said, 'In jail? Mr Rance, what exactly do you mean?'

'Why, merely that Mister Gilbert is behaving in a most regrettable fashion, Miss Morrisey. If he goes on as he did last week, he'll most certainly be apprehended as a felon.'

'Last week . . . ' Caroline came back into the room, and speaking in a low, grave way that did not in any way hide her sudden, painful anxiety, she said: 'Please, sir, tell me where you saw my brother? And why is he in danger of arrest?'

'I saw him on a road between Waterford and Mount Sweeny,' returned the agent with a certain relish. 'And as to why he may be arrested, Miss Morrisey, it stands to reason he is in grave danger. He was trying to hold up my carriage when I saw him. There was really no mistaking that bright head of his, Miss Morrisey, even with a hat pulled down over his eyes.' The agent looked deliberately at Caroline's head in its prim white cap, which so effectively hid her own thick fawn-gold hair, and added, 'Really no mistaking it, at all.'

'He robbed you? Gilbert did?'

'He certainly meant to, Miss Morrisey. But of course I saw through his disguise. There have been several highway robberies of late, you know, and no doubt your brother would be asked some exceedingly awkward questions if he were taken up by the authorities. . .'

Caroline knew very well that there had been a spate of highway robberies in recent months. The Dublin newspapers had been full of them, and though more than one writer blamed the trouble on the recent decline in trade and the resulting unemployment and poverty in the south of Ireland, there were others who took the view that the only way to stamp out this wave of crime was to punish the criminals with the utmost rigour and savagery.

She looked at the agent, feeling suddenly a little sick. How could Gilbert have sunk so low, Gilbert who was always so comfort-loving and given to taking the easiest way out of any situation? 'He must have been doing it for a wager,' she said. 'I can think of no other possible reason.'

'It's close on four years since you saw your twin brother, is it not? People can change a good deal in four years, Miss Morrisey.' There was no mistaking the spite in the agent's eyes as he looked her over. 'You've changed yourself, if you don't mind my saying so.'

The tall girl looked back, and said nothing. She had a clear skin, and a thin, pale face which was only redeemed from downright plainness by a pair of fine eyes. There was something about Caroline Morrisey's eyes which made Mr Rance wonder uneasily if she could read his thoughts. They were neither grey nor green in colour, but a mixture of both, with long dark lashes. She went on looking at him in the same thoughtful way which he found disconcerting, and said, 'Are you saying that you will inform on Gilbert unless I do as you ask? Is that it?'

He found himself disliking her more than ever. 'I prefer to say that one good turn deserves another, Miss Morrisey. And, indeed, I have done the Morrisey family several good turns in my time.'

She said nothing, but nodded in grave acknowledgement of this assertion.

He said in a nettled tone, 'I could quite well have informed on Mister Gilbert already.'

'Then why didn't you do so?'

'Don't tell me you would have wished it, Miss Morrisey?'

She knew very well that her wishes had nothing to do with it. She said slowly, 'No, sir. I would not have wished you to betray my brother; but neither do I wish to go to Mount Sweeny to look after Lord Vale's little girl. Surely there is someone else?'

The agent smiled in his sidelong way and said, 'You shock me, Miss Morrisey. I thought you would be prepared to go to some little trouble to save your twin brother from the gallows.'

She said doggedly, 'You told me that Gilbert had not succeeded in robbing you. What has he done, then, to deserve hanging?'

He said, 'There's still that business of the exciseman's death to be cleared up, remember? But more than that, he's in with some fellows . . . he's joined an organization . . . ' The agent broke off, and added with deliberation, 'Believe me, Mister Gilbert is in greater danger now than ever he was.'

For some reason she did believe him, and the very vagueness of his hints terrified her. She said in a shaken tone, 'What are you trying to say, Mr Rance?'

He did not answer for fully a minute. At last, he said curtly, 'I am not at liberty to tell you anything. All I can do is to give you a chance to help Mister Gilbert. Come to Mount Sweeny as Lady Jemima's governess, and you can try to persuade Mister Gilbert to go back to America. It could be fatal for him if he stays in County Waterford, Miss Morrisey.'

She said slowly, 'But what makes you suppose that Gilbert would come near Mount Sweeny, sir? It does not seem likely.'

He found her objections irritating beyond bearing. He said sharply, 'You are bound to meet your brother at Mount Sweeny. I can't tell you why,' he added, as she opened her mouth to ask for an explanation, 'But he'll be there, he or . . . or one of his accomplices . . . ' He broke off, and added severely, 'You'll have to be careful, Miss Morrisey.'

'Careful of what, sir?'

'I've already said, I cannot tell you,' he retorted. 'But these people your brother has joined are not playing games.'

Caroline quelled a nervous urge to laugh, for Mr Rance's hints of dire danger were rather ridiculous, for all that they made her shiver inside. She said, biting her lip, 'No wonder you found it difficult to find another governess, Mr Rance. What happened to the last one? Was she murdered? Or did she run away after listening to your dreadful warnings?'

'Miss Prendergast left,' he said, looking at her with renewed dislike. Of course, she could not possibly know about the accident, or of his urgent need to replace the last governess before there were questions asked. He fidgeted in his chair, one hand in the pocket of his brown coat. Caroline heard the subdued chink of metal as his restless fingers stirred the coins. 'Miss Prendergast left suddenly. If you are wise, my girl, you will ask no questions about her.'

Naturally, this was enough to make Caroline curious, but before she could pursue this tantalizing matter, he surprised her by taking his hand from his pocket and holding something out to her.

'Take this,' he said, pressing something flat and metallic into her palm and closing her fingers over it. 'Keep it by you. It will be safer, so. You'll need some form of identification, if you are to reach your brother without mishap.' He muttered, as though to himself, 'I don't want any more mistakes . . . '

She wondered if he was a little mad. 'It may be four years since I saw my twin, sir, but I don't think we'll have trouble identifying each other.'

He retorted, 'That's as may be, but you may not come upon Mister Gilbert in the first place. How should I know which of them you will meet, and you'll need some form of safe conduct . . . ' He broke off, and added in a hectoring tone: 'And you'd best tell them exactly who you are.'

'Them?' she echoed. 'I wish you would explain . . . ' She peered at the little coin he had given her. She had thought it was a guinea, but though it was about the same size, it was something rather different. It was a medallion, engraved with what looked like a heraldic device – a sort of snake. She turned it over, and saw the same serpentine device engraved on the reverse side.

'Hang it round your neck,' the agent told her, getting to his feet. 'That way you'll be sure to have it with you when you need it. And if it is one of the others you meet, make sure that they display the same sign before you trust them with a message.'

'What is this thing, sir? Some sort of snake?'

'It's the sign of the serpent, Miss Morrisey. Don't lose it, whatever you do. Now, how long will it take you to pack your things?'

She had not said that she would go to Mount Sweeny, of course, but this time she did not try to say she would not. She merely said doubtfully, 'I'll have to speak with Mrs O'Mahoney, sir. She may not find it convenient to release me at present. Today, she isn't even here, you know.' A fugitive smile came and went on her pale face.

'Just as well she's not here. Mrs O'Mahoney would not approve of my spending so long in here with you, sir. Her lady governesses are not encouraged to receive visitors.'

He said sourly, 'You must be ready to leave today, Miss Morrisey.'

'I couldn't possibly . . . '

'Of course you can. I'll send the carriage for you at noon, and mind you don't keep it waiting. You may leave a note for your employer. Tell her that you have trouble in the family. All too true, if I may say so,' he added, with a return to his spiteful manner. He rose rather ponderously to his feet, and made his way to the door. Once there, he turned to add, 'Think yourself lucky to be conveyed in his lordship's carriage, my girl.'

She stood aside as he went out into the dingy hall, and went after him. In spite of her profound distrust of Mr Rance, she felt a stirring of something like excitement. She had for so long yearned to go home. Mount Sweeny was not home, certainly, but it was only five miles away from Whitefield. She would once more see the blue hills and hear the surge of the sea and the cry of the gulls. She wondered why Mr Rance was so anxious to make her go to Mount

Sweeny. There must be some other reason, something more than his concern for Gilbert's safety. Mr Rance would not have travelled so far just to aid her brother.

She helped the agent on with his coat, and said pensively, 'I'd give a deal to know, sir, why you want me to go to Mount Sweeny. You must be desperate, indeed.'

'You flatter yourself, Miss Morrisey,' said Mr Rance coldly, as he buttoned his coat. 'Almost anyone with your qualifications would have done.'

'Still, you came nearly a hundred and fifty miles to find me,' she murmured, her thin face lighting up once more with that brief, glimmering smile. 'You've given me quite a new conceit of myself, Mr Rance.'

Two

THE HOUSEKEEPER AT MOUNT SWEENY was not slow to depress any signs of conceit in the new governess. She was no less stonily forbidding than the great house itself. Her hair was tightly pulled back from a bony forehead. Her eyes with their crinkled lids gazed coldly at Caroline.

'You are young for the post, Miss Morrisey,' she said in a voice as dry and colourless as her appearance. 'I cannot understand why Mr Rance selected you.'

Caroline could think of nothing to say to this daunting overture. She waited, her eyes downcast.

Mrs Datchet sniffed balefully, and the bunch of keys at her waist jingled as she fingered them. 'Well, I only hope that you will be more use than the last governess; and that you won't go off without a word to anyone the first minute your mother is ailing.'

'My mother died some years ago, ma'am.'

Mrs Datchet sniffed again, as if to say that Caroline's lack of maternal parent was all very well, but that she need not think it would make up for the disadvantage of her youth. The housekeeper seemed to be suffering from a sense of grievance. She lost no time in informing Caroline that she was in charge at Mount Sweeny, not Mr Rance, for all he may have taken it upon himself to engage a new governess. And if Caroline meant to behave like that inconsiderate Miss Prendergast, going off in the carrier's cart one evening, without so much as a word, she would be wise to say so at once.

'It was all very well for Miss Prendergast to write to Mr Rance, letting him know where she'd got to, and why. It wasn't Mr Rance who was left to deal with Lady Jemima.' She darted another doubtful glance at the new governess, and added, 'Did Mr Rance tell you what your duties were to be, Miss Morrisey?'

'He told me that I was to look after Lord Vale's little girl, ma'am,' said Caroline in her gentle voice. 'But I shall look to you to tell me more particularly how I must go on.'

A faint tinge of warmth crept into Mrs Datchet's manner. 'You will have to be firm with the child. Start as you mean to go on.'

'Is she very naughty?'

'Naughty? She's a little devil. Bad-tempered, too. Many's the time in the past ten days that I've itched to slap her.' Mrs Datchet frowned and jingled the bunch of keys again. 'She's hardly got a civil word for anyone, a sullen, ugly little madam. But you'll see for yourself. What she needs, of course, is half a dozen brothers and sisters to put a bit of life and fun into her; but of course with her ladyship dying, and in such a way . . . ' Mrs Datchet broke off, darting a questioning glance at Caroline. 'You've heard how Lady Vale was killed, no doubt? We don't speak of it here, of course . . . '

Caroline waited. Plainly, the housekeeper was dying to tell her about the shocking business of the late Lady Vale's death, and the storm of speculation and scandal that surrounded it. However, she did not succumb to the urge, and said merely, 'So it stands to reason Lady Jemima is an oddity. If she'd been a boy, it'd been different, I daresay. His lordship spoils her, when he takes time to see her at all; but most of the time she's packed off to one or other of her aunts or uncles, while his lordship gallivants in London or at Vale Park. He hasn't been at Mount Sweeny since her ladyship's funeral. There were things said then . . . I think the accident must have given him a distaste for the place.'

Caroline felt that this was good news. She had no wish to

18

lay eyes upon the Earl of Vale; and if she could only find Gilbert and prevail upon him to go back to America, she might never have to do so.

'Mind you,' the housekeeper was saying, 'if Lady Jemima was a good, biddable sort of child, or even a pretty one, it would be easier for everyone. As it is, none of her aunts or uncles are able to put up with her for long. She was sent down here without a single word of warning; and within a week, that tiresome Miss Prendergast took it into her head to leave. Really, it's too bad!'

Caroline tried to look suitably sympathetic, but she was feeling tired after two days on the road and was longing to escape. All the same, she could not help feeling a little sorry for the nine-year-old daughter of the wicked Earl of Vale. No one seemed to want her, or to love her; and Mrs Datchet went to some pains to make it clear that Caroline's duty was to keep the child out of everyone's way. The household had too much to do, Mrs Datchet also had too much to do, and she was not going to allow that little hoyden to interfere with the smooth running of the house. They might use the book-room in the mornings, since this was where all the Sweeny children had always done their lessons. Apart from this, Caroline and her charge were to stay in the schoolroom wing.

'I won't have her racketing all over the house, Miss Morrisey, making trouble for the servants and turning us all upside down. Please see to it that you remember that.'

Caroline made a suitably co-operative reply, wondering at the same time how the small army of flunkeys she had seen on her way upstairs could be much affected by the gyrations of one small girl. Then, to her relief, the schoolroom maid was sent for, and this young woman led Caroline down a bewildering series of corridors, down a short flight of steps, across a gallery, and eventually deposited her in the room which was to be hers.

It was a relief to learn that Jemima was out riding: and even more of a relief to find that she was not expected to share a bedroom with her charge. After nearly four years of sleeping in an alcove at one end of the smallest girls' dormitory at Mrs O'Mahoney's, the large quiet bedroom was a haven of luxury. Thankfully, Caroline stripped off her gloves and her grey hat. She threw them down upon the bed. She hated that hat. It was a cast-off from Mrs O'Mahoney, who had condemned even Caroline's most sober bonnets as being far too frivolous.

There was hot water in a jug. Caroline poured some into a basin, and washed her face and hands. She could hear the sound of the sea through the open windows, but they were too high for her to see out of them. She was about to put a fresh white cap over her severely braided hair, when there came a sound at the door.

Caroline turned. A small girl was sidling into the room. She stood just inside, regarding Caroline in a solemn and suspicious manner.

'You must be Jemima,' said Caroline, smiling. 'How do you do?'

There was no answering smile on the pale, unchildlike, shuttered little face. Jemima said in an abrupt voice, 'I came to look at you.'

'Indeed? Then, why don't you come closer? I'm quite tame, you know.'

Jemima came forward slowly, in the manner of one who suspects some kind of ambush. Caroline stood still, suppressing a tendency to laugh. She did not think this solemn, antagonistic little girl would like to be laughed at.

At last the child said, 'You are not like the others.'

'Your other governesses, you mean?'

Jemima nodded.

'I am sorry if I am a disappointment to you,' said Caroline in her soft voice. 'But you may get used to me after a while, don't you think?'

Jemima shrugged her thin shoulders. She was wearing a mud-bespattered riding dress and carried a whip in her hand. She said bleakly, 'It makes no difference. You won't stay. None of them do.'

'Why is that?'

Jemima shrugged her shoulders again. Caroline thought she could see why the child had failed to endear herself to Mrs Datchet. There was something both haughty and sour about her expression, and it was almost as if she did not know how to smile. 'How should I know why they don't stay,' she said. 'They just don't.'

'Well, if my stay is to be short,' said Caroline amiably, 'let us waste no time. Will you show me the schoolroom, and your own bedroom? Mrs Datchet was coming to make us known to one another, but she will not mind if we get a little acquainted before she comes.' Jemima looked mulish and far from enthusiastic. 'But perhaps, first, you'd like to change out of your riding dress?'

'No,' said Jemima. 'I like these clothes. I wear them all the time.'

Caroline thought that it looked as if the child slept in the same dress, as well. She looked grubby, crumpled and smelled quite noticeably of the stables. However, Caroline merely said, 'Do you have a pony of your own?'

Jemima's sallow face looked a shade more cheerful. She did have a pony. His name was Robbie. 'I ride him every day,' she said, eyeing Caroline coldly as she said this. Then, when Caroline merely looked interested, she ducked her tousled, matted head and said, "My papa has given orders that I am to ride every day. So you'll have to let me do so. If my papa gives an order, everyone has to obey.'

Caroline looked down at the child, a smile dawning. 'Oh? And do you obey your papa, too?'

Jemima looked momentarily surprised. 'Usually I do,' she conceded grudgingly, as though she suspected some sort of trick. And then suddenly she growled, 'You can't stop me from going riding.'

'If I had my way I'd ride with you, Jemima,' said Caroline, speaking no less than the truth. 'Do you suppose it would be possible to find a mount for me?'

Jemima looked perfectly astounded. Staring, she said, 'Miss Prendergast did not care for horses. She said they were dirty, smelly animals.'

'Oh?'

Glowering up at Caroline from under strongly marked brows, Jemima added in a challenging tone, 'I like horses better than people.'

Caroline nodded, and turned to pick up a fresh white cap to tie over her hair. She said mildly, 'I'll grant you that horses are easier to deal with than people, on the whole. Now, if you were a horse, I would know just what to do.' She tied the strings of her cap, and turned back to look at the unkempt child who was to be her charge. Jemima took a small step backwards as though fearing some assault upon her person; and then stood her ground, still glowering.

Caroline eyed her consideringly. 'I wonder at Miss Prendergast saying that horses were dirty, if she let you go around looking as you do this evening.' Jemima opened her mouth to make some retort, but Caroline forestalled her by saying, 'But perhaps it is only since Miss Prendergast left that you have had no one to brush your hair and keep you clean and comfortable?'

'Miss Prendergast only gave me lessons,' said Jemima sullenly. 'Maura looks after me otherwise.' Maura was the schoolroom maid who had recently shown Caroline to her room, flouncing away again as soon as she had done so. Caroline had not been favourably impressed by Maura, and perhaps something of her thoughts must have been reflected in her expression, for Jemima went rather pink in the face, and said, 'You need not blame her. I told her not to brush my hair. She pulls it, and it hurts.'

'Does she? Horrid for you. Would you let me try to get the tangles out if I promise not to hurt you?'

But before Jemima could give an answer, Mrs Datchet's voice snapped from the doorway. 'Lady Jemima! I told you that you were to come to me as soon as you came in.' She rustled over and grasped Jemima's thin arm and shook it.

22

'Just look at you! You're a disgrace! Whatever will Miss Morrisey think of you, I'd like to know.'

'What does it matter what she thinks,' retorted the child, pulling herself free, and moving hastily out of reach. 'She's paid to look after me, isn't she? She's just a servant, the same as you, Datchet.'

'Servant I may be, milady,' retorted the housekeeper, her thin lips pressing even tighter together at this piece of impertinence, 'but I'm taking you to your room, and Maura will bath and change you out of that filthy riding dress. She's bringing water up now. Come along, and no nonsense.'

But her stately advance upon Jemima was without the desired effect. Quick as a mouse, the child ducked past the housekeeper, and was out through the open door before she had time to do more than gasp. Caroline heard her running footsteps die away, and a door slammed in the distance.

'There!' Mrs Datchet made an exasperated sound in her throat. 'What did I tell you, Miss Morrisey?' She seemed to unbend a little under the stress of her chagrin. 'That child's nothing short of impossible! I'll need to send one of the footmen after her, for she'll have run out into the garden, and even Maura cannot catch up with her there. Of course, she ought to be whipped, but his lordship won't have it. Miss McTavish, she was the governess who was with her longest, was turned off for taking a stick to the little demon. Doubtless the child deserved it, but his lordship sent her off within the hour. Wouldn't listen to what Miss McTavish had to say, even. So, naturally the child's been worse than ever since then. She takes care to remind us all of what happened to Miss McTavish. Servant, indeed!'

Caroline said quietly, 'I am sorry she was rude to you, ma'am. I'll go and look for her. I'd rather not call on one of the footmen. Not straight away, at least.'

Mrs Datchet looked astonished. 'You'll not want to go haring round the shrubbery, Miss Morrisey. That's where she'll be, if she's not gone down to the shore.'

Caroline felt that she would like nothing better than some

23

fresh air, and she said with soft-spoken firmness, 'I'd like a walk, Mrs Datchet. And perhaps Jemima will change her mind after a while, and come in again. If you'll excuse me . . .'

There was no sign of Jemima in the gardens, nor in the shrubbery beyond. At first Caroline was so relieved to be out in the fresh air that she merely strolled about, hoping to see some sign of the runaway. But by the time she had returned from the shrubbery and skirted the east side of the great grey house, she was beginning to grow anxious. It was already growing cold, and the sun was low on the horizon. What if Jemima decided to stay out after sunset?

She went through a gate, and a stiff cold breeze hit her, so that she drew her shawl around her. She found herself on a stone-flagged terrace, and peering over a high crenellated stone wall she saw a shining expanse of sea and, closer in, a rocky cove with steep cliffs flanking it at both ends. And to her dismay, she also saw Jemima.

There was a heavy sea rolling in among the rocks. That beach was no place for a child of Jemima's age to be on her own. Caroline called out, realizing as she did so that Jemima would never hear her. She began to run along the terrace, looking for a way down to the cove, and met a startled looking man in livery standing in an archway, who answered her hasty question by pointing to an iron gateway at the end. Gripped by fear for Jemima's safety, she sped down an uneven flight of stone steps and was soon scrunching and stumbling along the shingle beach.

She was quite near to Jemima before she saw her again. Rounding a rock, she checked, gasping with relief to see her safe.

Jemima did not look round. Her whole attention was on something quite different, and as Caroline stood there watching, the child took a step forward into the edge of the water. It was then that Caroline saw the puppy.

It was a soaked, scrawny mite of a thing, marooned on a flat rock, but as Jemima took another step forward, trying to reach it, an incoming wave swept over the flat barnacled surface where the puppy was whining and darting backwards and forwards. The puppy was rolled over by the water, righted itself, and made another frantic dart towards Jemima.

Caroline splashed into the sea and dragged Jemima back, dumping her unceremoniously on the wet shingle. 'Stay there!' she said. 'Don't move!'

Then, without staying to see whether Jemima was going to obey her, she waded into the edge of the surf for the second time. Another huge wave was rearing itself at the mouth of the cove, and Caroline only barely managed to scoop the puppy up into the crook of her arm and turn back before the force of the breaker buffeted her behind the knees. She half fell, half crawled to the edge of the water, and thrust the soaked, shivering puppy into Jemima's outstretched arms.

Three

 DIRTY MONGREL FROM GOODNESS KNOWS WHERE!
Surely you don't mean to bring it in here, Miss Morrisey?'

'He's not dirty, Datchet,' said Jemima belligerently. The
housekeeper, along with a crowd of onlookers, had met them
at the top of the cliff steps. 'He's just been in the sea, and is
probably cleaner than you are.'

'Well, I'm not having it in the house, so don't think it,'
declared Mrs Datchet with quite as much determination as
Jemima's. She added, 'And you know very well you're not
allowed on the shore by yourself. I've told you over and over.'

'Miss Morrisey was with me,' retorted Jemima. 'She's in
charge of me now, so it's nothing to do with you.'

Mrs Datchet looked coldly at the third member of this
bedraggled little party. The new governess looked, if possible, more tousled and wet than either Jemima or the puppy
in her arms. But whatever quelling remark the housekeeper
might have made was deflected by one of the stable hands
who suddenly realized where the puppy had come from.

'It'll be one of them tinkers' pups, ma'am,' he said. 'There
was six or seven down at the gate, and likely they were after
drowning them before they moved on.'

'Then it will be crawling with fleas, no doubt,' said Mrs
Datchet, staring at the little creature who was venturing to
give a timid lick at Caroline's hand. 'I don't know how you
can bear to touch it, Miss Morrisey.'

'All he needs is a bath,' said Caroline. 'And something to
eat.'

'Well, he's not getting either in my house, Miss Morrisey.'

'This is my papa's house . . . ' Jemima began hotly, but paused in surprise when her new governess laid a hand on her shoulder and told her quite crisply to hold her tongue.

Caroline said gently to the housekeeper, 'Jemima will catch cold if we stand much longer in this wind, ma'am. Would you allow someone to take this poor little urchin somewhere warm and dry, and we can think what to do with him later?' There was a pause and an awkward stir in the motley throng of footmen, housemaids and grooms who had come to watch the fun. No one felt quite equal to offering their services with Mrs Datchet's cold eye upon them. Caroline was just wondering what to do next, when one of the youngest-looking footmen said timidly that he'd see to the pup if Miss wanted.

'Would you?' said Caroline, smiling at him gratefully. 'Just a bowl of warm milk and a box of straw to lie in. That's all he needs.'

'And just who do you think you are to be giving orders to my staff?' demanded the housekeeper, now stiff with affronted dignity. 'Walter is employed here to look after the downstairs fires and clean the upper servants' boots. It's no part of his duties to wait on stray animals which you choose to bring up from the shore.'

'Miss Morrisey saved the puppy from drowning, Datchet,' said Jemima, her teeth chattering so much that she could hardly get the words out. 'He's ours, and we're going to keep him. Just you try to stop us!'

'That's enough, Jemima,' said Caroline quietly, but with such a quelling look in her grey-green eyes that Jemima gave a quick gulp of surprise. 'Naturally we cannot bring the puppy indoors unless we have Mrs Datchet's approval.' And before the housekeeper had time to rally, she added, 'Please allow Walter to take the little dog for a while, ma'am. Jemima seems to be turning blue in front of our eyes. I'd like to get her into a hot bath directly.'

'If her ladyship had gone to her bath when I told her to,'

said Mrs Datchet sourly, 'none of this would have happened.'

'If you want to keep that puppy, Jemima,' said Caroline, kneeling by the schoolroom fire and brushing out the child's newly washed hair, 'you'll have to do as I ask. On the other hand, if you don't want to keep him, there's no more to be said.'

'I do want to.'

'Then you must keep to your side of the bargain,' said Caroline.

'I don't see why.' Jemima's pinched little face was flushed pinkly by the heat of the fire, and though her muslin dress was too tight and too short, she looked clean and fit to be seen. She said sulkily, 'I don't see why I should say I'm sorry to Datchet. It's quite true she's a servant.'

'As I am myself,' said Caroline, sitting back on her heels and looking at Jemima gravely. 'But it was neither kind nor civil to say so.'

'Why should I be kind to Datchet? She's not kind to me.' Jemima stood back and ventured a bleak, assessing glance at her new governess's face. 'Datchet said she'd like to beat me, and she would do, if she dared. She doesn't dare, though. My papa will not allow anyone to hit me.'

'All the more reason for you to treat people gently, it seems to me,' remarked Caroline. Then she laid the silver-backed hairbrush down and said calmly and pleasantly, 'I'm not going to argue with you, Jemima. If you want to save that puppy, and keep him in the house, you'll need my help. Maura doesn't want to look after him. She's already said so. If you want my help, and if you want me to talk to Mrs Datchet, you must first do as I ask.' Jemima's tightly closed, mutinous little face showed little sign of change. Caroline added, persevering, 'We'll be so busy taking Ferdy for walks and feeding him and brushing him and playing with him,

28

you know, that we won't see much of Mrs Datchet, once she's agreed to let him stay.'

For a moment it looked as if Jemima's mood of frozen obduracy was undergoing a slight thaw; but all she said was, 'Datchet has no right to stop me keeping him!'

Caroline glanced at the clock over the fireplace. They were to meet the housekeeper downstairs in the bookroom within ten minutes. She wondered how she could coax Jemima into a more conciliatory mood in so short a time. But she forgot even this in her surprise. She said in a startled voice: 'What's that . . . that emblem on the clock, Jemima?' She pointed to the coiled serpent on top of the gilt clock. 'That snake thing?'

Jemima craned her neck to look. 'That's ours,' she said, with a touch of surprise in her voice that anyone should not know it. 'It's the Sweeny serpent, my papa's crest.'

'Oh!' said Caroline, looking rather blankly at the odd emblem, and trying to think what it must mean. It was almost an exact replica of the serpent which was engraved on both sides of Mr Rance's medallion, the one which he had insisted she was to wear at all times. It was attached round her neck on a silk thread, hidden away under the bodice of her grey gown. It was all totally bewildering to Caroline's weary mind. Why should her brother Gilbert's friends choose to take the Sweeny serpent for their secret sign?

Jemima watched her new governess, and becoming alarmed by her sudden silence, said in a small voice, 'I'll come and see Datchet, Miss Morrisey. But if she dares to say Ferdy's a dirty mongrel once more, I'll kick her.'

The bookroom was a spacious apartment, about as different from Mrs O'Mahoney's bare, spartan schoolrooms as was possible to imagine. The walls were lined on three sides with leather bound books, the curtains were of rich brocaded silk, and a fire blazed cheerfully at one end, and, as they went in, candles were being lit by two footmen in livery.

'Where's that boy with my puppy?' demanded Jemima of one of them. 'Do you know where they are?'

'Now Milady,' said Mrs Datchet from the doorway. 'I've told you before not to interfere with the men at their work.'

'I'm not . . . ' But suddenly she recollected her promise to Caroline, for she said quickly, as though gabbling a lesson learned by rote, 'I'm sorry I called you a servant, Datchet. Please will you let me keep Ferdy in the house?'

Caroline had some difficulty keeping a straight face. The housekeeper looked so perfectly astounded by this sudden apology. She moved forward quickly and said: 'Believe me, ma'am, she is truly sorry.' With one hand she held on to Jemima's left shoulder, and added in her soft, low-pitched voice: 'And I've a notion that Jemima will be happier and more agreeable if she has a pet to love and care for. We'll make sure that he's not the least trouble to anyone, won't we Jemima?'

The housekeeper said doubtfully, 'Well, I don't know, I'm sure . . . '

Jemima said tensely, 'I'll write to my papa. He'll order you to let me keep Ferdy.'

'Now Jemima!' said a man's voice behind them. 'What's this?' They all turned, and Caroline saw a dark gentleman in a caped overcoat regarding them. He strolled over and patted Jemima's mousey head. She flinched and jerked away. He seemed to expect this, for he smiled slightly and said, 'What shenanigans are you up to now? Nothing too bad, I hope? Your Aunt Maria sent you a doll from London, but you're only to have it if you've been a good girl.'

'Lady Jemima's always a good girl,' said Mr Rance unctuously, appearing at the gentleman's side all of a sudden.

Jemima gave the agent a disparaging look, while the newcomer studied Caroline in a puzzled fashion.

Jemima said, 'This is my new governess, Uncle Richard. She saved one of the tinkers' puppies from drowning in the sea, and we want to keep it. You'll tell Datchet that it will be all right, won't you?'

'I should not presume to tell Datchet anything of the sort,' retorted the dark man, smiling at Caroline. He bowed civilly. 'Richard Sweeny, at your service, ma'am. I'm Vale's half-brother, and uncle to this graceless scamp you've taken in hand.' He said curiously, 'Whatever did you do to rid your-self of Miss Prendergast, Jemima? She seemed quite set to stay when I was here last. What subtle and dreadful persecu-tion did you devise to drive her away?'

'No! No, sir!' said Mr Rance, his reddened eyelids blinking as he came forward to explain. 'Poor Miss Prendergast was called to her mother's bedside in Waterford. It was all most sudden, and inconvenient. And then I had the happy notion of offering the post to this young woman.'

'A happy notion, indeed,' agreed Richard Sweeny, looking at Caroline with such a droll look of sympathy that it took the sting out of Mr Rance's disparaging introduction. Lord Vale's brother was good-looking in a rather stern, dark way; and Caroline found herself liking his quietly humorous air. She wished, all of a sudden, that she did not look so distres-singly plain in her white linen cap.

'Well, what's all this about a puppy?' demanded Richard Sweeny. 'Are we going to be allowed to inspect it?'

'It's a mongrel, sir,' said Mrs Datchet earnestly. 'I'm sure you'll agree that it's not at all a suitable animal for her ladyship to keep as a pet. Now, if it was one of your own spaniels, that would be different.'

'I don't want a spaniel,' said Jemima, beginning to glower, 'I want Ferdy.'

'So the puppy has a name, has he?' murmured Richard, glancing at Caroline. 'Do I understand, ma'am, that you are willing to accept this ill-bred creature into your schoolroom?'

'I am willing, sir,' replied Caroline gravely, 'but it must, of course, depend on what Mrs Datchet says.'

'Of course,' he agreed, a twinkle in his very blue eyes. 'I wonder if you know what you are taking on?'

'I have looked after puppies before, sir.'

He said dryly, 'That wasn't quite what I meant.' He

31

looked down at his niece who was waiting, taut with hope and anxiety, and added curiously, 'Why is he to be called Ferdy? Any particular reason?'

'He's Ferdinand, really,' Jemima explained seriously. 'Miss Morrisey says there is a prince in a play who was rescued from the sea. She's going to read the play to me, she says. . .'

Richard Sweeny chuckled. 'So this is the syrup that masks the medicine, I see? A new way of introducing the Bard?'

Caroline smiled at him and shook her head. 'I'll not allow Shakespeare to be classed as medicine, sir.'

Jemima tugged at Richard's sleeve. 'Come and see Ferdy, Uncle. Then you'll see for yourself what a beauty he is!'

'Where is he now, your princely fugitive?'

'The bootboy has the animal downstairs, Mister Richard,' said Mrs Datchet, adding in a long-suffering tone, 'If it is your wish, sir, I will send for it to be brought here.'

Richard Sweeny turned his attention to the housekeeper, smiling at her in such a warm and friendly manner that Caroline could not see how even the dour Mrs Datchet would deny him anything he might ask. 'You must do as you think best, Datchet,' he told her. 'Do you think you could bring yourself to let Jemima keep her puppy? She does seem to have set her heart on it, doesn't she; and you know how tiresome we Sweenys can be, if we don't get our own way?'

Mrs Datchet's thin lips stretched into something that was almost a smile. 'Well, I don't know, sir . . . What will his lordship say?'

'I'll write to his lordship and take the blame, if that will comfort you, Datchet. I doubt if he'll mind. For that matter, I doubt if he'll read my letter. It's some months since I've heard from him.'

So the matter was settled, and Richard took his leave of them. He shook Caroline's hand, his blue eyes thoughtful and kindly: 'You must let me know if there is any way I can serve you, ma'am. Don't let this bad niece of mine plague you to death.'

32

She smiled at him gratefully, and the smile seemed to light up her thin face. 'Oh, as to that, Jemima says I won't be here long. She expects her governesses to leave from time to time.'

Richard laughed, and advised her not to pay too much attention to what Jemima said. 'At all events, please don't go away without letting me know your intention. I find these constant changes most unnerving.'

When they were alone, Jemima said in a gruff voice, 'Don't you want to stay, Miss Morrisey?'

'I don't know, Jemima,' said Caroline, looking down at her. 'I've only been here a few hours. It depends.'

'What does it depend on?'

Caroline hesitated, seeking the best answer to this question. Jemima looked back, her closed-in little face devoid of expression. She certainly was an unprepossessing little thing. Still, Caroline thought, it was not everyone's good fortune to be blessed with charm. Her own brother Gilbert had more charm than was good for him, and so had her late father. Caroline had long ago ceased to think of charm as altogether a blessing.

She said thoughtfully, 'I suppose you could say, Jemima, that it depends on you. If you are not happy in my care, I shall not wish to stay.'

'Pooh!' said Jemima, shrugging those skinny shoulders. 'I don't care if you stay or go. They'll always find another to take your place.'

Four

THE COMING OF JEMIMA'S PUPPY to Mount Sweeny eased Caroline's entry into the household as nothing else could have done. Mrs Datchet, certainly, went on looking on the little dog with a jaundiced eye, and the schoolroom maid showed a marked reluctance to do anything for him; but everywhere else he was welcomed and made a fuss of. It soon became an established part of the daily routine for Jemima and her governess to call in on one or other of the many different departments of the great house – visiting the cavernous, crowded kitchen, going to the dairy with its great wooden churns and smiling, bare-armed dairymaids, or to the still room, or the leather-scented harness room where the head groom held sway. There were so many places to choose from; and wherever they went, the puppy trotting confidently ahead and Jemima proudly holding his leash, there was never any member of the household too busy to cast aside whatever they were doing, and to enter joyfully into the business of entertaining Prince Ferdinand and his small mistress.

Caroline was not surprised at this loving enthusiasm for the child and her pet, for she had always been sure of just such a welcome in her own childhood days at Whitefield. But she was glad of it, and as she watched Jemima beginning to shed some of her sullen, frowning ways, and to greet these people with shy smiles and a growing assurance – admiration of Ferdy was a sure way to Jemima's good graces – Caroline was thankful for the lucky chance that had brought the little creature into their lives.

Mount Sweeny boasted its own blacksmith, who plied his trade in a low, stone-built shed adjoining the stable yard. Jemima loved to watch the brawny smith at work, to be allowed to help to blow up the fire, or to watch – schooling herself not to wince in sympathy – while the smith clamped one great leg after another firmly between his leather-clad knees and pared the hoof with deft strokes of his razor sharp knife, before hammering in the nails. Of all the places they went to, the smithy was Jemima's favourite; and but for the fact that her puppy had to stay outside for fear of getting burned, Caroline would have had trouble getting her charge to come away from that fascinating, hot, reeking paradise.

Waiting outside with Ferdy, Caroline suddenly heard her name spoken. The voice and the words were familiar, so familiar that she felt herself transported back in time. She swung around, and saw Slattery standing there.

The old man looked as if he had seen a ghost. 'Miss Caroline? It's never yourself . . . ' He moved towards her, doubtfully, and she almost ran to meet him, dropping the puppy's leash, and holding out both her hands. Both his gnarled paws clasped hers, holding on to her as if he needed this reassurance that she was real. 'Miss Caroline . . . '

'Oh, Slattery!' she said, laughing rather shakily, for it was both wonderful and painful to come across her father's old servant so unexpectedly and suddenly. 'It is myself, indeed! And I am so happy to see you, I could almost cry!' She saw, as she spoke, that the old man's rheumy eyes were brimming with tears. She said warmly, 'What brings you to Mount Sweeny, Slattery?'

But he did not seem so overjoyed to see her, after all. He frowned up at her – she stood a head taller than he – and said in a grumbling tone, 'I'd ask you the same yourself, Miss Caroline. This is no place for you, I'm thinking.'

'Now, Slattery,' she said in a rallying tone, 'You must not speak so to me. I am the governess here, you know, and must be treated with respect.'

35

He grunted, still holding fast to her hands. He said gruffly, 'Governess, is it? The colonel'd turn in his grave, if he knew.'

'No such thing,' retorted Caroline, smiling down at him. 'Papa would think it a grand joke to see me here, to be turning all those tedious mornings in our schoolroom to good account.'

But the old man refused to share her amusement, for all that he had aided and abetted Caroline and her twin when they tried to evade their lessons in the old days. He fell to muttering, instead, and she caught the sound of Mr Rance's name, and something about it being wickedness, downright wickedness.

She was not wholly dismayed at this reception, however, for she had realized that Slattery was more than a little drunk. There was no doubt about it, for his speech was slurred, and there was a strong smell of home-brewed on his breath. She supposed he must have been refreshing himself in the Mount Sweeny buttery. She asked him once again how he came to be there, and he told her that he was waiting for one of Richard Sweeny's horses to be shod.

'Mr Sweeny's horse?' she echoed in surprise. 'You are working for Mr Sweeny, now?'

'These three years or more,' he admitted, adding with distinct sheepishness, 'and I'm a married man now, Miss Caroline. Mary O'Connor was after coming to keep house for Mr Richard – so with myself not wanting to leave Whitefield, and always having a fancy for Mary . . . '

He rambled on, and she was silent, and scarcely heard the rest of his tale. She was feeling stunned; not so much at the seventy-year-old Slattery having found himself a wife, but at the sudden realization that Vale's half-brother was living at Whitefield. It was a shock – a most disagreeable shock.

But she was given no time to dwell on the thought of Richard Sweeny living there, for Slattery was tugging at her arm, muttering again. She bent down to catch what he was saying, and he whispered beerily in her ear; 'That's what you must do, Miss Caroline. You just tell Mr Rance you're leaving.'

36

She straightened up, tired of his gloomy mutterings. 'I shall tell him no such thing. I did not want to come, at first; but now – ' She broke off what she was saying, for it occurred to her that if anyone could put her in touch with her brother, it would be Slattery. She could not imagine Gilbert being in the district without going to see Slattery. She said quickly, 'Mr Rance says that Gilbert is here. Have you seen him, Slattery? I must speak with him.'

But to her disappointment, he shook his head, and went on with his tiresome refrain. 'You didn't ought to be in this place, Miss . . . ' She was just going to cut him short, when he added with apparent irrelevance: 'And that Mister Gilbert's a limb of Satan, always was.'

'So you have seen him?' she said accusingly. 'Pray tell me where he is?'

'I'm not knowing where he is,' said the old man with sudden angry petulance, 'and I'd not be telling you, if I did.' And with that he vanished into the smithy shed. By the time Caroline had succeeded in recapturing the puppy, Slattery had gone.

By the time Caroline had been a week at Mount Sweeny, she had the feeling she had been there for ever. And she began, against her will, to grow fond of Jemima. She knew it would not do to grow attached to Lord Vale's little girl. She was only at Mount Sweeny to find Gilbert, and to persuade him to leave the district. But somehow it was impossible to hold herself aloof.

For Jemima was unlike any other child she had known. She was by no means easy, and all too often rude to people. She was in some ways spoiled, yet in others quite shamefully neglected. Even her clothes bore this out. They were shabby, outgrown and few in number. It seemed that none of her aunts or her previous governesses had felt it their business to see to them. Her life was run on the same haphazard lines. She was shifted from place to place like an unwanted piece of baggage, and Jemima seemed to accept this state of affairs, regarding it as natural that everything should be liable to sudden change – not least her governesses.

Jemima's own moods were as changeable as the spring weather, too, for she would be pert and disagreeable one minute, and the next as obliging as could be. Sometimes, as the days went by, she grew quite affectionate in her manner towards Caroline; yet she could veer in seconds to sullenness and mischief. She was quick to learn when she wanted to, and stubbornly stupid if a lesson did not take her interest. As the days went by, it seemed to Caroline that there were only two things about Jemima which were constant. The first was her love of her pony and her puppy. And the second was her unswerving adoration of her father.

Feeling as she did about the wicked Earl of Vale, it came as something of a shock to Caroline to learn that in Jemima's eyes he was the model of perfection. She was forever singing his praises, quoting his often unsuitable opinions, and wistfully recounting what they had done together on the rare occasions when Lord Vale took time to see her. Jemima seemed to take it for granted that her papa had wanted her to be a boy; and that since she had failed him in this regard, the advent of a stepmother was a necessary evil.

'Miss Prendergast said that my papa was a Great Catch, Miss Morrisey,' she remarked on one occasion. 'But none of the pretty ladies who came to Vale Park seemed to stay long. I don't think my papa liked them nearly as much as they'd hoped. Miss Prendergast said he was a better cardplayer than a lover.'

'Well, I shouldn't repeat that, if I were you,' said Caroline, bending over her sewing. Some of Miss Prendergast's opinions were as unsuitable as Vale's. 'At least I wouldn't repeat it to anyone but me, Jemima.'

Jemima looked surprised and retorted that she had already repeated it to her papa, and he hadn't seemed to mind. 'He laughed, and said Miss Prendergast wasn't quite such a fool as she looked, Miss Morrisey.' And when Caroline did not look up from her task of setting a sleeve in Jemima's new muslin dress, the child said insistently: 'It's true about those ladies wanting to marry Papa, Miss Morrisey. I always know. They bring me toys, and tell me I'm clever and pretty, and ask silly questions.'

'Horrid child,' said Caroline laughing, though in a way Jemima's precocity gave her an aching feeling inside. 'It will be a brave lady who takes over the task of being your stepmother. You'd best watch out! Stepmothers aren't so easily got rid of as governesses, you know.'

'N . . no.' Jemima seemed to consider this. 'If only I'd been a boy. Still,' she added, hunching her thin shoulders and looking like a little gnome, 'Papa says that I ride as well as most boys.'

So the days went by, and between conversations of this kind, and feeding the puppy five times a day, and making Jemima two muslin dresses, and taking both child and puppy for walks along the sea shore, Caroline found that she forgot about Gilbert for quite long stretches of time. When she thought about meeting her twin brother, it was almost with reluctance, for she was growing more and more interested in the Sweeny family and had less and less wish to go back to Dublin or follow her brother to America. For the first time since her father's death, Caroline really felt that someone needed her; and when she learned about the night people, and Jemima's fear of them, she was determined that she would stay at Mount Sweeny until this particular mystery had been solved.

Jemima had a way of becoming more truculent and tiresome in the evenings. Caroline put this down to her being tired, and tried to make sure that the routine of going to bed was always calm and free of stress. However, one evening Caroline grew weary of watching Jemima dawdling over her supper and she started to blow out the candles in the schoolroom.

Jemima got down from her chair. Caroline turned to look at her, and something about the way the child was standing, rigid and still, gazing towards the window, made Caroline say: 'What's the matter, Jemima?'

Jemima did not move. Caroline went to her. She looked very small and white-faced. Without turning her head, she said, 'Leave some of the candles burning, Miss Morrisey. Please . . . '

Caroline was bidden to take tea with the housekeeper that evening, so she did not mean to come back to the schoolroom. She said slowly, trying to puzzle out the cause of Jemima's evident panic, 'Leave them burning, Jemima? Why?'

'Maura always does . . . ' The child ducked her head away, but not before Caroline had seen that she was close to tears. 'Maura says they watch for the lights to go out.'

Caroline wondered what tales the schoolroom maid had been telling. The child looked positively terrified. Caroline grasped her thin arms and turned her about, forcing the child to stand beside her and look out once more into the darkening trees. She said gently, 'There's nothing to be afraid of out there. Nothing but an owl or two, and there's no harm in them.'

'Not owls,' whispered Jemima. She began to shudder as though with sudden cold. She felt like a thin, frightened bird in Caroline's arms. 'Not owls, Miss Morrisey. It's the night people. Maura says they hide out there, waiting until we've all gone to bed; waiting to come in . . . '

'Maura talks a great deal of nonsense,' said Caroline curtly. 'You must not believe all she tells you, you know.'

'That's what Miss Prendergast said. She didn't believe Maura when she told her the night people don't like being seen; and they took her away, Miss Morrisey.'

'But Jemima,' said Caroline, holding the child's quivering little body close. 'This is all untrue. Miss Prendergast's mother was taken ill, and she was obliged to go and nurse her.'

Jemima's voice was so low that Caroline barely caught the words. 'Miss Prendergast didn't have a mother to go to. She was an orphan, Miss Morrisey. She was always telling me that she had no one left in the world, and that I was luckier than her, having Papa.'

'Frightening her with stories, is it, Miss?' retorted the schoolroom maid, by no means abashed when Caroline took her to task next day. She was a rosy-cheeked girl with bold black eyes, rather like a robin. She tossed her head and said darkly, ' 'Tis better Lady Jemima be told, than to end up like poor Miss P.'

'Maura!' said Caroline sternly, 'if you know anything about Miss Prendergast's disappearance, you ought to tell Mrs Datchet.'

'And what'd I be doing that for?' demanded the girl scornfully. 'It won't help Miss P. And . . . and anyways, I'm not after knowing anything, Miss.'

'Then please don't speak of it to Jemima. I am persuaded she has been having bad dreams, dreaming that she's seen strange men in this part of the house. The best thing for her is to forget it, and I forbid you to tell her any more stories.'

'Just so long as she keeps her eyes shut when they pass, Miss.'

'That's enough, Maura,' said Caroline, exasperated. 'If you say any more to Jemima about these . . . these night people, I shall complain of you to Mrs Datchet.'

'Shall you just?' The schoolroom maid's eyes held a look of sly animosity. 'I'd not do that, Miss, if I were you. There's them as wouldn't like it, if you make trouble for me.'

'What exactly do you mean by that, Maura?'

But the girl would not say any more. She looked scared and pleased and mutinous all at the same time, as though the secret she was hugging to herself was almost too much for her to bear. Caroline could well understand how Jemima had been frightened. She did not more than half believe in the truth of the girl's hints; but all the same she was left with a horrid feeling of unease.

41

'Anyone could see that he's a prince, really,' said Jemima, bending over the chair where Ferdy was lying with his paws in the air. Jemima was tickling his bloated tummy. 'Of course you're a prince, aren't you, my beauty?'

'Stand up straight, do!' said Caroline, who was trying to pin up the hem of the second muslin dress, considerably hampered by this puppy worship. 'If you don't keep still, we'll have no time to take Ferdy on the shore before your ride.'

Jemima straightened herself. 'Maura says that sand is bad for his coat.'

'Not if we wash it off him when we come in,' said Caroline. 'Turn a little more towards the window, please.'

'Maura says she wouldn't bath him, not if you begged her to, Miss Morrisey. I don't think she can realize how royal he is, do you?' Then she added in her deep, unchildlike voice, 'She doesn't like us going on the shore, because she goes down there herself to meet someone.'

Caroline said nothing. She thought it was more than likely true that Maura was in the habit of slipping out to meet someone from time to time. Probably she ought to tell Mrs Datchet of these suspicions, but she shrank from doing so: just as she had so far said nothing about the night people, or of Jemima's fears. She had been wrestling with doubts and fears for a couple of days, wondering whom to approach, or what to do. If there was any truth in what Maura hinted, or if Miss Prendergast had really gone in pursuit of an intruder on the night she disappeared, plainly something should be done. On the other hand, the whole thing could be imaginary. If this was the case, the last thing Caroline wanted was for the child to be questioned, or encouraged to recall it. So the days went by, and she did nothing. Nothing, that is, until she met Richard Sweeny again, and it seemed only natural to confide in him about her worries.

When old Slattery first told her that he was in service with

42

Richard Sweeny, and that Lord Vale's half-brother was living at Whitefield, it had been a distinct shock. Somehow she had thought the house would have remained empty, and the thought of a member of the Sweeny family actually in possession gave her a pang.

Yet, when she saw Richard again, it was not so very dreadful. She had sent Jemima off on her daily ride, when she saw him walking towards her along the terrace. He looked transformed. He wore a dark blue military uniform, and there was a quantity of gold braid at his shoulders and on the cuffs of his tunic.

She smiled at him and said impulsively, 'How fine you look, sir! I scarcely knew you!'

He was looking at her gravely. 'Miss Caroline,' he said, giving her her old Whitefield name. 'I have only just learned who you are. I hardly know what to say. . .'

She smiled at him more warmly, liking him all over again, and said, 'There is no need for you to say anything, sir.'

'I only wish—' He was looking past her out to sea, as though reluctant to face her. But he turned back directly, and said, 'Don't answer if you do not wish it, ma'am, but . . . did Colonel Morrisey leave you utterly without provision?'

She nodded, and he burst out with a sort of repressed violence, 'It's a wretched, disgraceful business! What I would give to undo it all! I wish my brother had never come into Ireland that time!'

She had wished this often enough herself, but some contrary whim made her say, 'My father always had a shocking propensity for the card tables. His affairs were in a bad way long before Lord Vale took a hand in them, sir. Well, I'm sure you are aware of it, since all the world knew at the time. My father lived for cards, and was close to ruin a dozen times. It was unlucky that he chose to stake Whitefield.'

'Unlucky indeed!' Richard Sweeny echoed with considerable feeling. He took Caroline's hand and pressed it briefly. 'As you may know, I am the present occupant of your old home, Miss Caroline.'

'Yes, I do know, sir.'

He looked at her intently, his blue eyes troubled. 'You do not mind?'

Somehow it was easy to answer him. There was something so warmly sympathetic in his manner, yet a certain restraint too. Caroline found herself speaking of Whitefield as though it was something she did every day. 'I admit it gave me a turn at first, sir. But now that I've met you again, I find I do not mind.'

'You make it easy for me, Miss Caroline,' he said quietly. 'Will you allow me to call you that? They always speak of you so at Whitefield. I find it comes more naturally than that stiff Miss Morrisey.' And when she gave a nod of consent, he said gratefully: 'I hoped you'd give me leave, ma'am; and I'm hoping too that you'll allow me to take you over to Whitefield one day. I've done some things there, and I've plans to do still more. I feel myself to be merely a steward, keeping Whitefield in good order until the rightful owner comes home.'

'The rightful owner is Lord Vale,' said Caroline perversely, 'though with this house and several others already in his possession, he hardly stands in need of Whitefield.'

'If I knew what Vale was in need of . . . ' Richard began bitterly. Then he broke off and shrugged his broad shoulders ruefully. 'You've not met my half-brother, so it cannot interest you to hear my complaints about him.'

'Lord Vale is my employer,' she replied primly. 'Jemima thinks him wholly marvellous; though he never troubles his head to write to her, I notice.'

'When you've met my dear brother, Miss Caroline,' said Richard, still in that bitter tone, 'you'll discover that he never troubles his head about anyone or anything. He's fond of Jemima in his way, I suppose. I wish I could see some small sign that he cared even a jot for his lands and his tenants here at Mount Sweeny.'

Caroline looked at Richard Sweeny curiously. Here was yet one more person who had little good to say of the wicked Earl of Vale. With the exception of Jemima, it was the same wherever she went. Mrs Datchet had as good as said that Vale had murdered his wife, and that only Richard Sweeny's efforts had saved the Earl from being accused of it. The catalogue of Vale's faults grew daily; murderer, absentee landlord, gamester, heavy drinker. No one had a good word for him.

'If only Vale would come here occasionally,' Richard was saying grimly. 'If only I could prevail upon him to spend a few weeks in the district; this countryside would be less of a hotbed of discontent, and a safer place to live in. We can't afford to have disaffected people, and there are ever-growing numbers of them on the Mount Sweeny lands. With the danger of the French invading . . . ' He broke off, gave a sharp, exasperated sigh, and added: 'All these poor wretches know of Vale is that his agent is forever demanding higher rents, and does nothing at all to improve their lands or their dwellings. They're being squeezed dry to feed Vale's horses, to bedeck his expensive women in new finery—' He suddenly seemed to remember who he was talking to, and said, 'Forgive me, Miss Caroline. I should not speak so to you, I know. But there are times when I cannot blame Vale's people here for being troublesome and surly. Truly, I cannot blame them.'

Caroline could see that he felt very deeply indeed about his half-brother's shortcomings: and it was at that moment that she decided to confide in Richard Sweeny about Jemima and her fears. He was so quietly dependable, yet so caring a man, that she did not think she would turn to him in vain. Diffidently at first, and then with growing confidence, she told him of Jemima's conviction that her last governess had been spirited away by the night people.

He did not laugh at her, as she feared he might. Indeed, as her tale unfolded, his dark, handsome face looked a trifle grim. Presently, he said: 'It's the very devil, Miss Caroline. If

45

I had the time, I'd take Jemima to England, and throw her at Vale's head. Of all the criminally foolish times to send the child here! We're all in a turmoil arming and drilling the new Volunteer regiment, making preparations to repel the French, if they decide to land here. Vale knows this, too, for I've written to him several times on the subject. I cannot spare the time to take Jemima away; but neither can I be sure of her safety here.'

She stared, startled by his vehemence.

'You think I exaggerate, Miss Caroline? I assure you I don't.' He turned and pointed out to sea. 'You see those masts on the horizon? Those are French ships. They sail unhindered round these shores these days; and if there is a serious attempt at invasion – and our spies tell us there's one in the offing – who do you think will defend us?' She shook her head. 'We would have to defend ourselves, ma'am; and a poor job we'd make of it, if all landlords in these parts were as heedless and selfish as my brother Vale.'

She said in a low voice: 'So you think Jemima and Miss Prendergast really saw someone, sir?'

'I fear they may have,' he returned soberly. 'And if they are the people I suspect, Miss Caroline, it won't do for you or Jemima to stay at Mount Sweeny. The trouble is, though,' – Caroline had the feeling that he was speaking more to himself than to her – 'the trouble is that if I have you removed too hastily, it may put them on their guard. It could ruin all . . .'

'You know who these night people are, sir?'

He said quietly, 'I've had my eye on them for some time, ma'am. They are ruthless men, believe me.'

Caroline felt cold. She drew her shawl closer about her shoulders. 'C . . could they really have taken Miss Prendergast away?'

His dark eyes narrowed thoughtfully, but he made no direct answer to this question. Rather, he seemed to retire behind a wall of reserve; and shorty afterwards he went away, leaving Caroline more uneasy than ever.

Five

I MUST INSIST ON AN ANSWER, Mr Rance,' said Caroline,
standing between the agent and the door of the bookroom.
'You claim that Miss Prendergast wrote to you after she left.
If this was so, may I see the letter?' She paused, looking
across at Mr Rance's resentful, blotched face, and added
sceptically, 'If there ever was such a letter, sir . . . '

'Certainly there was a letter,' he retorted haughtily. 'Miss
Prendergast was called to her mother's bedside.'

'Jemima tells me that Miss Prendergast's mother and
father are both dead.'

'Lady Jemima is just imagining things, Miss Morrisey;
and if you know what's good for you, you'll say you don't
want to hear about Miss Prendergast.'

'Oh? And do you think Jemima is also imagining that she
has seen some of the night people, Mr Rance?' Caroline had
asked this question out of curiosity to see how the agent
would react: but she had not expected her quietly spoken
words to have quite such an effect. The man looked at her,
dismay and indecision in his bloodshot eyes. She said with
mild malice, 'Oh, so you know about the night people, do
you? I rather thought you might do so.'

The agent looked at her, frowning and blinking. 'You must
keep the child in her room, Miss Morrisey. Lock her in if
necessary . . . ' When Caroline said that she would do no
such thing, he added, glaring at her and biting his thumb
nail, 'It's not my fault that the child was sent here.'

'Who are these night people, sir?'

'None of your business, Miss Morrisey. Besides, the less you know, so much the better for you. You've got that medallion with you, I trust?'

She said slowly, incredulously, 'Is . . is Gilbert one of these men, sir?'

He smiled a little at that, and the sight of that malicious smile made Caroline feel still more uneasy. He said softly, 'You've guessed rightly, Miss Morrisey. Your brother is deep in with the night people, and if you don't succeed in talking sense into his head, he'll end up with a hangman's noose around his neck. It's all a game to him, still. I told him to hold his tongue, but it seems he cannot.'

'Why, sir? What has he been saying?'

The agent said seriously, 'He's been publicly threatening to kill Lord Vale. Raving and swearing he'd get even, he was, only last evening in the tap room of the inn he's staying in.'

'Oh, so you know where he's staying? Pray tell me . . . '

He cut her short. 'You'll see him soon enough, Miss Morrisey. They'll be coming here any day now.'

'Do you really think Gilbert will come here?' she said, wondering if she dared to believe him.

'He may do.' The agent lowered his voice. 'Some of them are bound to come. They'll be back any day now. The tides will be right, and there's a run due in just over a week. They'll come a few days before, to get all ready.'

'Oh?' It dawned on Caroline just what manner of men the night people must be. 'Free traders? Is that who they are?'

'It's no business of yours to ask who they are,' he retorted in his former hectoring way. 'Just do as I say, and ask no questions, my girl. And for mercy's sake don't forget to show them that medallion I gave you.'

'It's Lord Vale's crest they use, isn't it?' said Caroline distastefully. 'I wonder if Gilbert is aware of that. Well, if they're engaged in smuggling, it's only fitting for them to use the Sweeny serpent for their sign. The Sweeny fortunes were made in the trade, weren't they? Gilbert and I used to row

48

past the rocks here and tell ourselves tales about the wicked Sweenys and their adventures . . .'

But the agent was no longer attending to her. There were sounds of hoofbeats on the gravel outside, and he pushed past Caroline and went to see who had ridden up.

Mount Sweeny was beseiged by a storm that night. Shutters rattled, doors slammed and the rain seemed to hurl itself against the window panes as loudly as pebbles from the sea shore. Caroline lay in her curtained bed listening to the surf booming against the rocks below, unable to sleep, and unable to escape from her scurrying, tormented thoughts. It really did seem that Gilbert was one of the night people. What was he doing? Why had he joined such a sinister band of men?

In the small hours of the morning, the wind dropped somewhat. Caroline climbed wearily out of bed, and peered through the curtains at the clouds scudding across the lightening sky. She lit a candle from the embers of her bedroom fire, and carried it back to her bedside. If she could not sleep, she thought it would be better to read. Anything would be better than to lie there, a prey to forebodings about her twin's activities.

But her book was not on her bedside table. She gave an exclamation of annoyance. She remembered. Her copy of *Pilgrim's Progress* was where she had left it, on the bookroom mantleshelf. It was still too early for any of the servants to be about, so Caroline pulled the silk bedcover off the bed, wrapped it around herself, and sped like a ghost down the corridor.

A log crashed on the hearth as she stood in the bookroom doorway. She saw herself reflected in a gilt floor-length mirror at the far end, a tall girl with hair falling in a golden cloud about her face and shoulders; her rioting hair blending with the deeper sheen of the silk damask bedcover.

The little book was where she had left it. She reached up,

49

her candle in one hand, when something soft and damp under her feet made her glance down. It was a man's coat, muddy and wet. Even before she turned and saw the man lying on the sofa, some subconscious part of her mind was already expecting him. He lay there, sprawled in sleep, within yards of where she stood.

She was aware of a variety of thoughts, in layers one on top of another; disappointment that it was not Gilbert, dismay that she should be alone with one of the night people, and the sudden hope that she could creep away before this man woke and saw her. Her fingers went to the silk thread round her neck, and she began to move stealthily sideways. But she was too late. The candle wavered in her hand, and with a groan and a yawn, the man on the sofa opened his eyes and saw her. For a moment he did not move. He just lay there watching her; and then he said softly: 'How delightful! Juliet in search of her Romeo? What's that bit about teaching the torches to burn bright?' He clambered rather clumsily from the deep, cushioned sofa, and stood there swaying. 'Well, Juliet? Can you remember your lines? I'm damned if I can remember mine.'

He was drunk. Even without the strong aroma of brandy, she would have known it. The knowledge heartened her rather, for she had more than once dealt with Gilbert and her father in the same sort of state. Perhaps this man would be too drunk to notice that she was wearing her bedgown and a silk bedcover, and must present a very odd appearance.

The man ran a hand over his eyes, as if trying to clear his vision. As he did so, Caroline saw the heavy gold ring on one of his fingers. The Sweeny serpent seemed to wink at her, mocking, unmistakeable, the forked tongue plainly visible in the intermittent light from the fire and the single candle in her hand. She knew, then, what she had to do. Hampered more than a little by the folds of her wrap, she pulled at the thread at her neck. In her trembling haste, the thread snapped as she pulled the little medallion out of its hiding place.

'There, sir,' she said, holding it out to him, and finding that her voice was breathless and none too steady. She drew a quick breath and added, 'Mr Rance said that I must show you this when you came.' The man did not seem to have heard her, so she went on in her soft hurrying voice, 'I need to speak with Gilbert, sir. Please will you help me to find him?'

He took the little gold coin, screwing up his deepset eyes as though it was hard for him to focus on it. 'What the devil's this?'

'The sign of the serpent, sir . . . ' She waited, giving him time to find his fuddled wits. He showed no sign of having taken in what she had said to him. He stared down at the medallion as though mesmerized by the sight of it.

She thought she would have to repeat her request; but he suddenly looked at her, smiling crookedly in a way she did not like. He had the strangest eyes, deepset, slanting, golden in the candlelight; yet somehow cold despite their warm colour. 'Gilbert?' he said softly. 'Is he your lover?'

She could not think what to answer, and while she hesitated, she felt the warm blood flooding her face and neck. She dared not tell this man that Gilbert was her brother, so what should she say? She said stiffly, 'That need not concern you, sir. Please tell him to come and see me as soon as may be.'

He smiled at her again in a way that made her wish very much that she had been more properly clothed: and she wondered whether he was going to be easy to handle, after all. When he next spoke, she knew there'd be no handling him. 'Rance gave you this trinket, did he? Sly fellow. I've often wondered what he gets up to when no one's watching him. Still, I don't quarrel with his taste. Your hair is the colour of honey, you know.'

Caroline felt helpless in the face of his leering smile. She drew back, clutching the slippery silk of the bedcover round her, and said as quellingly as she was able, 'If you'll be good enough to give Gilbert my message, sir, I'll take my leave of you. It's cold in here.'

'Oh, don't go away, Juliet,' he said, lurching forward and putting a heavy hand upon one of her shoulders. 'Stay with me. I'll help you to keep warm.'

'If you were not in your cups,' said Caroline, coldly, 'you would realize how exceedingly silly you sound.'

He chuckled softly. 'You should have seen me before I went to sleep, my dear. If you think I'm in my cups now, I assure you I was as drunk as a wheelbarrow then. Stay with me, and I'll try to amuse you. I may be a trifle disguised, but I'm not incapable.'

'No,' she agreed disdainfully, 'I can see you are not, and I believe I would find you less disgusting if you were.'

'Tell me, Juliet,' his voice was as bland as hers, 'do your other lovers stand for these missish airs of yours?'

'My other—' She broke off, realizing how foolish and undignified it would sound to say there were no others. She stamped her bare foot on the hearth rug and said crossly, 'You may think what you like of me, sir, but if I did have a lover, he would certainly be a man who could hold his wine like a gentleman.'

He gave a great shout of laughter. Involuntarily, she told him to be quiet. She said severely, 'Do you want to bring the household down upon us? I assure you, I do not.'

He stopped laughing. 'Indeed it would be a pity to be interrupted too soon.'

'Then, please be careful. The servants start stirring around six o'clock. You should go now, if you wish to avoid being seen, sir.'

He said softly. 'So you have a kindness for me, after all, Juliet?'

'No such thing,' she retorted tartly. 'I am thinking of my own safety and reputation, if you must know. I cannot afford to be found here, particularly looking as I do.'

He smiled, and the cold, slanting eyes seemed to rake her from her head to her cold bare toes. 'You look very charmingly, my dear. But why are you so sure I do not wish to be seen? Do you know who I am?'

This was dangerous ground, she knew. Drunk he might
be, but he was one of the night people. What was it that
Richard Sweeny had said of them? Ruthless men, he had
called them. Finding a sudden difficulty in breathing, she
said with a sort of gasp, 'I don't know your name, of course;
but they say you treat Mount Sweeny as though you own it,
you and all the other night people.' She saw a faintly startled
look on his long, bony face, and added impulsively, 'I wish
you would take more care, sir! Your carelessness has
frightened one small child half out of her wits.'

'What small child?'

She wished she had not spoken. 'It does not matter.'

'So Jemima saw me, did she?'

She gazed at him, wide-eyed, seized by a feeling that this
man could see all her thoughts. He did not seem drunk any
more. If only he would stop looking at her in that cold,
penetrating way!

'What was the little monster doing that she saw me?'

'I . . I don't know. I was not here when she saw you. But if
you harm her, sir,' Caroline said, with a sudden fierceness
born of desperation, 'if you harm Jemima, I'll make sure you
go to prison for it.'

'What makes you think I'd harm her?'

Her throat felt tight, as though her fear of this man had
put a constriction about it. She stared up at him, unable to
tear her frightened gaze away. He had a long, closed-in, bony
face which was unlike any other she had seen. His nose was
crooked, one eyelid drooped lower than the other over the
intent, amber eyes. She said jerkily, 'Jemima did not mean to
see you. She knows you do not like to be seen, and she will
not tell anyone. . .'

'She told you, however. . .'

She was shaking. Her whole being was possessed by this
quaking feeling, and suddenly she could bear it no more. She
began to run to the door; but tripped over the bedcover, and
was saved from falling headlong by strong arms around her.
She turned, sobbing with fright and mortification, and struck

out at him with her clenched fists. He gave her a shake, and caught both her flailing hands.

'Enough, little fool,' he said irritably. 'You'll break your neck if you run about in that thing. Here. Come back to the fire.'

The spirit seemed to have gone out of her. Numbly she went with him, and found herself being pushed into a wing-chair. A glass of some amber liquid was thrust into her hand.

'Drink that, before you have another fit of the vapours,' he said. 'I never could abide hysterical females.'

She took the glass and sipped at its contents. It was brandy, very good brandy if smoothness was anything to go by. No doubt the night people had the run of the Earl of Vale's cellar, as they did of the rest of his house. She watched the man pour himself another, fuller glass, studying him with an odd sort of detached interest.

He seemed content enough to be the object of her study. He sat down on the edge of a nearby table, a tall, loose-limbed man in mudsplashed buckskins and boots. He was coatless, and his crumpled shirt had lace at neck and wrists. He looked like a man who had ridden hard, and she realized that he must have ridden through last night's terrible storm.

He smiled at her suddenly, in that crooked way that she was beginning to know. Everything about him was crooked, off centre. He was, perhaps, the ugliest man she had ever seen; yet his ugliness had a certain charm.

She wondered for the second time if he could read her thoughts, for he raised his glass, and said, 'A truce, Juliet? Let's drink to that, shall we? I won't harm you. You're far too charming. Not pretty, exactly, but something out of the common way. What are you doing in this house?'

She gave herself a mental shake, and said coldly, 'I am the governess, sir.'

'Ah! And who do you suppose me to be?'

She wanted to startle him. She thought she owed him that. She said, 'You're one of the night people, are you not? Mr Rance told me that you would come soon.'

His hands were long and thin, like the rest of him. He raised his glass to his lips again, sipped, and said thoughtfully, 'Yes, you certainly are something different from the common run of governesses, are you not? How did they come to engage you?'

She might have taken this chance to ask him about Miss Prendergast, whose place she had taken. Somehow, though, she did not quite dare. She said, 'You know, I really should go. Please will you tell Gilbert that I must see him, sir?'

He smiled more crookedly than ever. 'Let's forget about Gilbert. You might do better with me, Juliet. If we disposed of the inquisitive Jemima, you would be free to take up some employment better suited to your . . . your talents. You are hopelessly miscast as a governess, my dear.'

'I must suppose that you are joking,' she said, rising to her feet. He made no move to stop her this time. She sketched a curtsey, holding the bedcover tightly round her. 'I don't find it amusing, this talk of disposing of Jemima. I'll bid you good morning.'

'Don't tell me you've developed a fondness for the sulky Jemima?'

'She's not sulky with me. Not very often, at least . . . '

'Well, she's no beauty, even at the best of times.'

Caroline was already tired of hearing people make slighting remarks about Jemima. Coming from this intruder, it was too much to bear. She said hotly, 'It's not Jemima's fault that she's not beautiful. She is not responsible for her looks. And if she had ever been given affection or proper attention, instead of being pushed here and there, she might have learned how to show affection and consideration for others. She cannot copy what she has never known! Jemima has courage and character, sir, and those things will stand her in better stead than all the beauty in the world—'

She broke off suddenly, knowing she had made a fool of herself. The intruder was watching her with that intent, amused regard. She said more calmly, but for some reason wanting to convince him, 'You may have heard that Jemima

Sweeny is a pampered, rich man's child. I have heard it said myself. But it's not true. She is deprived, sir, starved of love and attention, and of people who truly care for her happiness.'

'You seem to care about her, at all events,' he remarked coolly.

His tone sobered her. She tried to smile. 'You think me demented, I dare say. But it makes me angry when people speak slightingly of Jemima.' She sighed, and added seriously, 'I have no reason to love Lord Vale, but since I've been here at Mount Sweeny, and have come to know Jemima, I truly think him despicable. He's made Jemima feel that she's failed him; failed him by not being a boy, by not being a beauty like her mother. I cannot forgive him for that! And the worst of it is, Jemima adores him!'

'Why don't you tell Jemima what a worthless fellow Vale is, my dear?' he suggested. 'It's something she's sure to find out sooner or later.'

'She wouldn't believe me,' said Caroline, picking up her glass and draining it in one gulp.

'What a way to treat my best brandy, Juliet.'

She gave a splutter of laughter, choking a little over the potent draught she had swallowed. 'It's not your brandy, sir. However much you treat all things here as yours, they still belong to the wicked Earl of Vale, you know . . . '

She saw, as she spoke, that his face was wearing a shuttered look. She gazed at him, fascinated, wondering why his really remarkable resemblance to Jemima had not struck her before? Feeling oddly calm, she said in a ghost of a voice: 'So that's who you are? It would have been more honest if you had told me, my lord.'

'Yes, but think what boring lives honest men must lead?' retorted the Earl of Vale, smiling appreciatively down at her flushed, accusing face. 'Now, tell me, Juliet? Why have you taken me in so strong a dislike?'

But he learned no more. The tall girl cast him a look of furious reproach, gathered the fallen folds of her golden silk bedcover around her, and ran to the door. A moment later he heard it slam shut.

He stood for a moment or two, gazing down at the embers of the fire, smiling faintly all the while. Somewhere a clock struck six times. He bent down to pick up the coat which he had flung down. Presently, with his coat and waistcoat over his arm, a decanter in one hand and a glass in the other, the Earl of Vale went in search of his bed.

Six

'MISS MORRISEY! You'll never guess what's happened! My papa has come!'

Jemima had just made this momentous discovery, and came dancing into the schoolroom to tell Caroline all about it. 'He's really and truly here, Miss Morrisey! Imagine! He rode in during the storm, and no one knew he was here 'til one of the maids found him sleeping in his bed.'

Caroline did her best to make a suitably appreciative reply, but she felt that even Jemima must sense that her enthusiasm was on the limp side. She was feeling weary and wretched after her sleepless night. She could still raise a wry smile, however, for the thought of how marvellously Vale's household had been caught out. Mrs Datchet had more than once declared that any member of the Sweeny family could arrive suddenly, with any number of guests or attendants, and everything would be ready for them. Lord Vale might not have been to Mount Sweeny for four years. This did not prevent the house being kept in readiness, as though he were expected hourly. That, at least, was Mrs Datchet's boast. Still, none of Lord Vale's servants had been so finely caught out as she had been herself.

Her head felt wooden, numb. Her mind did not seem to be working properly at all. Try as she might to think out the implications of her meeting with the Earl, to decide what it would mean in terms of danger to Gilbert and to Mr Rance, or to herself, no real answer seemed to come to her feverish surmises. Jemima gave her no peace for quiet reflection. The child chattered away, animated, rejoicing about Lord Vale's arrival, confident that Caroline must also regard this as a high treat. Caroline found herself reflecting sourly that even the most neglectful of parents had an unfair hold upon their offspring's affections. This brought to mind how she had told him to his face that he was a heartless, uncaring father. She flinched inwardly. Whatever else he might condone, she did not think he would forgive her for that.

Mrs Datchet arrived, much aggrieved about Vale's unheralded arrival. She blamed the gatekeeper, the night footmen, the grooms in the stables who had never heard his lordship ride in. In short, she blamed everyone except herself.

'Mrs Datchet,' said Caroline, resisting the temptation to defend any of these people; 'Mrs Datchet. Do you think I might have a word with Lord Vale?'

The housekeeper was immediately on the defensive, her pale eyes sharp with affronted suspicion. 'What do you want to see his lordship for, pray?'

'A private matter, ma'am.'

'If you have any complaints to make, Miss Morrisey, you may make them to me. Though what you have to complain of, I cannot imagine.'

'No, ma'am. It's nothing like that. But I should like to see his lordship as soon as may be.'

'Miss Morrisey, his lordship is still in his bed, asleep. Are you suggesting that I should wake him up for your convenience?'

'When he wakes, then?'

'In this house, Miss Morrisey,' said the housekeeper grandly, 'it is my duty to see that his lordship is not troubled by importunate persons. You will have to wait until you are sent for. His lordship may wish to see Lady Jemima, more than likely.'

When the housekeeper had gone, Jemima said wistfully, 'When do you think he will want to see me, Miss Morrisey? I want to show him Ferdy, and Robbie, and how I can jump the double bank in the long acre field.'

Caroline was of course unable to tell her. She thought she ought to give Jemima a hint that Vale would probably send her packing. Once or twice she was on the verge of saying some such thing, but each time she shrank from it. Watching the child lying on the floor with Ferdy, giggling when the puppy chewed at her hair, wrestling with him just as though she were another larger puppy herself, Caroline could have wept. It was all very well to tell herself that Jemima must take her chance. No one could save her from what life had to offer; and no doubt there would be a score more governesses before she had grown to womanhood. By then she would discover that her much adored father was not all she thought him, and Jemima would grow cynical and armoured.

It did not help much, either, to tell herself that Lord Vale's own behaviour had been more reprehensible than her own. He was her employer, and no doubt thought he had a right to amuse himself with any female who came his way. And he would think himself equally entitled to expect his daughter's governess to dress and behave with propriety. If only, if only she had not gone to look for her book at that ungodly hour! If only her mind had not been so full of the night people!

She got to her feet rather abruptly. 'Come along, Jemima,' she said in a reproving tone. 'Did you think to lie there all the morning, playing with Ferdy? If we don't get started, you'll still be doing sums when your papa sends for you.'

'My dear Vale!' cried Richard Sweeny, striding into the dining room with his spurs jingling. He clapped his half-brother strongly on the shoulder and said, 'So it's true? I hardly believed it could be, when they brought the news to Whitefield. Have you come to take Jemima away?'

The Earl flinched visibly, closing his eyes for a moment as though in pain. 'Good morning, Richard. I wish you would express your ecstasies in a less physical way. We are not all

60

as full of joy at this time of the day. And why the military aspect?' he demanded, having by this time reopened his eyes and observed his brother's style of dress. 'Are you taking part in theatricals again?'

'I'm on my way to a Volunteer parade. And as for the time of day, it's well past noon,' retorted Richard, with the cheerful scorn of the early riser for the sluggard. He glanced at his brother's somewhat sallow complexion above the gold brocade of his dressing gown, and added: 'Feeling a bit hagged, are you? Well, a day or two in the sea air will put you to rights. If you mean to stay that long, that is?' Vale made no answer to this oblique question, so Richard added rather drily, 'I suppose you may stay on a day or two, if only to rest the horses?'

'I mean to stay longer than that.'

'Oh?' Richard looked surprised. Then, perhaps feeling that he had not sounded very welcoming, he added, 'Forgive me, Hugo, but you cannot wonder that I am startled. You've not been here for . . . for four years. What decided you to come now, if it was not Jemima?'

'What made me come? Well, what makes one go anywhere?' replied his lordship, sounding weary. He got up from the table with caution, as though fearing that the top of his head might blow off. A footman sprang to open the door for them, and they went into the marble paved hall, and across it to the long, sunlit morning room.

Vale said, presently, 'I've come from Lismore, where the company was a dead bore. There was that fellow Carrick. I doubt if he ever washes, and his waistcoats gave me the headache. Yes, if any one thing decided me to come here, it was Carrick's striped waistcoat. That, and the news that we were all to take part in charades after dinner. I've never shared your taste for theatricals, Richard. So I left.'

'Do you mean to say, Vale, that you just got up and left? That you told no one. My dear Hugo . . . '

'What was there to say?' Vale sounded surprised. And when his brother did not answer, he added with a small

61

crooked smile, 'I left a note for Augusta, which she will have received before she went to bed. Augusta is never short of a word. No doubt she will think up something to say to the Hartingtons. Our dear sister is so resourceful.'

Richard tried to picture Lady Augusta Appleby's reaction when she found out that her graceless brother had left her flat in the middle of Lady Hartington's party. He gulped, and began to grin, saying in a shaking voice, 'Hugo, you are abominable! Still, whatever brought you here, I'm very glad to see you. Did you read my letter? The one I sent to Vale Park?'

Vale, standing with his back to the fire, said vaguely, 'Your letter? Which one was that? I seem to remember a score of letters from you, all of them somewhat . . . er . . . agricultural in tone. I almost fancied I could smell the farmyard as I broke the seal, dear boy.'

'When did you last break the seal on a letter from me, Hugo?' demanded Richard, raising his dark brows scornfully. 'Not since you had Hargreaves to do it for you, I fancy. Hargreaves wrote to say that he had brought that particular letter to your notice, which was why I ventured to think you might remember.'

'Hargreaves is constantly bringing things to my notice,' said the Earl sighing. 'Damnably hard to shake off, Hargreaves. Almost as bad as you, dear boy,' he added, as Richard took a hasty stride towards the window. 'Come to think of it, I did read your letter. You seemed to suggest, did you not, that Rance has been feathering his nest at my expense?'

'Quite,' said Richard curtly, coming back from the window, 'and he's been doing so for some time. I hoped that you'd have at least enough sense of self-interest to come and look into the matter.'

Vale smiled crookedly. 'Well, now you behold me. You have no more cause for complaint. Now, why are you so glad to see me, all of a sudden? I find myself quite touched at this outburst of brotherly affection. Four years' absence has indeed worked wonders.'

There was a pause: 'You have not changed much, Hugo,' said Richard evenly. 'Well, I wouldn't expect it. Let's say that your arrival is opportune, shall we?'

'Certainly. I am willing to say just whatever you wish, dear boy,' sighed the Earl, yawning.

Richard took no notice of this tiresome interjection, but went on to say crisply, 'You've heard that we've been warned to expect a French invasion? It may come any day now. Well, we're augmenting the Volunteer regiments, and there's urgent need for both money and more officers. You ought to join, Vale.' He paused, but finding the Earl's expression anything but enthusiastic, went on to say with renewed earnestness, 'If every landowner in the district would just stay on his estates, rouse his people to vigilance, give them the leadership they need, we'll stand a good chance of holding off the French, if they come . . . '

'Mm. Very eloquent, Richard; but you fill me with foreboding. What do you want me to do? Must I rig myself out in that badly-fitting uniform? I really don't think Fallow will care for it, you know. It really would not do to offend Fallow.'

Richard knew very well that Fallow, Vale's valet, would have no choice but to put up with whatever Vale chose to do. Moreover, he knew that he was being baited, and was already tiring of it. He said coldly: 'You may have your uniform tailored where you pease, Hugo; but you're perfectly right in thinking I'd like you to join the Volunteers. No doubt you would find it a great bore, less amusing than dicing or playing at cards.'

'Oh? Is there anyone hereabouts who can play a decent hand at cards?'

'Please, Hugo! Hear me out, I beg of you,' said Richard with scarcely concealed impatience. He watched his brother lower himself into a chair and cross one exquisitely booted leg over the other, and said in his blunt sensible voice, 'As you must know, Vale, you are far from popular in this district. You've been here very little, and the last time . . . '

63

Richard paused. Vale glanced at him, a cold, waiting glance. 'The last time, you scarcely endeared yourself to our neighbours, let's face it. Since then you've not been near the place, and your prolonged absence has made matters worse.'

'I am perfectly well aware that my name stinks in these parts.'

'Quite so,' said Richard, his voice drier than ever. 'I bear the same name as you do, remember, so I am also aware of it. More so than you, since I am obliged to live at Whitefield. People have not forgotten the disgraceful way that Whitefield came into Sweeny hands. It has taken me a deal of trouble and hard work to live that stigma down.'

'I won Whitefield in fair play. Morrisey would not have held it against me, had he lived.'

'He died within hours of that game, by his own hand. They blame you for that.'

'I know it,' said Vale coldly. 'Well, go on. I suppose you must have some motive for delivering this dose of home-truths so soon after telling me you are glad to see me?'

Richard nodded. His blue eyes were grave. 'Yes. I have a motive. I want to see you reinstated, your good name restored . . . '

'Vaulting ambition, indeed, dear boy.'

'Listen to me!' said Richard sharply. 'Don't you see what I'm getting at? This is a time of crisis in the south of Ireland. You have a chance to re-establish yourself with your neighbours; perhaps the only chance you'll ever get!' Richard's voice had taken on a ringing tone, and his blue eyes seemed to flash with enthusiasm. He went on, earnestly, 'Now is the time for you to prove that you have the public welfare at heart, that you care more for your tenants and your labourers in their hour of peril than for your own selfish amusements. I want to see you at the head of the Mount Sweeny Volunteers, preparing to defend your own land against a foreign invasion!'

'Such eloquence!' murmured the Earl in soft-voiced mockery.

Richard looked at his brother and said reproachfully: 'If only you would take this chance. If only you would play your cards carefully, Hugo, you might repair the damage which has been done.'

'If it were only a matter of playing cards,' sighed the Earl, 'I might find it rather more in my style. Can you really see me playing at soldiers, dear boy?'

There was a short silence. Richard sighed in his turn, and said: 'All right. Don't join the regiment, if that doesn't appeal to you. What I implore you to do, though, is to declare yourself willing to raise men and arms here at Mount Sweeny. Rance says he won't do so, since he's had no instructions from you. This has, of course, been interpreted as your having refused to support the Volunteers in any way. I want to see that tale refuted, Hugo. Come with me to Mannering's house. You remember Giles Mannering? He's the colonel of the new regiment, and a good sort of fellow. If you'll take the first step, he'll be willing to forget the past.'

'Mannering? Yes, I remember Mannering. He was a crony of Morrisey's was he not?'

'Then, you'll come?'

'I'll think about it,' said the Earl maddeningly. 'Now, tell me something I want to know, Richard. Who are the night people?'

Richard looked down at his brother sharply. 'What's this? What are you getting at, Hugo?'

'You heard my question.'

'How did you hear of the night people?'

'Does it matter how I heard?'

'I think it does matter,' said Richard gravely. 'It's important for me to know how you heard of the night people, within hours of getting to Mount Sweeny.'

'I was taken for one of them.'

Richard stared at Vale's ugly, crooked face in something like consternation. 'Taken for one of those ruffians? How? Who by?'

'By a young woman who claims to be Jemima's new gov-

65

erness. She's an improvement on the grim Miss Prendergast, I must say.'

Richard was silent for fully half a minute. He was about to demand a fuller explanation of this astonishing assertion, when Rance came in, bowing, rhapsodizing and apologizing by turns.

'My lord! Such a surprise you gave us! I must offer my profound apologies for not coming earlier, but the news only just reached me! On behalf of the staff and tenants of Mount Sweeny, may I say how delighted we all are to welcome you!'

'You may say it, Rance.' said Vale coolly, 'but I have just been told by my brother that I'm regarded as an ogre in the district. Which of you am I to believe?'

'Mr Richard likes to have his little jest, my lord.'

'It's no jesting matter, Rance,' said Richard curtly. 'There has been growing disaffection lately, not to mention outbreaks of rick burning and maiming of cattle on the Mount Sweeny estates. It is right that his lordship should know it. His lordship also wanted to know,' he added, eyeing the agent very straightly as he spoke, 'his lordship has just asked me to tell him what I knew about the night people. What do you think of that?'

The agent's red face grew visibly redder and more mottled. He seemed to have difficulty in speaking. Then he said uneasily, 'How in the world did you hear tell of them, my lord?' He looked across at Richard's expressionless face, as though seeking his aid, and said rather helplessly, 'I hardly know what to say . . . '

He was saved from further speech by the sudden opening of the morning-room door. Caroline Morrisey marched into the room.

'Lord Vale,' she said, in a crisp, clear voice. 'I wish to speak with you, if you please.'

'Dear me, what a momentous morning this is, to be sure,' murmured the Earl, leaning back in his chair. He watched her walk toward them down the long room.

'My lord,' said Mr Rance hurriedly, 'this is the new gov-

66

erness. The last one left suddenly, my lord, so I took the liberty of engaging this young lady . . . '

'So you engaged her, did you?'

'Yes, my lord.'

'Well, let's hear what she wants to say.'

Caroline was taken off balance. This was not the reception she had been nerving herself to meet. She expected rejection, dismissal and public disgrace. She had come downstairs because the suspense had grown unbearable. And after all this, she found Lord Vale lounging in a chair, dressed in a garish dressing gown and smiling up at her as though he was really quite pleased to see her! It was distinctly undermining. She had been so determined to get the worst over with dignity and speed. She blinked at him, and said breathlessly, 'May I speak with you alone, Lord Vale?'

'I have no secrets from Rance, or from my brother, ma'am.' he said casually. 'Come and sit down, and tell us what you want.'

'I prefer to stand, sir. I have come to say that I wish to leave your employ.'

'But you've only just come. What's the matter? Is Jemima out of sorts today?'

Mr Rance glared at Caroline, trying to catch her eye, and said, 'Now, Miss Morrisey! Don't be hasty!'

Caroline was just wondering, dazedly, whether the Earl could possibly have been so drunk that he did not remember their early morning meeting, when he said: 'What did you call her, Rance?'

'Rance called her Miss Morrisey,' said Richard with a certain relish. 'Allow me to present Miss Caroline Morrisey, Vale. She is Peter Morrisey's daughter, you know.'

Vale looked at Caroline appraisingly. 'Yes. She has a look of him, doesn't she? At least, she would do if she weren't almost extinguished by that appalling cap.' He smiled up at Caroline in his crooked way, and added curiously, 'Why do you wish to leave, ma'am?'

Caroline was dumbfounded. She had taken pains with her

appearance that morning, putting on her forbidding starched cap as though it had been armour for the coming fight. Not so much as a scrap of her hair was visible. She knew herself to be a veritable vision of respectability. How dared he speak so coolly about her likeness to her father, and at the same time make slighting remarks about her appearance! She raised her chin, warmed by a heartening sense of anger. 'If you remember my father and what you did to him, my lord, you can surely understand why I would not wish to stay in your house!'

'You accepted the post in the first place,' he pointed out, with a coolness that infuriated her still further. 'Now that I find much harder to understand.'

'My lord!' put in Mr Rance, palpitating with unease. 'If I had known that your lordship might have some objection to employing Miss Morrisey . . . '

'It's Miss Morrisey who objects, not I. She seems rather a promising young woman to me. Why should I object to her?'

Caroline stared down at his ugly, faintly smiling face, unable to make him out at all. She had an illogical feeling that she had been given a reprieve. She stammered in her bewilderment, 'I . . . I thought you would tell me to go, my lord.'

'Not at all. Not until you have satisfied my curiosity, at least. Why are you here, ma'am? I mean to find out, you know.'

She looked at him blankly, but before she could feel more than a vague alarm at what he had just said, he added calmly and dismissively, 'Bring Jemima to the stable yard in half an hour's time, will you? I am taking her riding.'

'Oh, sir!' Her soft voice was warm with gladness. 'Jemima was so hoping that you would!'

For a moment she thought there was a glimmer of warmth in the cold amber eyes. He said, 'Very well. In thirty minutes, then.'

She turned to go.

'And one thing more . . . '

'Yes, my lord?' Relieved she might be, but she did not care for his peremptory way of commanding her attention. She raised her chin, and said in a carefully colourless tone, 'What is it, sir?'

'Get rid of that cap, ma'am,' he told her coolly. 'It is an abomination.'

'Well, really!' cried Richard, coming to Caroline's defence with an air of half-laughing indignation. 'Miss Caroline must be allowed to wear whatever she pleases. You cannot dictate to her in everything, Hugo!'

'I pay her, don't I? Why should I allow her to offend my sight?'

Caroline said crossly, 'I am just removing myself from your sight, my lord. I am indeed sorry if my person offends you.'

'I've no complaints about your person, Juliet,' he returned, smiling in a way that reminded her vividly of their encounter in the bookroom in the early hours of that morning. 'Really none at all. It's only your cap that I object to.'

Seven

CAROLINE WATCHED JEMIMA and the Earl clatter off down the avenue, and turned back towards the house. Maura met her at the door of the schoolroom. Her expression was sullen.

'You've to go down to the beach, Miss. Someone wants to see you.'

Caroline's eyes widened. Her pulses began to race with excitement. 'Who is it, Maura? Who gave you this message?'

There was no mistaking the malevolence in the girl's glance. 'Find out for yourself, Miss. I'm not after knowing what he wants with you.' The maid turned on her heel, and flounced off down the corridor.

Caroline lost no time in going down to the shore. When she reached the bottom of the steep, uneven steps she paused, uncertain which way to go. It was just like Gilbert to send for her, but to leave no precise instructions as to where she would find him. Then it occurred to her that it might not be Gilbert after all. What if it were one of the other night people? She had no little medallion to show. She had left it in the bookroom, and had never thought to look for it.

She walked along the beach a little way, worrying about this. It was not surprising, then, that she heard Gilbert's voice before she saw him. She looked up the face of the cliff. There he was, perched on a slab of rock above her head, grinning mischievously.

'Well, Car? I thought you were never coming.'

'I came as soon as I got your message,' she said, trying to speak calmly, trying to ignore the delighted thumping of her heart. 'How did you know I was here? Did Mr Rance tell you?'

'Rance? Not he.' Gilbert slid down the side of the rock, and a moment later she found herself clasped tightly in her brother's arms. 'Aren't you going to bid me welcome, sister? What does it matter who told me you were here?'

'Oh, Gil!' she said, clinging to him. 'Gilbert! I have so longed to see you!'

'Well, there's no need to strangle me,' he said rather impatiently. Gilbert had always hated to be hugged or held in any way. 'Tell me, what the deuce are you doing at Mount Sweeny?'

'I'm Jemima Sweeny's governess,' she said, glancing up at the dark slate roof and smoking chimney stacks of the house, all that could be seen of Mount Sweeny from where they stood. 'I've been there almost two weeks.'

'That's what I heard. But why? I couldn't believe my ears when Maura spoke your name. Why did you come?'

She smiled at him fondly and said in a laughing tone, 'One must eat, after all. Lord Vale pays twice as much as Mrs O'Mahoney did, you know.'

'For God's sake, Car, I don't know how you could bring yourself to enter that man's house.'

She was suddenly serious. 'I came here because of you, Gilbert. Mr Rance made me come. He said he was worried about you.'

For a moment Caroline's twin brother stared back at her in utter consternation. She returned his gaze lovingly, reflecting that he had lost none of his good looks. Even with his jaw dropping in amazement, Gilbert was an exceptionally handsome young man, and the last four years seemed to have sharpened and defined his features, hardened and matured his appearance. He shook his fair head, as though trying to clear his mind. He repeated in a tone of disbelief: 'Rance made you come? Rance?'

71

Gravely she assured him that this was true. She might also have told him that Lord Vale's agent had all but blackmailed her into coming, but she knew Gilbert's hot-headed ways, and had no wish to have him dashing off to wreak his anger on the agent at this point. It was much more important to find out what Gilbert was doing, and to persuade him to go away, if it was as dangerous as Mr Rance had tried to make her believe.

She said, 'Mr Rance told me that you held up his carriage, and that he had recognized you.'

'Oh, he told you about that, did he?' Gilbert grinned. 'You should have seen his face, Car, when I called to him to stand and deliver! I thought he'd burst a blood vessel.'

She did not smile back at him. She said soberly, 'Mr Rance also told me, Gilbert, that he'd heard you uttering threats against Lord Vale.'

His smile faded. 'Damn Rance and his tattling! Still, what if I was speaking against Vale? I'm not the only one round here who hates him, and wishes him dead.'

'It cannot be wise to go around saying so,' retorted Caroline. 'If he came to harm, people might blame you. Besides, I am persuaded that you don't mean it, Gilbert. I'm not suggesting that you should approve of Lord Vale, or have anything to do with him; but what happened at Whitefield is over and done with. It's no good looking back, torturing yourself with regrets, growing bitter. You must try to forget it.' She saw that he was looking distinctly annoyed, and added quickly, 'Why did you come back here, Gilbert? I know it must pain you to be so near White-field, with no right to go there any more. Why not go back to America? Mr Rance thinks you should do so.' She looked at his coat of blue cloth and his breeches and shining boots, which were of the finest leather. She said fondly, 'You must have done well there. You look very fine and proosperous.'

He looked down at the sleeve of his coat, which she was fingering with her work-roughened hand, and said ruefully, 'You talk as though it had been easy, Car. It was not, I assure you. It was little better than hand to mouth for the first two years. After that I fell in with a fellow who breeds horses, and things were better. Don't judge my condition by my clothes, though. I had this coat made in Waterford, only a week ago; and I wouldn't be in Ireland at all if I hadn't had a deuced good run at the card table.'

'Gambling again? Oh, Gil!' she exclaimed distressfully. He stiffened, and she knew she had been foolish to let the words escape her. It had never done anything but harm to oppose her menfolk in their passion for games of chance. Gaming was like a fever with them, and opposition only served to drive them to further excesses.

Gilbert shook off her arm. 'If you must know, it was the first game I'd played in over a year. Caleb does not hold with such things, and it was only that I met some men in Boston . . .'

She did not ask him who Caleb was. It seemed more important to retrieve her mistake, to placate him. 'Please, Gilbert,' she said in her soft voice, 'don't be vexed with me. I did not mean to scold, truly.'

He grunted, but looked a little mollified. 'I should think not, indeed! You're in no position to take a high moral tone. You're not so particular yourself, are you, working for our father's murderer!' She flinched, wounded by his ready condemnation. He did not notice. He was still wrestling with a sum which did not seem to add up. He said in a muttering sort of way, 'Damn me if I know what that fellow Rance is playing at. Why should he wish to bring you here?'

'I don't know, Gil.' She had been puzzling over this herself. Slattery's incomprehensible mutterings had made her uneasy, and she certainly could not bring herself to believe that Mr Rance's main concern was for Gilbert's safety. She said slowly, 'All I know is that he came all the way to Dublin to fetch me, and would not take no for an answer.'

'The devil he did!' Gilbert shook his bright head. 'Rance has always been damned devious. He was too friendly by half, considering I'd tried to rob him. Yet, I have no option but to trust him.'

Caroline said soberly, 'He's done me more than one kindness, too, but still I cannot like him. All the same, Gil,' she added, rather sadly, 'it might be best for you to follow his advice, and return to America. There's no going back to the old, easy ways – not for either of us.'

'What, Car?' he said, with a quick, mischievous grin. 'Are you tired of me already?'

She smiled back at him. She had never been able to resist Gilbert when he smiled, or when he spoke in that funning tone. 'Now you are being foolish beyond permission, dearest. I'd give anything to keep you here with me. You know that. For that matter, I'd follow you to America, if only it were possible.'

'Would you, Car?' He looked at his sister rather searchingly, 'I wonder what you'd think of Caleb? He's a rough sort of fellow, plain-spoken, with no book-learning – unless you count the Bible, which he can spout by the hour, when he's in the mind of it. Caleb's a New Englander, born and bred,' he added, as Caroline looked at him in some surprise. He read her thought rightly, and answered it with a chuckle: 'You're not the first one to think it's odd that Caleb and I should be partners. At least, he's offered to go into partnership with me, when I go back . . . '

'Ah! Then you intend to go back to America, after all?'

He jerked his shoulder, and said irritably, 'Intend? It costs nothing to have intentions; but I've no longer the means of carrying them out.' He sighed sharply, and Caroline began to realize that much of Gilbert's irritability was a mask for his pent-up anxieties. 'I tell you, Car, I had absolutely no choice but to take up with Rance's offer.'

She watched him gravely, waiting for him to unburden himself of his troubles.

'I was robbed, you see. When I first set foot in Ireland I had enough money to do my business, and pay my passage back to Boston. It was Caleb who made me come. Caleb,' Gilbert explained, in answer to his sister's curious look, 'Caleb and I have done well together, breeding and selling horses – all-purpose animals, the sort that can pull a carriage or draw a plough. We're almost partners now, though I worked for him as a paid hand at first. But Caleb had this odd notion that I must come back to Ireland, and set my affairs to rights. He said it never did any good to embark on a new life when there was unfinished business still to be done. He's like that, Caleb,' Gilbert said, looking at his sister earnestly, as though he very much wanted her to understand. 'He's like a father to me. I used to talk to him about Whitefield, and the way it was lost to us; and when I won that money, Caleb insisted that I should use it to come back here . . . ' He grinned rather sheepishly. 'Well, he was in a position to dictate terms, for I've a notion to wed his daughter.'

'Oh?'

'So here I am. Caleb thought I'd just come to settle that affair of the exciseman who was killed; but to tell you the truth, I was more interested in proving that Lord Vale cheated at cards.'

Caroline looked at him blankly. He smiled at her evident surprise, a grim twist of the lips. 'That surprises you, does it? Had it never occurred to you that Vale might have fuzzed the cards during that game with Father?'

'Never, Gil,' she said bluntly. 'There was never a whisper of it.'

He looked disappointed, but he shrugged his broad shoulders. 'Whispers can be hushed up. It stands to reason that Mannering and all those landowning nobs wouldn't want to stir up trouble for themselves by offending the great Earl of Vale.' He sounded bitter. 'I went to see old Mannering, and he told me to keep my mouth shut. He absolutely denied that there had been anything havey cavey about Vale's amazing run of good cards. I could see I wasn't going to get any help from him.'

'Sir Giles was at Whitefield when Father was playing Lord Vale,' said Caroline, shaking her head. 'If there had been anything wrong, he would have seen it.'

75

'Turned a blind eye to it, more like!' said Gilbert, bitterly. And before Caroline could say more, he added: 'But it makes no matter. I've found a better way of dealing with his fine lordship – and to line my pockets, at the same time.'

She looked at him doubtfully. 'Oh? This offer that Mr Rance made you?'

The young man said, 'Rance put me in the way of it, but my first piece of good luck was in meeting Slattery. I'd had my purse slit, and was in flat despair, when I came upon Slattery reeling along the waterfront. He'd been celebrating after fair day – you know how he likes a noggin or two – and when I told him of my trouble, he insisted on lending me some of the money he'd got from selling cattle. Poor old Slattery, he fell on my neck and wept to see me. So I saw him back to Whitefield. He was in a bad way, and it seemed the least I could do; and on the way back to town I saw Rance's carriage bowling along the coast road, and took a notion to milk that fat rascal of some of his ill-gotten gains.'

'Gilbert!' she exclaimed, between dismay and laughter. 'What a risk to take! Mr Rance might have shot you, or had you arrested.'

'Not he! He looked like a stuffed badger when I held my pistol to his ribs, and the two bully boys who are supposed to guard him came down off the box like frightened sheep. But he hadn't much money on him, more's the pity – and worse still, he recognized me. He gave me a sharp scold, which from a robber like Rance was hard to swallow, and sent me on my way empty-handed. He must have thought better of it, though, for next day he came to my lodgings.'

Caroline said nothing. She watched her twin's face while he told her of this second encounter with the agent, and felt a chill which had nothing to do with the sharp sea breeze at her back.

'Rance took me to that ruined chapel up there on the cliff,' Gilbert went on, wagging his head upwards to where this building stood, roofless and open to the skies, surrounded by gravestones of generations of Sweenys. 'It was eerie among

76

the gravestones, I may tell you, but not half as weird as what came next. We went down into the crypt, a small underground cavern where they used to hold secret masses in the old penal days. It was the strangest feeling, Car, talking with someone I couldn't see. It was just a voice, not much more than a whisper, which seemed to come from where the altar was. Rance warned me that it would be like that, so I just sat still as he'd told me, and only spoke when I had to.'

Caroline's eyes had widened with foreboding. Gilbert went on with his tale.

'Rance didn't give a name to that voice, but the other night people have a name for him. They call him the Serpent, after that sign he uses. And then,' Gilbert's voice sank lower, as though he were unconsciously copying the whispering voice in the crypt, 'then the Serpent said he'd help me to pay my way back to Boston. He offered me money to kill Lord Vale . . .' He saw the look on his sister's face, and added defensively, 'Don't look like that, Caroline! It's not like killing just anyone. Vale's our enemy, the villain who drove us out of Whitefield, and caused Father's death!' And when her expression did not change for the better, he added earnestly, 'And you needn't think there's much danger in it. Rance vouched for this Serpent fellow. He told me I couldn't go wrong, so long as I kept a still tongue in my head, and obeyed orders. What's more, Rance gave me a hundred guineas on account. The Serpent's orders, he said.'

Caroline did not know quite what to say. She knew that money was important to Gilbert. Even in their young, affluent days, her brother had been impatient of suggestions that he should study even minor or temporary economies. But even so, it seemed incredible that his need for gold was so urgent that he would agree to commit murder to get it. She said carefully, 'Why does the . . . the owner of this voice want Lord Vale killed?'

He shrugged his shoulders, annoyed at her question. He had lived for so long with the notion that the Earl of Vale was his prime enemy, that it seemed – or it had seemed until that moment – perfectly natural that others regarded him in the same light. 'How should I know why he wants me to kill him? It's damned convenient, at all events, for I was getting nowhere at all trying to prove that Vale cheated at cards. Mannering told me to go away and cool my head. He just refused to help, Caroline, for all that he professed to be Father's friend. So I'm not complaining now that the Serpent has offered to pay me three thousand guineas to do what I've been wanting to do these four years, or more!'

He saw that she was still regarding him in that grave, unsettling fashion. He said defensively, 'Caroline, I'll never come by that sort of money in the normal way! If I do what this Serpent fellow wants, I can pay my way back to New England, join Caleb on equal terms. After we are wed, Clemency and I might buy some land out west. There's grand, fertile country out there in what they call the Ohio valley . . .' He was visited by a new notion, and added generously, 'I'll tell you what, Caroline. I'll take you with me. Clemency is the sweetest creature. She'll be overjoyed if I bring her a new sister.'

She felt helpless, unable to reach him. She said soberly, 'You talk of that money as if it is already yours. What if you are caught trying to kill Lord Vale?'

'I shan't be caught.'

She said gravely and fearfully: 'Everyone will know it is you, Gilbert. Why, even Mr Rance told me that you had been threatening to kill Lord Vale. He was fearful for your safety.'

'Rance cares nothing for my safety!' retorted Gilbert furiously. Then he said more quietly, 'You don't think I'd shoot Vale at Mount Sweeny, do you? Give me the credit for a little sense. I'll be sent word when he's about to leave Lismore, and I mean to waylay him on the road. Vale never travels in a carriage if he can help it, but makes a habit of riding ahead on his own. So, you see . . . '

'Gilbert . . . ' she began, despairingly.

'Oh, cease your fretting!' he said, cutting her short. 'This Serpent and his men have got it all planned. I shall be on board a French ship and on the high seas within hours of doing their business.' He kicked at a pebble with his shining leather boot. 'The night people are all back in the district now, getting ready for the next run. All I'm waiting for now is to hear that Vale is setting out from Lismore.'

'Lord Vale is already at Mount Sweeny,' Caroline told him, rather grimly.

She had the satisfaction, if only a forlorn one, of seeing her brother go white with shock. So he was not so cool about doing this murder? She added quietly, 'I wish you would come and talk with his lordship. I don't know what to think of him, truly; but he is Jemima's father, and perhaps not as black as he is painted . . . ' She added, before he had time to argue, 'He rode in last night; and I met him and talked with him. What's more, I mistook him for one of your horrid night people.'

He stared at her blankly, and then gave vent to a nervous sputter of laughter. 'Trust you to do something idiotish, Caroline! How shocked Vale would have been, if he knew he'd been taken for a common free trader!'

'Oh, he knew,' said Caroline ruefully. 'I asked him to take a message to you.'

'The devil you did, Caroline!'

He sounded so alarmed and angry, that she felt obliged to explain how this mistake had come about. 'He was wearing a serpent ring, you see, and Mr Rance told me that the night people always carry that sign on their persons.'

He gripped her arm. 'What did you tell him?'

She did not answer at once. She could feel the tremors of his fright and fury pulsing through his tightly clutching fingers. She said quietly, 'Lord Vale does not know that you are my brother. He chose to think that you were my lover, and I let him think it.'

He tried to digest this, to fathom what it might mean. He said with some severity, 'I wish you had not interfered. You should not be here.' Then he added, 'How long does Vale mean to stay at Mount Sweeny?'

'I don't know, Gilbert.' She eyed him bleakly. 'You cannot mean to go on with it. I wish you would be sensible, and have nothing more to do with the night people, or their . . . their leader.'

He sighed sharply, and took his hand from her arm. 'If only I could afford to . . . ' He looked at Caroline, and said in a resentful tone, 'I wish you would try to understand. Why should you make such a pother about my wanting to punish Vale? He had no scruples about ruining our father. And besides, this whole district would be better off without him. He's the worst sort of absentee landlord – and that fat villain Rance is hated everywhere. Such people ought not to be allowed to flourish, for they'll be the ruin of this country . . . '

He broke off, for it did not seem that his twin sister was much impressed by what he was saying. He added seriously, 'I know what I'm talking about, Car. I've been riding in the hill country between here and Lismore, and I've seen people living in hovels you would not wish to house a pig in.'

'I know,' she said gently, 'But . . . '

He cut her short. 'Now, don't try to tell me that Lord Vale is not aware of how his tenants are treated . . . that Rance does things in his name and that he knows nothing about it! Vale is to blame for putting Rance where he is, and if he knows nothing about his agent canting the rents, and enclosing common land that people have grazed and dug by right since time began, he damned well ought to know it!'

Caroline nodded. 'I know, Gilbert. But what would you achieve by trying to kill Lord Vale, now he is come into Ireland at last? You'd do better to come and tell him what you've just told me.'

Gilbert gave vent to a disgusted sound. 'Talk? He'd not listen to me. Such people believe what they want to believe, and see only what they want to see. I tell you, Caroline,' he went on earnestly, 'the whole system in Ireland is rotten. Vale and Rance and their like would be given short shrift in

New England. We believe there that no man should pay taxes without a proper say in how the money shall be used. In fact, men have died defending that belief – better men than Vale.' He drew a breath, and came down off his high plane of oratory, saying with a reluctant grin, 'Come, Caroline! You're just being contrary. Don't try to pretend that it would break your heart if Vale came to harm!'

She said evenly, 'No, Gilbert. I won't pretend that; but even Lord Vale has a right to speak in his own defence.'

He opened his mouth to answer, but seemed to check himself, for all he said was: 'I need that money, Car, and I've undertaken to kill him. I cannot back down now. I've entered into a business arrangement, and I must keep my word.'

'Better to break your promise, surely, than to be hanged as a murderer?'

He did not speak for a moment, and when he did, he said urgently and coaxingly, 'Caroline, listen! Don't you want to come to America with me? It's a fine beautiful place, with land and opportunities for a man with gold in his pocket. Don't you want to start a new life, to wear pretty clothes again, to find yourself a husband?' He frowned at her, noticing consciously for the first time that she was looking drab and worn, anything but charming, with a grey bonnet that made her look older than her years. He felt that it was somehow spiritless of her to look like that. He said scornfully, 'Surely you don't want to spend the rest of your life being a drudge in other people's houses?'

'No, I don't want that, but—'

'Then you must help me to come near Lord Vale. You'll be helping yourself to escape, Car. As soon as I have dealt with him, we'll be off.'

'No!' Her tone was one of violent repudiation. 'No, I won't do it, Gilbert, and if you've any sense at all, you'll find another way of paying your passage back to America. It's one thing to engage in free trading, but murder is quite another matter . . . '

He glared at her. 'You know nothing about it, Car. Free

81

trading's hardly what you'd call a gentlemanly occupation. There's not many of the night people who would think twice before doing murder, if it suited them.'

Caroline thought of Miss Prendergast, and said curiously, 'Jemima says that her last governess was taken by the night people. She went after some intruders, and never came back. Could your friends have done her a mischief?'

He looked at her blankly. 'I know nothing about a governess. It's outside of enough that you should pretend to be one, Car! I wish you'd never come here. If you're not going to help, you'd best go back to that seminary you were in.'

'I cannot do that. Mrs O'Mahoney would never take me back, after I left her so suddenly.'

'Well, there must be other places . . . ' He broke off, eyeing his sister doubtfully. He wished that Rance had left her in Dublin. Come to think of it, it was extraordinary that the agent should have brought her to Mount Sweeny. He said imploringly, 'Please, Caroline, don't you see that your being at Mount Sweeny might ruin all. I am committed to do this for the Serpent . . . '

'Then, I am just as committed to stay at Mount Sweeny, and to do my best to prevent you, Gilbert,' she said firmly, wondering at the same time how in the world she was to achieve this aim. She added imploringly, 'Only say that you will give up this horrid, dangerous task, and I'll promise to do everything else you want!'

But he merely grunted, pulled his watch from his waistcoat pocket and looked at it. That watch and chain had belonged to his late father, and Slattery had pressed it into his hand. The old man had saved it when all the rest of Colonel Morrisey's effects had been sold or taken in charge by the new owners; and he had kept it hidden, giving it into Gilbert's hand only weeks before. It still gave Gilbert a warm feeling of pleasure to handle it.

He frowned at his sister uncertainly. It had given him a jolt to learn that the Earl of Vale had actually arrived at Mount Sweeny. It was one thing, he found, to promise to kill an enemy he had never seen. During his four years of exile, he had come to think of Vale as the author of all his misfortunes. But he saw, all of a sudden, that the Earl of his imaginings had been a token figure, more of a symbol of injustice and absenteeism than a flesh and blood man. Caroline's horrified reaction to what he meant to do had succeeded in awaking some uncomfortable qualms.

But there was no time to dwell on such things. He had an appointment which he dared not miss. 'See here, Caroline,' he said hastily, 'I cannot stay. I wish you would go away from Mount Sweeny. You'll do nothing but harm, if you try to interfere.' And without waiting to hear what she had to say in reply, he walked away down the shore.

He found Rance sitting in his room. The agent was comfortably ensconsed by the fire, a tankard on a table beside him. When Gilbert came in, he turned his head and said sourly, 'You're late. I've been sitting here half an hour or more.'

Gilbert crossed the room without speaking and poured himself a tot of brandy. He felt in need of it. He tossed it down.

The agent said, 'No wonder you've been heard talking foolishly, if you've been drinking that stuff, Mr Gilbert.' He added, before Gilbert could make any retort: 'I've got news for you. I've come to say that Lord Vale is now arrived at Mount Sweeny. That's put paid to your plan to waylay him on the road. However, it should be possible to come at him as he rides about the estate; and it will make it all the easier for us to get you away afterwards.' The agent saw that Gilbert was frowning, and hastened to explain his meaning. 'The next run will take place at the dark of the moon – in less than ten days. It will depend on the weather and the tide, of course. The Frenchies will come inshore in the night, and they've already agreed to take you on board with the rest of the cargo.'

Gilbert set his glass down on the mantelshelf with a click.

83

He said curtly: 'Rance, I've been thinking. I cannot do it.'

The agent sat where he was, his eyes on Gilbert's troubled, handsome face. Gilbert found this lack of response unnerving. He said rather too loudly, 'You must not suppose that I am afraid to kill Lord Vale, or that I hate him any less than I did . . .' He broke off, and added awkwardly, 'I've just come from seeing Caroline.'

'Ah.' The agent rubbed his hands together, and looked satisfied. 'I thought that was it. And did she try to persuade you to go back to America? I told her to do so.'

'Told her?' Gilbert's voice was indignant, but in truth he was glad of this small diversion. 'It's none of your affair to tell my sister what to say to me, Rance. In fact, you'd no right to bring her to Mount Sweeny at all.' He frowned down into the agent's face, and added curiously, 'Why in the world did you bring Caroline here, Rance? She had some rubbishing notion that you brought her here on my account. Of course I told her that it was no such thing . . . '

The agent smiled, pursing his lips together and looking smug. 'Your sister was right, in a way. Mind you, I needed her to replace the other governess; but I'd an idea that Miss Morrisey would prove doubly useful, and I'm already being proved right.'

Gilbert saw no reason for the agent to look pleased with himself. He said abruptly, 'Look, Rance. Stop talking in riddles about my sister, and attend to what I say. I cannot kill Lord Vale. You'll have to tell that Serpent fellow that I've changed my mind.'

The agent continued to look quietly satisfied, though he made a reproving clicking noise with his tongue. 'It's not like you to turn down a chance of earning three thousand pounds, Mr Gilbert.'

Gilbert moved jerkily across the room, and said, 'I don't want to turn it down, of course: but Caroline was so upset at the notion of my doing this murder . . . '

'Naturally she would be,' said the agent smoothly. 'But then, she is a female, and females are always squeamish. It was uncommonly foolish of you to tell her what you meant to do, Mr Gilbert.'

'If you had not brought Caroline to Mount Sweeny, I'd have had no opportunity to tell her anything,' retorted Gilbert with considerable resentment. 'Far from being useful to you, Rance, it's my sister's presence that has overset all our plans. Even if I did try to shoot Vale, Caroline has threatened to stop me. She'll put Vale on his guard, at the very least. D'you call that being useful?'

The agent looked at Gilbert, no longer smiling, and said with deliberation: 'If your sister tries to interfere, it will be the worse for her. The master does not brook interference. Nor,' added Mr Rance solemnly, 'nor will you be allowed to back away from your commitment, Mr Gilbert. With your sister at Mount Sweeny, you have no choice but to perform your task. No choice at all.' And when Gilbert gazed down at him in slowly dawning comprehension, he added in case Gilbert had not fully understood, 'The last governess met with a sad accident, you know. If you try to go back on your word, Mr Gilbert, I could not answer for your sister's safety.'

Gilbert opened his mouth to speak, but no words came. He knew something of the Serpent's way with erring members of the organization. There had been some ugly tales. He made an effort to focus his mind on what Rance had said about that last governess, and said rather shakily, 'Caroline said that the night people might have done away with that last woman. Did they do so?'

'No such thing,' replied the agent, shaking his balding head. 'It was an accident. The silly female fell down the cellar steps, as it happened.' He saw that Gilbert looked relieved, and hastened to add, 'But don't run away with the notion that you can afford to play us false, my boy. I brought your sister here because, with things as they stand, I could not afford questions, or anything in the nature of a search of the cellars. But now that she's at Mount Sweeny, you must see that she would be in a vulnerable position, if . . . if the master decided to punish you for backsliding.'

85

'Damn you, Rance! Just you leave Caroline out of this!'

The agent shrank back in his chair, as Gilbert lunged towards him. But he said steadily enough: 'I've no wish to harm Miss Morrisey, my boy. She'll be safe enough, just so long as you continue to carry out your present . . . commitment.'

Gilbert turned away, as though he could no longer bear to look at the agent's complacently smiling face. He said, after a pause: 'I see that I've no choice in the matter. But how do I know that Caroline will be safe? She'll have to be got away, after I've killed Vale.'

The agent shrugged his heavy shoulders. 'I'll try to arrange that she can go with you on the French ship. You may leave that to me, Mr Gilbert.' He lumbered to his feet, and said briskly, 'You are to leave this inn tonight. I'll pay your shot here. All you've to do is to take your coat and your hat and go out of the door. Mick's waiting for you on the street corner.'

'How do I know you'll pay my shot, you old niggard?' demanded Gilbert, disliking the idea of being taken in custody by the night people, and having to leave his comfortable lodgings. 'It'd be just like you to forget to pay it, and leave me to be locked up for debt!'

The agent shrugged his shoulders for the second time. 'You may rest easy on that head, Mr Gilbert,' he said smoothly. 'We mean to take the greatest care of you. Mick has strict orders not to let you out of his sight.'

Eight

'I DON'T LIKE IT, SWEENY,' said Sir Giles Mannering, shifting awkwardly from one foot to the other as he warmed himself in front of the great, blazing hall fire at Mount Sweeny. 'It's more than four years since I came under this roof; and I swore at the time I'd never do so again.'

'I am aware of that,' said Richard Sweeny gravely and a little ruefully, 'and I'd not ask you to do so now, if it were not for this state of emergency. Don't think I'm unaware of what a generous concession you are making, sir, in agreeing to call on my brother in this way. I am indeed sensible of it, and believe me, I'm exceedingly grateful.'

'Save your gratitude until we see what comes of this meeting,' growled the other. 'If there ever is a meeting, that is.'

Richard turned his head and glanced up the main staircase once more. They had announced their arrival some thirty minutes since, sending word to the Earl that they would be obliged if he would see them. The word came back that his lordship was changing his clothes, but would attend them presently. Sir Giles had not been best pleased by this; and was showing signs of marked reluctance to stay and wait any longer. He had declined all offers of refreshment, and it did not look as if he was going to be in any mood to make concessions, if and when the Earl condescended to make his appearance.

Richard tried again. 'At least allow me to take your coat, Sir Giles,' he said in his quiet sensible voice. 'I can see it's positively steaming. Much best to let one of Vale's people

87

dry it for you. Lady Mannering will give me a fine dressing if I allow you to take cold. She'll be displeased with me already for delaying your return home after the parade.'

The older man smiled reluctantly, the first sign of thaw since he had allowed himself to be led through the door of Mount Sweeny. 'You know very well, Richard, that you can blarney my wife into doing just whatever seems best to you. Are you hoping to turn me up sweet, as you manage to do with nearly all the females of your acquaintance? You know, Richard, it's always been a bit of a puzzle to me that you've never taken a wife to yourself. There's a score of females on the catch for you. Have none of them ever taken your fancy?'

Richard's dark brows rose fractionally, but he said merely, 'You flatter me, sir. Take off that wet coat, I beg of you. I can only beg your further indulgence for my graceless brother. I'd go and fetch him out of his dressing room, if I thought it would serve; but I've a notion it would only make him dally longer over his toilet.'

'Ha!' The magistrate muttered something uncomplimentary about his lordship's foppish ways; but he did relent enough to hand his damp overcoat to a waiting footman, and he went with Richard into the bookroom and accepted a tankard of home-brewed. 'Damme if I understand how the fellow can spend so long furbishing himself up!' he exclaimed testily. 'What does he think he is, a man milliner? I've no patience with this sort of dandyism, Sweeny, and find it perfectly ridiculous.'

But oddly enough, Sir Giles found nothing to laugh about in the Earl's appearance when he joined them some short time later. He was dressed with elegance, certainly, and there was a foaming of exquisite lace at his throat and wrists. But there was nothing effeminate in the man's bearing, and he wore none of the fobs and seals and fol-de-rols that the magistrate had rather expected. His only jewelry was an eyeglass on a black silk riband, and the great gold Sweeny ring, which every Earl of Vale had worn for as long as anyone could remember.

'Well, Vale,' said the magistrate, bowing coldly. 'This brother of yours says you're willing to give us your support. We need money and we need men, as no doubt he has explained to you. Is it true that you are prepared to give us these things? And if so, why did Rance assure us that he was forbidden to do so?'

Vale's long ugly face might have been graven in stone. He said merely, 'Did Rance tell you who had forbidden him?'

The magistrate, a grizzled, burly gentleman with a craggy face and beetling brows, said evenly, 'He gave us to understand that it was yourself who had imposed this ban.' And when the Earl neither denied nor agreed to this suggestion, Sir Giles said gruffly, 'I tell you bluntly, my lord, I don't trust that man Rance. I don't trust him, or like him.'

'Why not?'

'Why not?' echoed the other, rather taken aback by having his bluntness returned in kind. 'Several reasons, my lord. Rance is said to take bribes, fawns upon his betters and bullies those who are weaker than he. But apart from all that, I've got my suspicions that he's behind a good deal of the gun-running and trafficking with the French, and other such treasonable on-goings. Rance is deep in with those villains that call themselves the night people, or I miss my guess.'

Richard's dark head came round with a jerk. Vale's long face showed no emotion. He was wearing a hooded, closed-in look. 'Go on, Mannering,' he said softly. 'What else can you tell us about the night people? And why are you so sure that Rance is one of them? Can you prove it?'

The magistrate agreed with some reluctance that he had no direct proof. 'I just mistrust that bowing, fawning way he has, and wonder what lies beneath it. And another thing, I asked to search the cellars here at Mount Sweeny. You should have seen the way he pokered up, my lord. He refused point blank. Said you had expressly forbidden him to show anyone the cellars.'

'Very proper,' said Vale coolly. 'Rance had no authority to let anyone down there. Our cellars at Mount Sweeny have always been closely guarded, Mannering. Our ancestors would turn in their graves, if they thought we were letting strangers poke about in them. Isn't that so, Richard?'

Richard grinned faintly before turning back to watch the magistrate's face. Sir Giles favoured Vale with a brief wintry smile. It was, after all, common knowledge that the Sweeny fortunes had been founded on wrecking, piracy and free trading. There were said to be a regular honeycomb of passages and caverns under the cliffs that surrounded Mount Sweeny cove. Some were so secret that they were said to be known only to the head of the Sweeny family; the secrets being handed on by the reigning Earl to his heir, and to none other. Sir Giles said in his brusque way, 'Look here, Vale. It's not kegs of brandy I'm looking for. I can turn a blind eye to that sort of harmless contraband as well as anyone—'

Vale said evenly, 'What do you expect to find, sir?'

Sir Giles said slowly, 'I'm not very sure. There may be arms stored there, my lord; though it seems likely that the night people would move these inland without delay. I hope, rather more realistically, to uncover some evidence that the cellars are being used, and that the night people have chosen the Mount Sweeny cove as their gateway to the sea. If I find such proof, my lord, I shall at least know where to set my lookouts.' The magistrate would have given a good deal, at that moment, to have had an idea of what thoughts were passing through the Earl's mind. But there was still no sign of emotion on his bony face. One eyelid drooped a shade lower than the other, and if anything, he had the air of a man who was half asleep. It crossed Sir Giles's mind, at that point, that it was no wonder he looked tired. Richard had told him how his half-brother had ridden through the storm on the previous night. Well, sleepy or not, the magistrate meant to leave the Earl in no doubt as to how things stood. He said bluntly, 'I don't mind telling you, Vale, that there are a dangerous number of discontented people on your estates. If the French come, as they very well may, there would be some who would look on them not as invaders, but as deliverers; for there have been some ugly happenings lately. Rance has served eviction orders on a score of families who have found it impossible to pay their dues. And all this in your name, my lord. This, you may say, is your affair. What concerns me is that, if the French use Mount Sweeny as their gateway to Ireland, they'll have a ready-made army of supporters awaiting them.'

'Are you suggesting,' Vale enquired acidly, 'that Mount Sweeny is unique in this respect? What about your own tenants, Mannering? Are there no malcontents on your property?'

'I am only suggesting, my lord, that Rance's methods have greatly exacerbated and inflamed what has always been a problem. If he were my agent, I'd look very closely into how he has been conducting himself.'

Lord Vale said coolly, 'You may rest assured that I shall do so, sir: but I believe I shall also do so in my own time, and in my own way. Not under duress.' Sir Giles drew in his breath, misliking the Earl's tone, but before he could say anything, the Earl looked at his brother, and said, 'Shall we let Mannering into the cellars, dear boy? What do you think?'

Richard did not answer immediately. He said in his deep, sensible voice, 'I've also had my eye on these night people. I think Mannering may be right. They may very well have been bringing in guns, and ammunition, but I'll still lay you odds that the main bulk of their contraband is exporting woollen cloth and goods from our Irish manufactories, and bringing in brandy and wines and the like. Trafficking with the French has only lately become a dirty word, Sir Giles: and however much we may call it treason, to these traders it has long been their main means of making a living – and more necessary, being Irishmen, their sport. You know that, do you not, Hugo?' Richard grinned suddenly at his elegant brother. 'Confess, it was your main entertainment when you were at Mount Sweeny as a lad?'

There was a faint answering gleam in Vale's hooded eyes.

'Of course. I prided myself that I was O'Grady's right hand man. I was small for my age in those days, sir, and could shin up any mast like a monkey,' he explained to the magistrate who was frowning at him in a puzzled fashion. 'And I had my uses as a decoy. You know the kind of thing, lighting bonfires on Sweeny's head to draw the excisemen off while the cargo was run in past the harbour wall. Oh, I'll vouch for it being sport, Mannering, and it was well worth the thrashings it earned me from my father. Sport, indeed,' he added reminiscing, turning his eyes to the window where the setting sun had turned the sea to molten bronze. 'I've never found anything to match the excitement of rounding Sweeny's head with a full cargo, with the lights of the exciseman's cutter only fifty yards behind. O'Grady was a matchless seaman. He outwitted them every time.'

'Not quite every time, my lord,' said the magistrate drily. 'O'Grady ended up on the gallows, and such of his fellows as escaped the same fate have left the district. No, my lord, O'Grady lost the last round, fair and square.'

Vale's long, pale face was a haughty mask. 'He was informed against. If that's your notion of fair and square, Mannering, it is not mine.'

'See here, my lord,' said the magistrate, 'we are straying from the matter in hand. These night people are what concerns me now; and they're nothing like the traders you knew as a boy. Sometimes I wish we hadn't allowed the excise authorities to deal so harshly with the old lot; for it left a gap, and these new men who have come are of quite a different cut. They'll stop at nothing. Their leader, the Serpent, has somehow got the whole countryside in thrall, and I confess I'm at my wits' end. That's why I'd like fine to search your cellars here, my lord. Rance has the keys to those cellars. He claims to be the only person who has, apart from your lordship, that is.'

'You think Rance is the leader of the night people?' Vale's tone was sceptical. 'You'll need proof if you mean to accuse him, you know.'

92

The magistrate returned the Earl's cold look with an unflinching one of his own. 'I've wondered more than once if it could be Rance, my lord. The Serpent's activities do seem to bring us back to this district, time and time again. And here we come to a blank wall. No one knows anything. Nobody has seen or heard tell of the Serpent; though at the sight of that little medal they all carry on their persons, they freeze like rabbits in front of a stoat. No, I don't think it's Rance, but I believe your agent may know something of these people, something that the others do not . . . '

Vale was looking down rather pensively at the serpent ring on his finger. 'So we think the leader of the night people has some connection with Mount Sweeny, do we? Or is it merely that you hope to find this is so?'

'I want to find this Serpent, my lord, and it matters little to me where or how I find him. I must find him, if we are to root out the poison in our midst.' He saw Vale's crooked brows go up, and he said seriously, 'There's more to it than just free trading and running guns, though those things are bad enough, and my main concern at present. This Serpent has other . . . other interests. Blackmail, extortion, to name but two. There's a ruthless and dedicated mind at work at the centre of all this, my lord. If I could exact the same loyalty and obedience from my own men, I'd be mighty proud of myself.' He sighed, and scratched his head. 'There must be some chink in his armour, some weak link in the chain. Give me leave to search your cellars, my lord. I'll not hound your agent without proof of his guilt, I promise you.'

The Earl yawned, and began playing with some dice, throwing them deftly onto a small table at his elbow, and picking them up again between his long, white fingers. 'You relieve me, Mannering. It would not suit my convenience to have my agent clapped up within hours of my arrival.'

'Suit your—' The magistrate turned to watch his host, all his earlier prejudices returning in a rush, 'I'll take leave to remind you, my lord, we are at war with France. The national interest cannot always be set aside to suit your convenience!'

'No indeed,' sighed Vale, throwing the dice once again, 'the whole thing is a dead bore, one cannot deny. Still, it does give energetic fellows like Richard a chance to dress up and play the hero, does it not? I've never seen the dear boy look more flourishing.'

'Hugo!' said Richard, at the same time forestalling the magistrate's indignant riposte by laying a restraining hand on his shoulder. 'Try to be serious for just a few minutes together, I beg of you! I've prevailed on Sir Giles to come here, very much against his will, because I believe there is a good chance, now, for you to give your aid and support to this national effort, and thus to be reinstated with your neighbours.'

The magistrate said curtly, 'It's plain to me, Vale hasn't the least interest in any such thing. He's been playing with us, all this while. Well, my lord?' he said, in a challenging and far from friendly tone, 'am I not right? You don't give a rap for what your neighbours think of you . . . ' He broke off, remembering something, and added with deliberation, 'I'll tell you something you should know, Vale. Young Morrisey's back in the country. He came to my house a while back, asking to see me. He'd just landed, come back from America, and was harping on that gaming session you had with his father. Gilbert wanted to know if I thought you might have cheated?'

'Gilbert?' The Earl smiled faintly, as though something had amused him. 'And what did you tell him, Mannering? Were you able to give him the evidence he sought?'

'Damme!' exclaimed the older man, grimly amused in his turn. 'Does nothing shake that uncaring look you wear? If you must know, I told him that I had been present throughout that damnable game, and had no fault to find with the way it was played.' His smile had quite gone. 'I sent him about his business, advised him to look to his own affairs. He was in trouble before he skipped off to America, and even though they all said the man Gilbert killed had been the aggressor, the matter was never sorted out.' Sir Giles looked

94

at Vale very directly, and said, 'Gilbert means to come and see you, my lord. He wants to have the matter out.'

'Dear me. Do you think he will call me out?' sighed the Earl. 'How tiresome that would be!'

'God knows what he may do,' returned the other soberly. 'You must understand that Gilbert Morrisey is bitter, after all that took place, and I'd not put it past him to do you a mischief.'

Vale nodded, his face as unreadable as ever. 'I can certainly understand that he might wish to. What I find harder to fathom, though, is why Gilbert Morrisey's sister should be employed here as my small daughter's governess? Very much against her will, if I read her rightly, too.'

Sir Giles Mannering looked greatly astonished. He gazed into Vale's crooked, closed-in face for several seconds, before saying in a wondering tone: 'It stands to reason it would be against her will, my lord. Caroline refused point blank to let me write to you on her behalf after Peter Morrisey died. Said she wanted nothing to do with you, or your charity. Caroline is Gilbert's twin, and to my mind, the girl is worth two of her brother.' He appeared to be struggling with his thoughts, and presently said dazedly, 'Never tell me that Caroline Morrisey's playing at being a governess?'

'You couldn't have described her rôle better,' said Vale drily. 'Playing at governess, that's what she's doing. What intrigues me is what she means to do here?'

Richard said indignantly, 'You've got windmills in your head, Hugo. Miss Caroline is just what she seems to be. Rance engaged her. He's befriended her before, I believe.'

'Ha!' said Sir Giles grimly. 'That rascal Rance never does anything without some benefit to himself.'

Richard was still watching Vale, and was goaded into saying with a certain warmth, 'Miss Caroline is a nice, respectable young woman, with no nonsense about her, Hugo. She's clever with Jemima, too, which is more than you could say for that other snivelling woman. And . . . and Miss Caroline's not even pretty.'

'No? Would that detract from her respectability?' demanded the Earl, his amber eyes suddenly alight with laughter. 'I don't want to destroy your illusions, Sir Galahad, but you should have seen her as she was last night. All silken hair and shining eyes in the candlelight; an odd sort of governess, by any standards. But she wasn't trying to play a part, then ... ' He turned to Sir Giles, who was staring at the two brothers, feeling at a loss. 'Now, Mannering. You are used to sifting evidence. Why should this young woman deliberately try to make herself look drab and insignificant? Does that not suggest she is up to something?'

Sir Giles suddenly felt himself on firmer ground. 'I can vouch for Caroline Morrisey's honesty and good sense, my lord.'

'There!' said Richard, mildly triumphant. 'What did I tell you? Miss Caroline is innocent. I'd stake my life on it.'

'Have it your own way, Galahad,' murmured the Earl, unimpressed. 'For my part, I find it wiser to suspend judgement. I never judge a female by what she seems to be.'

'Now, see here, Vale!' The magistrate was growing impatient with this irrelevant talk. He would like to have taken time to see the daughter of his old friend, but there were more pressing matters to be attended to. 'Do you mean to let me into your cellars, my lord, or do you not? That's what matters now.'

It was only when the search of the cellars had taken place, and the magistrate had ridden away, disappointed that there was nothing more incriminating in those deep, labyrinthine corridors beneath the castle than a quantity of excellent wine, that Vale said suddenly:

'That Morrisey female was looking for her brother. She thinks he's with the night people. I don't think Mannering is aware of that.'

Richard stared. 'What are you saying, Hugo?'

The Earl said slowly: 'If he really means to harm me, the

96

wench is in a prime position to help him, is she not?'

Richard shook his dark head. 'I just can't believe that Miss Caroline would be party to any violence. She's such a gentle, level-headed person.' But there was a look about the set of Vale's thin-lipped mouth that made him add rather anxiously, 'Treat her gently, Hugo, I beg of you. You should hear how they speak of her at Whitefield. They all love their Miss Caroline . . . '

'So they know she's here, do they?'

'These things get around. All the more reason to treat her well, Hugo. It will do you no good to have it said that you'd mistreated yet another member of the Morrisey family.'

Vale laughed softly. 'Still trying to reinstate me, dear boy? What an optimist you are! Well, do not fret. I mean to learn more about what your Miss Caroline is up to before I pass judgement upon her. I can hardly do that if I lock her up on bread and water. One more thing. She wants to keep it a secret that she's here to meet her brother. We'll play along with her on that score, I think.'

Nine

OH, SO YOU'VE BROUGHT FERDY to meet my papa?'
cried Jemima joyfully. 'May I hold him? Look, Papa, isn't he an
angel?'

Caroline handed the wriggling puppy into Jemima's arms,
smiling rather ruefully. She had meant to be well out of the
way before Vale and his little daughter came back from their
morning ride, but had been caught crossing the hall. 'Be
careful, Jemima,' she said. 'His feet are still wet.'

The Earl tickled one of the puppy's ears with a long, white
finger. The serpent ring gleamed on his hand. The puppy
yawned widely. 'Bored with life already, Prince Ferdinand?
It'll be worse as you grow older. Besides, you shouldn't do it.
Yawning in company is bad manners, I may tell you. You
should bear that in mind, Jemima.'

'Strange advice from you, Hugo,' said Richard who was
with them. He smiled at Caroline, as though inviting her to
share his amusement. 'You know, ma'am, far from practising
what he preaches, my brother has just come from Lismore.
And there, rather than allowing himself to be bored for an
instant, he just walked out, leaving our poor sister to make
what excuses she could. It is beyond me to understand how
he dares to preach manners to anyone. Certainly not to
Jemima, when you are so well qualified to do it.'

Caroline quelled an urge to laugh, and said: 'His lordship
seems more concerned with the puppy's manners, sir. I
admit they leave a little to be desired.'

98

'Quite so,' agreed Vale smoothly. 'I should not, of course, dream of trying to tell Miss Caroline how to go on. It would be most improper.' Caroline gave an involuntary choke of laughter, and he looked at the puppy and added lazily, 'So this is the tinkers' cur? Have you been presented to Jemima's new love, Richard?'

'Certainly,' retorted Richard. 'I was here on the day he was rescued from the sea.'

'And outfaced Mrs Datchet when she tried to forbid us to keep him,' put in Caroline. 'Mr Richard was really most kind, my lord. Jemima and I are in his debt.'

Vale smiled at her crookedly, and said, raising his eyeglass and turning to Richard, 'I should have known you had a hand in it, dear boy, when they told me the puppy was called Ferdinand. I'd forgotten . . . '

'Forgotten what, Papa?' demanded Jemima curiously. She had been raining kisses on the small dog's damp fur, and had so far taken little part in the talk going on around her. She repeated: 'What had you forgotten about, Papa? Calling him Prince Ferdinand was nothing to do with Uncle Richard. He comes out of a play called *The Tempest*.'

'Quite so,' agreed Vale, still surveying his brother. 'Your Uncle Richard and your mama and all their chattering friends were acting *The Tempest* when I was last here. It was just before she was killed.' He flicked the child's thin cheek with a careless finger, and added, 'Your mother had a notion to have you for Ariel, but at barely five years old, you were too young for it.'

'Oh?' Jemima had very little recollection of her mother, so naturally any new thing intrigued her. She said slowly, 'I remember Mama in a play. She wore a green dress and her hair all long . . . '

Richard chuckled. 'Amazing, isn't it, how even the youngest females seem to notice what other women wear! I swear I never do; and as to recalling what someone wore four years since, I fear I am blind in that respect.'

'There are times when blindness could well be counted as

99

a boon,' said the Earl disagreeably. Still using his eyeglass, he had turned to stare at Caroline, who was wearing her outdoor clothes. 'I do not think I have ever seen anything worse than that bonnet, ma'am. You look a fright. Worse than you did in that shocking cap yesterday. Wherever did you find such a garment?'

Jemima let out a squawk of laughter at this, and Caroline said crossly, 'You don't suppose I wear this thing because I like it, do you, my lord?' She put a hand to her hated grey bonnet, and added, 'It happens to be the only one I own. My late employer gave it to me.'

'Good God!' said the Earl, staring. 'Then, as your present employer I reserve the right to give you another as soon as may be. I suppose that there is a milliner somewhere to be found? You may enquire about it.'

'Thank you,' said Caroline. She did not in the least want to laugh, but it was hard not to. The Earl looked so disdainful, as though it really gave him pain to see her in such an ugly hat. 'But I shall do no such thing, of course. It would not do for you to buy me things to wear. It would not be right.'

'Oh, and do you think that would stop me doing it?' he enquired in a dulcet tone, which further eroded her precarious composure. 'What an odd notion you have of me, my dear.'

She looked up at him, then, her grey-green eyes brimming with amusement. She really could not help it, with Richard Sweeny looking shocked, and Jemima staring at her in a puzzled way. It was too much! Meeting Vale's glance, she thought he knew very well that she would dearly love to have something new and pretty to wear; knew, too, that she could not accept it from his hands. She said in a shaking voice, 'I'm sure it would not deter you, my lord. If you decide to spend your money on a hat for me, I cannot stop you. But it would be a sad waste. I would not wear it.'

'Why not?'

'Why not?' She echoed his question, copying the mocking

100

inflection of his voice. 'Give yourself the indulgence of a little thought, my lord. Mrs Datchet and your whole household would be utterly scandalized. I shudder to think what they would say!'

'I never bother with what people say,' he said, sounding bored.

'Now that,' said Richard, 'is the first true word you have spoken among all this nonsense. Don't pay any heed to my brother, Miss Caroline. He's a shocking fellow.'

It was natural that Vale's unexpected arrival had a marked effect upon the entire household. A leisurely place before, there was a change in the tempo of the house, a new briskness, a hum of excitement and zeal among all the Earl's many retainers. There were constant comings and goings, sounds of carriage wheels, voices in the hall. It was said that the Earl had agreed to support the new Volunteer regiment, and meant to supply uniforms and equipment for up to forty men from Mount Sweeny. There were hopes that his lordship himself would take command of this platoon; but, it was found that this task was going to fall on Richard Sweeny's capable shoulders.

'I might have known it,' said Mrs Datchet, who, since discovering that the new governess was the daughter of the late Colonel Morrisey of Whitefield, had unbent amazingly. 'I sometimes wonder what his lordship would do without Mister Richard to stand at his back, and keep watch and ward. After her late ladyship was killed, you know, it was Mister Richard who persuaded his lordship to leave the district for a while until the fuss had died down. There were many that tried to say that his lordship had contrived the accident that killed her. Mister Richard was in a state about it, Miss Morrisey; you've no idea. Came to me, on the afternoon of her ladyship's funeral, looking grey as a stone. "Datchet," he said to me, "Datchet! You must help me. See to it that none of the maids go tattling about what they

101

heard, or saw! You and I know that his lordship is innocent, but there'd be many who might not be so sure." '

Caroline listened to these revelations, and to others; not knowing quite what to make of them. One thing was certain, however. Whatever people might say about Vale, however they might tell tales of his heavy drinking, his freakish humours and unreasonable demands; they all took a passionate interest in every single thing that he did. There was a good deal of pleasurable surmising about Mr Rance. It was said that Lord Vale had spoken to him for fully half an hour, and that the agent had left the house, looking as though the interview had been anything but to his liking. Caroline was ill-natured enough to share the general hope that Mr Rance had been brought to book, for once. She liked the man little enough on her own account, and had since heard tales of his rapacity and uncaring conduct that made her like him still less. She hoped, when the Earl had seen how things stood on his Irish estates, he might even consider looking for a more humane man to act as his agent. Surely even the most uncaring landlord would notice the tumbledown state of so many of the farm buildings, workers' hovels with rotting thatch, the white-faced children and the sullen looks of his tenantry; the deserted houses and broken jetty at Sweeny's Port, which had once been a thriving fishing community?

'Get up, Juliet!' said Vale, crossing the floor of Caroline's bedchamber and flinging back the curtains from the tall windows. It was still barely light. She blinked at him owlishly, holding the bedcovers up to her chin. 'Get up. We're going riding on the shore. Jemima is half dressed already.'

Caroline sat up, still clutching the sheets up to her chin, and said severely: 'You can't come in here, my lord. Please go, and I'll bring Jemima down to you.'

'Jemima can see to herself. I told you, you are coming with us. I want to watch the sunrise from the cliffs over Sweeny's Port.'

102

'I . . . I cannot ride with you,' she said crossly. 'For one thing, I've no suitable clothes to ride in. Please go away, my lord. You must not come bursting in like this.'

'Must not?' he echoed, his brows lifting in sudden hauteur, so like Jemima that it made it harder to go on being indignant. 'And who are you, Miss Caroline, to tell me what I must not do?'

She said quietly, 'Please go away, my lord.'

He smiled at her, his eyes travelling over her sleep-flushed face and streaming hair, resting on the fingers which were grasping the sheets so tightly. He said: 'Don't you want to come riding with me, Juliet? I'll bring you a riding dress, if you'll stop being missish and promise to put it on. Jemima is counting on your coming with us.'

She was still not more than half awake, or she might even then have demanded to know how he hoped to procure a riding dress for her at such an hour. But she did so very much long to go riding, and she could just imagine Jemima planning such a treat for her. She nodded. 'Very well, my lord. If Jemima wants me to come.'

There were to be other rides, other mornings, but to Caroline there was something magical about that dawn. By the time the three of them had breasted the hill and dismounted beside the ruined chapel, the hushed beauty of the morning had washed away her chagrin at being woken and ordered out in such a cavalier fashion. She felt cleansed and at peace with the world. A skein of wild geese passed over their heads, their wings gilded by the rising sun, their sad cries swelling in heartbreaking chorus, then dying away as they disappeared over the other side of the bay.

Vale spoke suddenly behind her, echoing her thought. 'At peace now, Juliet? Come. Admit you're glad you came?'

She smiled at him, grateful for this offered truce, yet unwilling to break the spell that lay upon her spirits. Jemima had been chatting with the groom who had come with them. The child came running over the grass, the skirts of her riding dress sodden by the dew, her thin face glowing with happiness.

'You can see for miles from here, Papa,' she cried. 'Paddy says they used to shine a light from the chapel tower in the old days, to show the free traders' ships when it was safe to come into harbour!'

'True enough,' said Vale: 'and to lure others onto the rocks, as well. Some of my forebears,' he added, turning to Caroline, 'were no better than pirates. The Morriseys of Whitefield, I believe, were more respectable.'

'I'm afraid so,' she agreed gravely. 'Sadly dull and unromantic, we used to think. You've no idea how we envied you wicked Sweenys your disreputable past.'

'We?' He looked down at her, waiting. 'You had brothers and sisters, Miss Caroline?'

'A brother, my lord,' she said briefly, turning away from him. Then, feeling the need to change the subject, she said in an interested voice: 'Oh, look! Miss O'Grady's awake already. I can see smoke coming from her chimney.'

He peered downwards in the direction of her pointing hand. The huddle of cottages looked like toy dwellings, but even at that distance the gaping roofs and blackened walls of some were all too plainly to be seen. The broken uprights of what had once been the jetty of Sweeny's Port ran into the edge of the sea like jagged teeth. The desolation was worse close to, as Caroline well knew. The village had been deserted until old Miss O'Grady and her son had come back to live there; appearing from goodness knows where, and setting up house in the ruin of what had once been the best house in the village.

She told him something of this, glad of an excuse to turn away from his too searching gaze. 'They all think she's a witch, my lord, and with her cats and her one goat and her chickens, she lives there all alone and unmolested. Except for Joey, of course. He's not quite right in the head, and can't talk properly.'

'Maura says Miss O'Grady's bewitched him,' said Jemima, who had been listening. 'She says the devil's got his tongue, and no one but Miss O'Grady can get it back for him.'

'Maura's a silly, unkind girl,' said Caroline reprovingly, 'talking of what she does not know. Did you tell her that we'd called on Miss O'Grady and Joey, and how pleased they were to see us?'

Jemima nodded, and said smugly, 'I showed her the shells Joey gave me, and she crossed herself and wouldn't touch them. I was glad. Maura's always touching my things, and moving them; so my shells will be safe.' She gave a tug at Vale's arm, and said, 'Come down and say good morning to Miss O'Grady, Papa. She likes to see people. She said she'll read the cards for me one day, if the wind is in the right direction.'

Over the child's head, Caroline looked at Vale. His face was averted. He was frowning. She said tentatively, 'Please don't be vexed, my lord. Miss O'Grady's old and wrinkled, but she's no witch.' He said nothing, but was staring fixedly at the village below. She went on, hurrying a little because there was a rigidity about his frowning stillness, and she sensed that he was angry. 'I thought the village was deserted. The fishermen had their boats seized by the excisemen, you know, as a punishment for smuggling: so they've all gone away. No one has lived there since. It's sad, a sort of ghost place, my lord; only when Jemima and I were exploring it, we found Miss O'Grady and Joey living there, in the same cottage where she used to keep house for her brother.'

He said with sudden harshness, 'O'Grady's? That house? We'll go down. I wouldn't go there before. I was wrong. You don't lay ghosts by shutting them away.'

She told him that they must take the old track, which was hidden from them by a rise of ground.

'I know that,' he said with asperity. 'Do you think yourself the only one who belongs here, Miss Caroline? I'll have you know I've been down that track more times than you. Sweeny's Port, for me, used to mean home. I knew every nook and cranny of that village.'

'Then you'll be shocked at the way it looks now, my lord,' said Caroline. 'It's been let tumble down, and Miss O'Grady and Joey live in what was once the boathouse of their cottage. The roof leaks when it rains, and they share their only living room with six cats and some chickens. All the same,' she added, smiling, 'we'll be made welcome, and be given new-baked bread and an egg to break our fast. And if you don't want to offend, my lord, you'll sit down and eat whatever she lays before you.'

He smiled at her suddenly, a smile that made him look years younger. 'And fresh mackerel—' He broke off, his brows drawing together. 'I was forgetting. There'll be no fishing boats now . . . '

She did not tell him that Joey had pieced together a flimsy coracle of hides stretched over a wooden frame, which they kept hidden in the gorse and scrub behind their cottage. They set off, making their way down the sloping, zigzag track to the village, riding in single file, picking their way down the rutted, grass-grown road, where so many laden waggons had gone in other days.

At the bottom of this road, Caroline came up with Vale. 'Stay here at this end of the bay with Jemima, my lord, while I go and tell Miss O'Grady that you're here. Please,' she added imploringly, as he looked at her haughtily. 'She's shy and proud, and would not wish to be found in . . . in disarray.'

Vale said curtly that she need not think she was the only person who knew how to go on. But he stayed at the end of the quay, with Jemima and the groom who had ridden with them. Caroline gave the reins of her horse to their attendant, and went on foot down the cobbled way to the huddle of houses that were once the dwellings of prosperous fishermen in Sweeny's Port. O'Grady's was the first house. Its four-square walls were still as solid as ever; but the empty windows of the second floor yawned darkly under the sagging thatch of the roof. Only the low, whitewashed annexe at the far end showed signs of life. A thread of smoke spiralled lazily into the still, morning air. There was a goat tethered to a post, and as Caroline pushed open the little wicket gate, a hen went past her and scuttled away with an offended cackle.

The door of the cottage was shut. Caroline paused, startled. Normally the top of the half door would be open; more often the whole of it. It was something of a shock to be confronted by the solidly closed door with its blistered paint. A dog barked inside the cottage, and as Caroline went forward and knocked, the barking became more excited.

There was a silence, broken only by the barking dog. Caroline knocked again and called Miss O'Grady's name, wondering whether the old woman was ill, or was merely skulking inside, thinking her early morning visitor to be one of Mr Rance's men. Caroline knew that Miss O'Grady lived in daily dread of a visit from one of these. Her tenure of the cottage was by no means safe, and if the agent or his men came demanding rent, or some other dues, Miss O'Grady had nothing to pay them with.

There was a shuffling inside. Caroline called out once more, and presently there came the sound of a wooden bar being lifted, and the door creaked open, just a little way.

'So it's yourself, Miss?' Miss O'Grady's short-sighted eyes peered past Caroline, and her manner was distinctly cautious. 'Well, come in then,' she said, after a pause. 'Come in, and shut the door.'

It was dark in the low, windowless room, and as the top of the door thudded shut and Miss O'Grady fixed the wooden bar back in place, Caroline peered into the gloom. There were two men in the room, one seated on the only chair, and the other standing at the far side of the fire, watching her from beneath the brim of a dark hat. The man in the chair turned his head.

'Good morning, Caroline,' said Gilbert. He had a pair of

107

pistols on a shelf at his side, and seemed to be engaged in priming one of them. 'Have you come to tell me how best to come up with Vale? I could do with a bit of help, I can tell you. I've got to finish the job and be off within a week.'

Caroline came back down the cobbled way that had once been the quayside of the little port. She was hurrying, running awkwardly and holding up the skirts of her riding dress. She came up to where Vale was sitting on a low wall, so out of breath that for a moment she seemed unable to speak. Fifty yards beyond Vale she could see Jemima chatting to the groom.

Vale watched her. She said breathlessly, 'We'll have to see Miss O'Grady another day. She . . . she's not well, my lord.' She glanced behind her as though fearful of what she might see, and added in a more controlled tone, 'I believe she would be pleased to see us some other time, but . . . but this is one of her bad days, my lord. Pray come away . . . '

He did not move. He, too, was looking along the ruined quay at the house which had once been O'Grady's. He was frowning.

She said, her voice shaking, 'We should go, my lord. Please.'

He looked down at her. Her face was pale, her grey-green eyes wide with shock and a sort of anguish. He said quietly, 'What's the matter, Miss Caroline? Did something frighten you back there?'

She disclaimed rather wildly. It had been nothing; merely that Miss O'Grady had been keeping to the house, which was not at all like her. And then, when he said nothing, but continued to watch her, she added on a wild inspiration, 'It's Joey that's bothering her, I think. He's generally quiet and gentle; but he has rages, sometimes, and grows quite violent.' It occurred to her as she spoke that she had not seen Joey in the cottage at all. Perhaps it was true that he was in the loft above that dark little room, sleeping off the effects of one of

108

these rare but alarming fits. She found herself stammering, 'We should go, my lord. All Joey needs, at those times, is rest and quietness. We'll come another time.'

To her intense relief, he accepted this, and within minutes he had helped her to mount her horse and they were off. She was grateful for the need to ride in single file, and gradually her hammering heartbeats steadied and her choking terror receded. Only when they were once more riding beside the ruined chapel did Caroline find the courage to look down at Sweeny's Port once more. She reined her mount, and Vale paused beside her.

'Better now, Miss Caroline?' he murmured. She did not dare to look at his face, but she thought he sounded amused. 'We must take more of these morning rides. They give one food for thought, do they not?'

'Do they, my lord?' returned Caroline raising her head and eyeing him somewhat belligerently. 'I should think they might do so. If I were the owner of Sweeny's Port, I should be ashamed to see it in such a shocking, run-down condition. Is there nothing you can do to make things better, to bring the fishermen back?'

'Ah,' he said, smiling at her, his amber eyes glinting with pleased malice, 'I can see you are very much recovered, Miss Caroline. But perhaps I should tell you that I never attend to sermons before noon at the earliest. Shall we ride on now, before you are tempted to deliver yourself of yet another?'

Ten

HEIR RETURN TO MOUNT SWEENY had none of the mist-wreathed enchantment of their setting out. It was broad daylight, and as the little party clattered past the rectory and the forge and the scattered collection of hovels that flanked these larger buildings, ragged children peered at them from doorways, two shawled women turned to stare, and the blacksmith shaded his eyes and pulled his forelock when he saw them. The Earl did not pause, however, and if he noticed the tumbledown condition of the buildings, or the sullen looks of the women, he made no comment.

The day passed in a bustle of comings and goings. Among the callers was Sir Giles Mannering, who came into the bookroom and stayed chatting with Caroline for some little while. He brought messages from his wife, and seemed concerned for Caroline, asking her several times whether she was content in her present situation, and reiterating the offer of a welcome for her in his household, should she stand in need of it. Lady Mannering, it seemed, was just that day setting out for County Limerick, where her daughter Perdita was about to be brought to bed with her second child; otherwise, the magistrate assured Caroline, she would have come to call herself. Caroline sent fond messages to Perdita, once her dearest friend, much warmed by this kindness and friendly affection.

He turned to go. She had been aware, all along, that he was uneasy, a shade distrait. Suddenly, he gave voice to one of the things that was bothering him. 'Has Gilbert been here?' he demanded. He added, before she had time to frame an answer, 'You've heard he's back from America, I fancy?'

She found herself holding tight to the edge of a table, as though to steady herself. The terror of the morning was still with her. 'Yes, sir,' she agreed carefully, 'I know he's back.'

For a moment she was almost tempted to confide in the magistrate, to seek his help. Yet, no sooner did the notion come to mind, than she dismissed it. It was too dangerous. She could not give Gilbert away.

There had been a moment when she had thought her brother would launch himself from the cottage, and try to shoot the Earl down. He had crouched there in the dark, smoke-filled cottage, his newly primed pistol in his hand, peering out of the half door at the figures at the other end of the beach. She had protested, terrified; and by some miracle had managed to persuade him that to murder the Earl there and then would implicate Miss O'Grady and Joey. He had turned back from the door, the fierce light dying from his eyes; and Caroline had taken this chance to flee. There had been no time to argue the rights and wrongs of it, and she knew he would try again.

She looked at the magistrate's craggy, sensible face, and said cautiously, 'Gilbert won't like me working for Lord Vale. You know how he feels about . . . about Whitefield.' Suddenly conscious of Jemima's stare, she added lightly, 'But I like it, you know, and am well on the way to being spoiled. We went riding today, and are going again tomorrow. His lordship lent me the loveliest little chestnut mare . . .'

'Nor do I like your being here,' said Sir Giles, ignoring the last part of her speech. 'It's no place for you to be, nor,' he added, becoming aware in his turn of Jemima's presence, 'nor should this child be here. We searched the cellars last evening, and though we found nothing, that's not to say that there is nothing going on.'

He paused, eyeing Caroline in a worried way, and might

111

have been about to say more, when they were interrupted by Vale and some other gentlemen entering the bookroom.

'And who is Gilbert?' demanded Jemima, when they had gone out again.

Caroline turned and smiled at her. 'Gilbert is someone I have known all my life,' she said, wishing that Vale's questions were half as easy to answer as his daughter's. 'You could almost say that we grew up together. Did I ever tell you, Jemima, of the time my father brought a baby fox home? We reared him with a litter of puppies. It was the dearest little creature . . . '

The notion of raising a platoon of Volunteers at Mount Sweeny was put in train that day, and with a speed and a sense of urgency that made Sir Giles Mannering realize that it would be unwise to judge Vale's character by the air of foppish weariness he chose to assume. Mr Rance was sent for, so were a number of Vale's tenants, the doctor, the parson, and a score of gentlemen who lived in the vicinity; not to mention purveyors of cloth, shoe-makers, saddlers and the blacksmith. Within hours there were scores of volunteers lining up in the forecourt, shouts and orders echoing up and down, sounds of horses and the crunching of wheels, and a general stir and bustle. There was hammering and the clanging of iron in the yard. The whole household was in an excited turmoil of unaccustomed activity. Housemaids became seamstresses, set to sewing up the yards of blue material which had been cut out by two tailors on the great gunroom table. Scullions turned into messengers, blacksmiths' assistants, the head cook was seen staggering across the east terrace bearing a hogshead of ale, while Vale's valet, Fallow, sat at a table in the servants' hall and wrote down the names of the volunteers – both these gentlemen forgetting their dignity for the time being, in their determination to be at the centre of these new and thrilling events. Even Mrs Datchet caught the prevailing infection, and offered to help

112

Caroline make a banner for the Mount Sweeny Volunteers.

Caroline had been casually informed by the Earl that this was to be her contribution; 'Nothing elaborate, Miss Caroline,' he had said, in passing, 'just our crest in gold on a dark blue ground. See to it, there's a good girl.' She had been racking her brains as to how to achieve this, and was much relieved by Mrs Datchet's offer of assistance.

They spent the rest of the day designing the banner, drawing it out, and rummaging through a veritable Aladdin's cave of silks and threads which Mrs Datchet had stored away, choosing just the right shades of blue and gold. It seemed no time before the evening had come, and it was time to take the puppy for his last run in the gardens.

Jemima and Caroline met Vale coming in through the main door. Caroline dropped a slight curtsey and told Jemima to say goodnight to her father. He handed his hat and gloves to a footman, dismissing the man with a nod, and said: 'No need to say goodnight yet, Jemima. You'll dine with me.'

Jemima gave a little skip of pleasure. 'Oh, good! May I stay up late and play cards with you, Papa?'

'If I'm in the humour for it,' he said, pulling one of the puppy's ears. 'We shall see. Go and put Prince Ferdinand to bed.'

Caroline turned to follow the child up the stairs. At the foot of them, she paused: 'What time do you dine, my lord? I'll bring Jemima down to you.'

'You'll dine with me yourself as well, ma'am,' he said, looking her over with the disparaging look she was beginning to know. She had changed out of the borrowed riding dress, of course, and was once more clad in one of her grey, governess gowns. 'And furbish yourself up a little, for goodness' sake.'

She said levelly, 'I prefer to eat upstairs, my lord. But, thank you.'

'Your preferences are no concern of mine,' he snapped impatiently. 'You'll dine with me. It is my wish.'

113

'My lord,' she began, pausing as the realization came to her that opposition in this matter would make him more determined. She said gently, 'I think it better if I don't dine with you.'

She saw his crooked brows rise, and the look of haughty enquiry on his long face, and tried to think of some way to convey to him that she could not do what he asked. She could almost hear the sly sniggers in the servants' hall, the whispering conjectures. She said nervously, 'Please try to understand, sir. It won't do for us to dine together.'

'My dear girl, I shall dine in whatever company I choose.'

'Yes, my lord, and it is kind in you to invite me to accompany Jemima. But it is better not.'

'You'll dine with me. Be here in an hour's time. If you're late, I shall come and get you, Juliet.'

'Very well, my lord,' she said meekly. 'I only trust I shall not bore you. I have no conversation.'

'Good God,' he retorted derisively, 'd'you think I want to dine with you because I want to hear you talk? I want only one thing, and that's to keep you under my eye.'

'Oh,' said Caroline blankly.

'In an hour's time, then. Don't be late.'

His talk of keeping her under his eye had made Caroline feel distinctly uneasy. What did he mean? What did he suspect? These conjectures occupied her mind all the way back to the west wing, but the sight of Maura and two other smirking housemaids standing in her room brought her back to reality with a bump. She demanded to know what they were doing; and when she saw what they had brought, and discovered whose things they were, her earlier unease was swept away by a gust of very different sentiments. There was little sign of the meek governess in the stormy-eyed girl who came upon the Earl in his private sanctum known as the rampart room.

He was reading a book, and looked up, frowning. 'What now, ma'am?' he demanded in an unwelcoming tone. 'It's

114

fair to tell you that I am not accustomed to being disturbed in this room.'

She said tensely, 'Nor am I accustomed to . . . to being treated like a mindless doll, my lord. How dare you send your wife's clothes into my room? You will tell them to take them away this instant, or . . . or I shall refuse to stay on here.'

'Will you, now?' he murmured, laying his book upon his knee. 'And where do you think you will go, Miss Caroline?'

'I . . . I don't know,' she stammered, 'but you may be sure I shall choose somewhere where I am treated better than in this house.'

'I wonder,' he murmured again, smiling faintly in a way that made her shiver. 'If you want to know what I think, ma'am, I do not think you will have any choice in the matter at all. If you leave here without my permission, you will certainly find yourself locked up in Waterford jail.' She gave a small gasp, and he went on in the same soft tone, 'I have not, so far, told Sir Giles Mannering of your connection with the night people. If you leave here, however, I might feel it my duty to do so.'

She stood as though turned to stone. The angry pinkness drained out of her face, leaving it paper white. Her eyes had grown enormous with shock. Her lips moved, but no words came.

He said, 'I see you take my meaning, my dear. Do not look so stricken. If you behave yourself I shall not hand you over to the authorities. But you should remember that there is an ugly spirit abroad just now, and anyone trafficking with the French is likely to be given short shrift, or so I'm told.'

She recovered her voice and said, 'I know nothing about trafficking with the French, my lord. I'm no traitor.'

'No?' She could not have told whether he believed her or not. 'Well, I'm keeping an open mind about that for the present . . . and about other things.' He paused, and added for good measure, 'The authorities may not feel so lenient. Even your good friend Sir Giles might not feel able to defend you, for with fears of an invasion running so high, there is an urgent need to find out more about those friends of yours; particularly about their leader. Sir Giles might not like the idea of handing you over for questioning. Some of these interrogators are not too particular about their methods, as he will know. But he would do his duty.'

Caroline shut her eyes, trying to rid her vision of that cruelly penetrating regard, groping for reason and some way out of this dilemma. She opened them again, and said quietly, 'That's blackmail, Lord Vale. I have suffered it already at Mr Rance's hands. I had not expected you to sink so low.'

'No? Hadn't you?' he enquired blandly. 'Did you never hear the expression, "Like master, like man", Miss Caroline? Besides,' he added, as she merely went on looking at him in the same clear-eyed, reproachful way, 'besides, blackmailers can only ply their trade when their victims have a guilty secret to hide.' He saw her flinch and added in a more kindly tone, 'Come, Juliet. Tell me what you are doing here? Tell me about this Gilbert, and why you need to see him so badly? I've no wish to hand you over to the authorities. If you'll be frank with me, I may even be able to help you.'

She looked down at the carpet, tracing the pattern with the toe of her shoe, trying once more to think rationally. Would it do irretrievable harm to tell Vale the truth, to seek his help? The urge to lay her burden on someone else's shoulders was almost overwhelming. She thought she could trust him. But, no sooner did she allow herself to think of trusting him, than she thought of what Gilbert had been hired to do, and her fears rushed back. At all costs she must stop Vale guessing Gilbert's identity – at least until she had talked with her brother once more, and if possible persuaded him to give up his wicked and dangerous commission. Vale assumed that Gilbert was her lover. He must go on thinking so, for as long as possible.

'I cannot tell you anything, my lord, except that . . . that I . . . love Gilbert, and assure you that he's no traitor. He's

116

only lately fallen in with the night people, and it's my earnest wish to find him, and persuade him to go away.'

'How did he come to join them?'

'I cannot tell you that, either,' she said.

'No? Well, tell me this. Have you made contact with him?' She nodded, eyeing him warily. Then, sharp as a swordthrust, the next question came. 'He was in Miss O'Grady's cottage this morning, was he not?'

She said in a shaking voice: 'I . . . I cannot say. It had nothing to do with Miss O'Grady. There is nothing I can tell you, my lord, so please do not ask me.'

'Nothing? Surely you can think up some tale that will satisfy me, ma'am?'

She shook her head, close to tears. 'No, my lord.'

For what seemed an age, he said nothing at all. His eyes were half closed, and he was staring down at the serpent ring on his long white hand as though there were something about it which displeased him. Then he said curtly: 'So. Keep your secrets, if you will, ma'am. I'm in no hurry to learn them. It's my experience that truth will out, given time and patience. In the meantime, I have you under my eye. You'll stay here and look after Jemima.' He smiled suddenly, a sharp, malicious smile. 'And as for wearing Sybilla's clothes, if you don't like the notion, we'll see about getting you some others.' She shook her head in wordless protest, and he raised his brows. 'No? Then if you won't accept new clothes, you may alter Sybilla's ones for the time being. I daresay,' he added carelessly, as she stood there looking at him in dumb dismay, 'I daresay your Gilbert will thank me for making you look more presentable. When he sees you looking less of a fright, he may not prove quite so tiresomely elusive?'

She shook her head again, but smiling a little this time. 'I don't think so, my lord. He'll think the worst, more like, and try to call you out. Come to that,' she added, looking at him beseechingly, 'everyone will think the very worst if I go around wearing your wife's clothes.'

'I have already told you, I don't care a rush for what

117

people think.' She started to speak, but he cut her short. 'Let's hear no more about it, Miss Caroline, or I'll be tempted to hand you over to Sir Giles's fellows, if only to stop your complaints.' He rose to his feet and patted her unresponding cheek. 'The night people have chosen to use my crest as their sign, they even dare to make free with my house. Your Gilbert may be as innocent as you claim, Juliet; but you'll stay here as hostage for his good conduct for as long as it pleases me. Be a good girl and go and furbish yourself up for dinner.'

Eleven

THE BANNER FOR THE MOUNT SWEENY VOLUNTEERS kept Caroline stitching away in the housekeeper's room whenever she had time to spare. It was for this reason – or perhaps because she wanted to avoid him – that she did not see Vale's half-brother for some days. She had come, she found, to value Richard's good opinion, and she did not somehow think he would approve of her new, transformed appearance.

Even so, she was startled by the look of stupefaction on his dark, handsome face when she saw him staring at her from the doorway of the bookroom. He had all the appearance of a man who has just sustained a severe shock.

She smiled at him nervously and curtsied. 'Good morning, sir.'

He came forward, and speaking jerkily, said, 'Forgive me, ma'am. I . . . mistook you for . . . someone. How do you do? How do you go on?'

She thought it best to take this hurdle straight on, and said, 'As you see, sir, I go on very prosperously; too prosperously for my position here, you may think. You see, Lord Vale did not care for my grey gowns; and he made me wear these, which are more to his taste.'

'Made you?' His voice was harsh. 'Surely, he did not coerce you, ma'am? Even Vale—' He broke off, evidently deciding that there was nothing his brother would not do to get his own way. He looked at her dress more closely, and said in a doubting voice, 'I can't credit it, ma'am. Is it poss-

119

ible that my brother has insisted on your wearing one of Sybilla's gowns?'

'He had all of them brought to my room,' she answered simply, looking down at the dark silk of her skirt because she could not bring herself to look any longer at the puzzled, hurt look on Richard's face. She said in a mortified voice, 'It's true, Mr Sweeny. I can find no excuse for myself agreeing to wear them, except that I did not know how to stop his lordship insisting.'

'Surely you could have refused,' he said in a low voice. 'Forgive me, ma'am. But it was surely not . . . what you wished? Your every feeling must be offended.'

She nodded, shamefaced, and said defensively, 'I tried to refuse, sir, but . . . but his lordship made it . . . difficult.'

'Why don't you tell him that I threatened to send you to prison if you didn't do as I told you, Juliet?' demanded Vale cheerfully, sauntering in and looking at her pink, ashamed face with amusement. 'That should arouse his knightly ire.' He took her chin in one hand and turned her face up. 'Yes. You look very becomingly today, my dear. Don't dare to pretend that you do not know it.'

'Hugo,' said Richard in a stifled voice, 'are you sunk beneath reproach? I cannot think why Miss Caroline has not packed her bags and left, after being treated so.'

'I daresay she'd have very much liked to,' returned the Earl, releasing his hold on Caroline's chin. She turned away from him and began to stack some books on a table with considerable vigour. 'It suits me to keep her here under my eye, however.'

Richard strode over and laid one of his hands on one of hers, imprisoning it. 'Let me say this, ma'am. I am yours to command. You may be sure of a welcome at Whitefield, Miss Caroline, at any time. If my brother's behaviour is insupportable to you, I will convey you there at once.'

'Well done, dear boy,' said Vale satirically. He said to Caroline in a congratulatory tone, 'You've made a conquest, my dear. I told you it would be so.'

120

She removed her hand from under Richard's hard, warm one, and said curtly, 'This is a foolish conversation. If it amuses you to continue it, my lord, I fear you must do so without me.' She moved to the door. 'Jemima has gone for the puppy, and we are going out.'

Richard caught up with her in the hall. 'I meant what I said, ma'am. You have no need to put up with such treatment, I assure you.'

Vale was standing a little way off, watching them. She said with a smile, 'Oh, I don't heed his lordship's nonsense. When gentlemen reach a certain age, sir, they take strange whims, behave like small boys. They cannot help it. It's due to a fear of growing older, I understand.'

'Viper!' said Vale with an appreciative chuckle. 'You see, Richard? She's not so defenceless as she seems. And she plays a good hand at cards, too. I disremember when Jemima had a governess with such diverse talents.'

'Pray excuse me,' said Caroline, as Jemima and the puppy came in sight at the head of the stairs. But as she spoke, there were sounds of commotion outside the front door, and two carriages were seen drawing up on the gravel sweep beyond it. Vale and his brother looked out, and Caroline saw them exchange glances, for all the world like two schoolboys caught out in some mischief.

'It's Gussie,' said Vale. His voice held no enthusiasm. Two footmen had already hurried past, and one was opening the first carriage door. 'I had hoped she would have been too offended to come here. Indeed, I was counting on it.'

'She's probably travelled all this way in order to give you a trimming,' retorted Richard with a certain pleased malice. 'Shall I stay and lend you my support, for what it's worth? Not that my presence will stop Augusta having her say.'

Caroline was also moving towards the stairs, intent on escaping, but Vale stopped her. 'Don't run away, my dear,' he said. 'Jemima must stay and pay her respects to her Aunt Augusta. Who knows, the sight of Prince Ferdinand may charm my dear sister out of her indignation.'

121

'So?' Lady Augusta Appleby stood in the morning room and began to draw off her gloves. 'So, what have you to say for yourself, Hugo?'

'What would you like me to say, Gussie?'

'I should have thought a word of apology might have been suitable,' she retorted. 'Never have I been so humiliated as when you left Lismore without a word! I did not know what excuse to make for your sudden disappearance. What the Hartingtons thought of you, I dread to think! And I have been obliged to travel that abominable road without company—'

'You were under no obligation to come here, Gussie,' said the Earl in a bored tone. He raised his eyeglass to survey her diminutive and elegantly gowned form, and her handsome but indignant countenance, then turned sideways to watch the comings and goings of a score of people through the morning room window. A phalanx of footmen were still bringing in Lady Augusta's effects, mingling with grooms and outriders. A darkly-clad lady's maid passed the window supervising the progress of a heavy leather box which contained her ladyship's jewels. 'Without company, Augusta? Short of travelling with an army, I should have thought you could hardly have been more heavily accompanied.'

Lady Augusta gave a snort, and said to Richard, 'I can see that Vale is determined to brazen it out, and I shall get no apology from him. Well, I did not expect it. Why should I?' She turned to look at Jemima, who was standing with Caroline near the door, her puppy in her arms. 'Well, child? Come and give me a kiss—' She broke off, suddenly taking notice of Caroline. She stared, and said sharply, 'And who are you, pray?'

'I am Jemima's governess, my lady,' said Caroline in her gentle way, curtseying to this high nosed, modishly-dressed little lady, who was eyeing her in some astonishment.

'Good gracious! You look far too young, and not at all as I

122

would expect. And where, pray, is that other simpering female who was with Jemima when I last saw her? I disremember her name.'

'Miss Prendergast left in a hurry, ma'am,' said Caroline. 'I have been here for some weeks.'

'Indeed?' Lady Augusta went on staring up at Caroline over the bridge of her nose, as though she was inspecting a tall piece of furniture. 'Extraordinary! And what makes you think you are qualified to instruct my niece, may I ask?'

'Don't be rude, Gussie,' said Vale. 'Treat Miss Caroline gently, I implore you. Even three weeks of Jemima's company may not have wholly prepared her for your specialized brand of incivility. Don't be dismayed, Miss Caroline,' he added kindly, as Caroline turned her grey-green eyes upon him in half-laughing reproach, 'someone once told my dear sister that holding back her curiosity might lead to her being carried off by a spasm. She never bridles her tongue, for that reason; and look how well it answers! Is she not the veritable picture of health?' Caroline gave a choke of laughter, and he added smoothly, 'You should strive to copy my sister's habit of frankness, Miss Caroline.'

'Yes, my lord,' said Caroline, biting her lip. 'I shall try to do as you suggest.'

'Good girl!'

Richard felt that it was time to intervene. He said, 'Enough, Hugo! Leave poor Miss Caroline alone. I must be on my way, Augusta, but I trust you will come to Whitefield when Hugo and his party ride over tomorrow? If you are not too done up after all your journeying, that is?'

'No such thing,' said her ladyship. 'I shall recover quickly enough. At least, I expect to do so, if only Vale would offer me some form of refreshment. I confess I am famished. When do you dine, Hugo?'

'If it will sweeten your disposition, Gussie,' retorted the Earl acidly, 'we'll dine as soon as may be.'

* * *

123

A night's sleep seemed to have done wonders for Lady Augusta's temper. The visit to Whitefield took place as promised, and a jubilant Jemima was allowed to ride beside Vale in his curricle. Caroline, condemned to travel alone in a closed carriage with Vale's sister, had been half expecting to endure a further sharp inquisition. Instead, she found herself being entertained. The lady had a wry wit and an intense interest in all that went on around her; and since she seemed to spend her life moving between Dublin and London – with occasional visits to fashionable watering places to recruit her strength – she was full of spicy on-dits about tonnish personalities. Laughing at these anecdotes, Caroline formed the opinion that Vale's eldest sister derived considerable enjoyment from her widowed state. Her children were all grown and married, and with ample means at her disposal, Lady Augusta could do precisely as she pleased, without the need to consult the wishes of anyone but herself. It seemed no time at all before the carriage was drawing up at Whitefield, and Richard Sweeny was greeting them at the door.

Caroline did not greatly enjoy the visit. She wondered, afterwards, whether her disappointment and sense of loss came from expecting too much. After all, she had longed for four whole years to go back to Whitefield.

It was not as she remembered it, and to make matters worse Slattery was still in his most surly humour, and did not speak to her at all. He seemed to be in charge of the horses, and went muttering after them when they were led to the stables, and was not seen again until they were brought back at the end of the visit. Slattery's new wife, on the other hand, was all smiles and curtseys. She led the ladies upstairs, where a couple of neatly dressed maids were waiting to attend to their wants. It was Mrs Slattery who later gave them a tour of the first floor rooms, and they were shown the elegant new furnishings from Dublin, and the bedhangings specially woven in Kilkenny. It seemed a different place entirely from the Whitefield of Caroline's childhood.

The difference showed again when they were served an

elegant nuncheon by two deft and silent footmen. It was certainly more peaceful than it used to be, when Slattery had been in the habit of keeping up a running discourse while he waited at table, and the two boys who helped him made a cheerful clatter in the background. Caroline, listening absently to Richard Sweeny and his sister arguing about the latest land reforms, came to the conclusion that it was the quietness that made Whitefield seem so unfamiliar – that, and the gleaming cleanliness of everything. Colonel Morrisey would have raised a furious rumpus if any item of saddlery or the carriage brasses had been less than perfect, or anything was lacking for the comfort of his horses; but none of the indoor servants had troubled much about cobwebs, or tarnish on the silver. And never, even when the colonel's luck was running high, had there been any thought of wasting money on furbishing the upstairs rooms.

But she had little time for reflection, for Richard seemed determined to go out of his way to show Caroline everything, and to seek her approval for all he had done. He was kindly, thoughtful, attentive to the wants of all his guests; but particularly to Caroline. She wished he had not singled her out so. She would have been more comfortable if he had allowed her to remain in the background, as she had meant to do. And although she said everything that was proper, and duly admired all that she saw, it was a relief when the Earl grew suddenly bored, and brought the visit to an end.

Their departure was delayed. Jemima was missing, and although she was found after a search, Vale was incensed at being kept waiting. He punished the child by bundling her into the carriage with her aunt; taking Caroline with him in the high, yellow-wheeled curricle, instead of Jemima.

Caroline felt that this was unjust. She maintained a stony silence all the way down the avenue. Vale said, at last: 'Vexed with me, Miss Caroline?'

'Not in the least, my lord,' she retorted coldly. She did not look at him, but when he said nothing, she could not resist saying, 'It's not my place to tell you how to deal with your own daughter.'

'No,' he agreed with maddening affability, 'I am able to deal with her well enough. She won't keep me waiting again, I fancy.'

'How was Jemima to know that you would suddenly take a notion to leave Whitefield?' demanded Caroline, turning to look at him crossly. 'It was most unfair to punish her for failing to . . . to anticipate your whim, my lord!'

'I have never laid claim to being fair, Miss Caroline,' he answered gently, steadying his horses for the Whitefield gateway ahead. 'You must know, better than most, that life is not fair. However, you must also know – for I think you are not stupid – that you've made a hit with Richard. It would redress the balance in your favour a little, if he were to make you an offer, my dear. He'll make a good husband. I hope you mean to have him?'

Angry at his cynical tone, confused, yet determined not to show her confusion, Caroline said sweetly, 'Thank you, my lord. I'd be more grateful, if I did not suspect that you only want to find a way of disposing tidily of Colonel Morrisey's destitute daughter. How inconvenient it must be, indeed, to have me here?' She saw that he was taken aback, and added: 'I shall not accept Mr Sweeny's offer, if he makes me one – which I think unlikely.'

'Doesn't being the mistress of Whitefield tempt you?'

She shook her head. She did not tell him that the neat, elegantly appointed house they had just left was a foreign place to her. She said instead, sadly, 'It is no good to go backwards, even if it were possible. I don't wish to be married for the sake of Whitefield, or indeed for any house.'

'What?' His tone was derisive. 'Do you mean to remain an old maid for ever, Juliet?'

She smiled a little, her eyes on the road ahead. 'I'd never marry as a means to find security, my lord. Four years ago, when I began to go about in society, it seemed a horrid fate to remain unwed . . . '

'And now?'

She smiled at him sunnily. 'Now, thanks to you, Lord

Vale, I have had four years to reflect. Yes,' she added thoughtfully, 'I do thank you. There is nothing like trouble and a lack of material things to focus the mind on what matters. It makes one appreciate luxuries, too. I'd never have taken such pleasure in riding that nicely mannered mare of yours four years ago; nor would I have enjoyed driving behind such a glorious pair of horses as you have here, my lord. I used, in the old days, to take these things for granted. Now, it is sheer delight.'

He looked at her, a twisted smile on his lips, and a look in his hooded eyes which might have been admiration. But all he said was, 'Trying to put me in a blush for my wicked deeds, Miss Caroline?'

She laughed back at him, her eyes shining. 'Has anyone done that, my lord? I think not. Besides, you can hardly boast of being wicked, can you? My father did not have to play cards with you—'

It was then that she saw Gilbert. He came out from behind a stone wall, masked, with a pistol levelled in their direction.

Everything happened at once. She must have cried out in protest. There was a shot. The Earl lurched, grunted audibly, and slewed sideways, half pinning Caroline against the side of the curricle. She made a grab for the reins. There was blood; blood spurting, blood slippery on her hands as she wrestled for control of the frightened horses.

There was no time to see how badly Vale was hurt, or to look backwards to find out what Gilbert was doing. The horses were snorting, plunging, then taking off in a mad gallop towards the junction with the cliff road. If she could not rein them back in time, make them turn that corner, they would plunge down the precipice into the sea.

She leaned against Vale's inert, swaying form, pushing him aside so that she could grasp the reins more firmly; and began to fight a desperate battle to stave off disaster.

Twelve

'*A* MIRACLE,' SAID RICHARD QUIETLY, taking one of Caroline's hands and raising it to his lips. 'Without you, Miss Caroline, Vale and his curricle and his horses would have been smashed to pieces. I thank heaven you were driving with him, instead of Jemima.'

'So do we all,' said Lady Augusta, closing her eyes for a moment. It did not help. She was still visited by the inner vision of that moment when she thought that nothing could save her brother; and the sight – only minutes later – when they all rushed towards the spot where the horses had come to a shuddering halt against a gate, to find Vale's inert form dangling half out of the curricle, his face a mask of blood. Lady Augusta said in heartfelt tones, 'She did what many men could never have done, Richard. Those greys aren't easy to handle at the best of times.'

'As I said,' repeated Richard, 'it was a miracle.'

'Not nearly such a miracle as Lord Vale's recovery,' retorted Caroline, who was finding this general acclaim increasingly tiresome, 'I thought he was dead at first.'

So had they all thought, until the Earl had opened his eyes and cursed them all roundly for standing gaping at him when they ought to be seeing to his horses. It seemed that the bullet had grazed his head just above the hairline, knocking him half-insensible for five minutes, and causing a positive fountain of blood. Next day, apart from a headache and bad temper, the Earl had suffered few ill effects from his

128

attempted assassination. The horses, indeed, had come off worst. One of them had strained a tendon, and the other was cut about the legs and neither would be on the road for some time. The masked man had escaped. After firing the shot which struck Vale down, he had vanished once more behind the wall; and by the time anyone had recovered enough presence of mind to go after him, he was nowhere to be seen. A trail of hoof marks led up the hill, coming to an end in the thick wood above. Richard and Sir Giles – summoned from his home – mounted a search, but no trace of the miscreant was found.

Caroline was divided in herself, and so odd and opposed were her thoughts that she was inwardly astonished that nobody seemed to notice. When the horses had at last ceased their wild course, and she could turn her eyes on Vale, she had thought him dead; and something inside her died at that moment. And when he suddenly woke into cantankerous life, she found herself holding a trembling Jemima; and weeping and laughing and shaking just as much as the child in her arms. The others were busy helping Vale to his feet, or obeying his behest to see to the horses. All Caroline could do was to clutch Jemima and cry – while the other half of her was praying that Gilbert had managed to get away, wondering where he was.

She soon had herself in hand again – at least outwardly – and once back at Mount Sweeny was able to bear with the questions, the congratulations, even read to Jemima before she went to bed, just as if there had been no twin brother hiding out somewhere among the neighbouring hills, hiding there with murderous intent which she could do nothing to avert. The doctor came and went. He pronounced that the Earl had escaped death by a fraction of an inch, and that he ought to lie in a darkened room for a day or two, until all signs of headache had abated. Vale retorted that he would do nothing of the kind, and demanded a glass of brandy; at which point the doctor retired, and on meeting with Lady Augusta in the hall, begged her to try to keep the Earl quiet, if it were at all possible.

Predictably, Vale was an impossible patient. He refused to stay in bed, refused to stay indoors; yet after half an hour in the stables, he came into the bookroom looking grey, and ensconced himself in a chair there, demanding that Caroline should pull the bell and send for the brandy decanter. She obeyed, inwardly terrified by his pallor, wondering if he was about to keel over in a faint. He stayed in the bookroom throughout most of the day, quarrelling with his sister, sending for various people and tiring of them within minutes, jumping down Jemima's throat whenever she made a sudden noise, or fidgeted to go out. The only person who succeeded in keeping him quiet was Caroline, with whom Vale insisted on playing at piquet, game after game, endlessly, until she was dizzy with fatigue, and felt that her head must ache as badly as his.

Towards evening, Richard came again; but he, too, incurred the Earl's displeasure. He utterly refused to arrange a parade of the newly formed Mount Sweeny Volunteers for the following day, saying that Vale would never be well enough to attend it.

'Stop behaving like an old woman, Richard,' said his brother irritably. 'D'you think a mere scratch is going to keep me from doing what I want? If you won't arrange the parade, I'll tell Rance to do it. Pull the bell, Miss Caroline. Rance is an idle fellow. We'll send for him.'

'Don't trouble yourself to pull the bell, Miss Caroline,' said Richard quietly. 'It's no use sending for Rance. He's ill. He's taken to his bed, so I hear.'

Vale frowned. 'So why wasn't I told?'

Richard shrugged, and said with a slight smile in Caroline's direction, 'Perhaps no one had the courage to tell you, Hugo. It's not everyone who has the stamina to put up with your ill humour . . . ' He broke off, looking more closely to where Caroline sat at the far side of the card table: 'My dear girl, you have no need to put up with it, either. You look worn to the bone, and I'm persuaded you have the headache. Will you not go upstairs and lie down for a while?'

'She'll go when I tell her to, and not before,' retorted the Earl, moving back to his place opposite Caroline, and seating himself once more. He moved slowly, and as he lowered himself into the high-backed chair, Caroline saw him wince. But all he said was: 'Will you cut, ma'am? You're interrupting our game, Richard. If you won't do what I ask, you might as well take yourself off. And take Gussie with you, for heaven's sake! She's forever sighing over her embroidery and looking sourly at the brandy decanter. She's almost as bad as Jemima: and unlike Jemima, I can't just send her out walking with the schoolroom maid.'

Lady Augusta gathered up her sewing and said she would be charmed to go with Richard. In fact, she had been thinking of moving herself over to Whitefield. Perhaps that would answer better than being cooped up at Mount Sweeny watching Vale drinking himself to death. She started rustling towards the door, and Richard paused to say: 'One thing Sir Giles and I were discussing, Hugo . . . ' Vale raised a crooked brow, and waited. Richard said seriously: 'After this last incident, you really must take care when you ride out. Don't go riding without a proper escort, I do implore you. We really cannot risk such a thing happening for a second time.'

'What are you suggesting?' demanded the Earl, with scant enthusiasm. 'That I should take the Mount Sweeny Volunteers with me everywhere I go?'

Richard said seriously, 'Something of that kind, at least. Promise me, Hugo, that you won't venture out on your own.' And when Vale hunched an impatient shoulder and turned back to his cards, Richard added more strongly: 'It's simply not safe, Hugo! For all our sakes, you simply must take elementary precautions!'

'Richard's quite right,' said Lady Augusta, putting her chagrin aside in order to add her mite to this request. 'Impossible though you may be, Hugo, none of us wants to attend your funeral just yet.'

Vale turned his head to look at his sister, a movement

131

which seemed to give him pain, and served to increase his already considerable irritation. 'You're like a couple of clucking hens, the pair of you! And why should Richard worry about attending my funeral? Once I'm disposed of, he'll have charge of all this; and everyone knows he'll make a better Earl of Vale than I.' Richard shook his head at his brother, and Vale added with asperity, 'I shall ride exactly where and when I please. So go away, and let me attend to this hand. Miss Caroline may be a bit absent minded, but she has a sly way of taking advantage if I allow myself to be diverted.'

When they had gone, stalking out without another word, he said with a quick frown: 'Does your head hurt? Richard's right, you do look worn . . . ' He added, after a pause, 'Why didn't you say you wanted to stop?'

'I'm all right, my lord. It's your turn to discard.'

He did not move. 'Go upstairs and lie down. I'll tell Datchet to see that Jemima does not disturb you.' And when she said again that there was nothing the matter with her, and she did not wish to retire to her room, he flung his cards face down on the table and said disagreeably, 'You must please yourself what you do, then. For my part, I've had enough of this game. I've a good mind to go upstairs and lie down myself.'

'Now, Richard,' said Lady Augusta, two days later, coming upon Richard Sweeny alone. With all the comings and goings due to the setting up of the Volunteers, this was a rare event. 'I wish you would tell me about this latest start of Hugo's? I can't make out that young woman at all. One moment I think her the demure governess, and the next she's laughing with Hugo and flaunting herself in Sybilla's clothes. Half the household are convinced she's Vale's latest doxy; yet, somehow I don't think it. Apart from anything else, he's always been so careful of Jemima; and the child goes with them everywhere.' She sighed, and shook her head in bewilderment. 'I'm almost tempted to think he's serious, for once;

132

that they might make a match of it.'

Richard looked startled. 'Certainly not, Gussie. Hugo's never serious.'

She looked at him thoughtfully, 'Perhaps not. One can never tell what Hugo is thinking. But I think he's taken with her; and as for that girl, she's in a worse case. She tries to hide it, of course, but it's my guess she's fathoms deep in love with Vale.'

'Nonsense, Gussie!' Richard's voice was still vehement. 'He's amusing himself, and Miss Caroline has quite enough sense to see it. It would take more than Hugo's clumsy efforts at flirtation to take Miss Caroline off balance.'

'Perhaps . . .' Lady Augusta did not look convinced, however. 'They seem to live in each other's pockets, and to tell the truth Hugo does not try to flirt with her, most of the time. Rather, he treats her like he might Jemima's older sister, scolding her for taking too little trouble with her appearance, and criticizing her card play.'

'Oh, are they still playing cards all day long, then?'

Lady Augusta shook her head, and said resignedly: 'Not all day, my dear Richard; but all night – for so late do they sit up that I find myself quite done up with watching them.' She saw that he was looking puzzled, and added: 'You know, that's what I find so hard to fathom. Hugo insists that I stay up to act as duenna for that young woman. That's not in his usual style, you'll agree?'

Richard said nothing at all. He kept his dark blue eyes on his sister's face, and waited for her to go on.

'And it's not only in the evenings that he avoids being alone with her. They have been riding all over the place for the past few days; but they never go without Jemima and a groom in attendance.'

'Just one groom!' Richard burst out. 'Do you mean to tell me that Vale has utterly disregarded what I told him about the risks of riding without a proper, armed escort?' He saw Lady Augusta nod, and added explosively, 'Really! Hugo is the most contrary . . . tiresome fellow! One might almost think he is going out of his way to attract another assassination attempt!'

'Don't! Don't speak of that!' Lady Augusta groped for her smelling salts, unstopped the small bottle and inhaled. She looked up at her brother's concerned face, and said shakily, 'I don't mean to turn all vapourish on you, Richard. As you know, I'm given to despising those who give way to their feelings. But that narrow escape of Hugo's . . . it put me so much in mind of Sybilla's dreadful accident! I don't know how it is, but Sybilla has been so much in my thoughts these past days. I can't seem to get her out of my mind.'

Richard bowed his dark head, and in a low voice he said: 'No more can I, Augusta. Nor can I.'

She looked at him comprehendingly. 'Of course. For you it must be even more real, since you were watching when Sybilla went over the cliff; watching, helpless, as I was the other evening . . . ' She gave herself a little shake, and said in something more like her usual brisk, decided tones, 'It stands to reason that Hugo might take it into his head to marry that girl. There's no doubt that she saved his life, for all that he was churlish enough to blame her for laming the greys.'

Richard raised his dark head, and said with a dawning grin, 'He had the nerve to blame her for that, had he? Good God!'

Lady Augusta smiled grimly, 'Oh, you needn't think she took his scolding meekly, however. She has spirit, has Miss Caroline Morrisey. I'm even beginning to think she will do very well as the next Countess of Vale.'

Richard seemed to have recovered from his earlier astonishment. He laughed, and said: 'Even if Hugo was in the humour to be leg-shackled again, Gussie, Miss Caroline would have more sense than to take him on. He made Sybilla a devilish husband, as you must very well remember.'

'All the same,' returned her ladyship, who had witnessed too many fights between Vale and his late wife to try to pretend that their marriage had been anything but a travesty, 'all the same, Vale might do well to try to persuade her. Such a match would improve his standing with his Irish neighbours; and for all that she's a beanpole, she's perfectly presentable. And the Morriseys, after all, were at Whitefield long before the Sweenys were even thought of.'

'I didn't say that there was anything the matter with Miss Caroline's lineage, Gussie,' he retorted, smiling at his sister as though she had said something remarkably foolish. 'I merely assure you that she will not marry Hugo. She's too good for him, by half.'

Thirteen

ILBERT CAME INTO MR RANCE'S SICKROOM QUIETLY. His breath was coming fast, for he had been running; and when he had satisfied himself that no one but the agent was in the room, he replaced a small pistol in his pocket.

'Good afternoon, Rance,' he said cheerfully, grinning at the agent's affronted expression. 'I hear you're not receiving callers? Did you contrive to turn even the great Lord Vale from your door? I saw them ride off.' Then, with a quick frown, he added: 'That's the third time I've had that devil Vale in my sights, and not been able to deal with him. Caroline was in the way. She never seems to leave his side, she and that brat she looks after.'

'So it seems,' said Mr Rance, sitting up in bed. He had indeed succeeded in sending the Earl away, having instructed his housekeeper to say that the doctor had forbidden him all visitors. He looked at Gilbert, who must have walked in without so much as a by-your-leave, and added unpleasantly, 'Your sister hasn't wasted much time with his lordship, it seems. They appear to find each other's company most entertaining.'

Gilbert took a hasty step towards the bed, his expression darkening. 'What the hell are you insinuating?'

The agent smoothed the sheet with one plump hand, pursed his lips as though savouring a pleasant taste, and said suavely, 'I'm insinuating nothing, my boy. Nothing at all. I merely hear things . . . '

136

'Damn you! What've you heard about Caroline?'

'Only that Lord Vale is with her constantly, rides with her, dines with her, plays at cards with her 'til all hours. He even encourages her to wear the late Lady Vale's finery, which has caused quite a stir at the house. But I daresay there's nothing in it . . . ' He smiled slyly up at Gilbert's taut, angry face. 'To tell the truth, my boy, I did not think your sister had it in her. When she first came to Mount Sweeny she looked quite plain; but when I saw her last . . . ' He smiled again, pursing his lips at the corners. 'Oh, it was a very different story. Very fine, she was, and laughing up at Lord Vale as though his very insults gave her pleasure.'

Gilbert said through clenched teeth: 'Insults her, does he?'

'There's nothing in that,' said the agent. 'His lordship treats everyone the same; says what he pleases, orders people about, and cares nothing for whether they like it or not. I got the impression, though, that your sister did seem to like it. Not all the time, I daresay; but for all she strives to guard that cool, untouchable look of hers, you could see that she was hot enough for his lordship underneath. If you take my advice, Mister Gilbert, you'll do your business quickly, and take that sister of yours away . . . '

'Damn you, Rance,' said Gilbert, glaring down at the agent, his hands clenched at his sides, 'keep your foul tongue off Caroline, unless you want me to strangle you in your sickbed. I don't know what she is playing at, but I'm willing to swear it won't be as you are hinting.'

'Oh, his lordship can be very charming, when he chooses.' And then, as Gilbert's expression darkened, he changed the subject by saying, 'You must not come here. I told you that before.'

'So you did,' said Gilbert, still frowning down at the agent as though it would give him pleasure to do him a mischief. 'I'm heartily weary of being told what to do by you, Rance. Take care you don't give me one order too many!'

'It's not my orders, Mr Gilbert.'

'So you keep telling me,' retorted the young man, narrow-

137

ing his eyes and regarding the agent's mottled face without favour. 'Tell me one more thing, then. Who is this damned Serpent? I'm certain you could tell me that, if you wanted.'

The agent's eyes turned, involuntarily, to the panelled wall beside the bed. Then he looked at Gilbert and said reprovingly, 'Don't speak that name here. You're in trouble enough with the master already. Of all the bungling fools! I don't know how you could have missed killing his lordship, the other evening. You had him at point blank range, they tell me . . . '

'Dammit, Rance!' protested Gilbert, nettled by this criticism from someone who had spent the past few days skulking in his bed. 'How was I to know that Caroline would be in the curricle with Vale, and that the silly chit would stand up and shout at me? One thing, the Serpent can't blame me for Caroline being at Mount Sweeny! That was your idea, not mine!'

'Listen to me, Mister Gilbert,' said Rance, sitting up and speaking with the authority of one who knows he has the whip hand. 'The master wants to see you. He's not pleased with you, my boy. Not in any way pleased.'

Gilbert showed no sign of being stricken with terror at these words. On the contrary, he was staring down at the agent, with the air of a man who knows himself on the verge of making a discovery. He said slowly: 'So he wants to see me, does he? Do you mean to rise from your bed, to escort me to the chapel, Rance? Or will you leave me to find my way there?'

'I shall come with you, Mister Gilbert,' said the agent, sounding prim and disapproving. 'I am obliged to do so. I am quite as much under orders as you are, I assure you. All of us must abide by the master's rules.'

'Rules?' echoed Gilbert thoughtfully. 'You know, it does seem to me strange that you are the only member of the organization who is able to interpret the Serpent's rules. How is it that the Serpent never shows himself to any but yourself? And you are always in the offing when he speaks to

his minions in that damned whispering manner. In the offing
. . . ' Gilbert paused, and repeated slowly, 'In the offing, but
never actually there . . . '

'I told you,' said Mr Rance, uncomfortably. 'The master
insists that things are done in a certain way. And it will do
you no good to question your orders. I have already warned
you about what happens to people who do that.'

'Indeed you have,' retorted Gilbert cheerfully. 'It fairly
made my blood run cold, the first time or two. Clever old
Rance! You've hit upon a capital way of staving off curious
persons, have you not?' The young man paused, and added
quietly, but with a measure of menace in his eye, 'Mick and I
have been together these past few days, you know, and we
have come to the conclusion that something ought to be done
about this Serpent. If we could discover his identity, we
could get together with some of the other fellows in the
organization, and confront him. The night people are heartily sick of this . . . this whispering terror that keeps them all
in subjection. What do you say to that, Rance? Isn't it about
time that someone unmasked the Serpent, and spoke to him
face to face?'

The agent made a hasty movement with both his hands, as
though imploring Gilbert to speak more quietly. He said
quickly and uncertainly, with a glance at the wall, 'No
indeed, Mister Gilbert! You must not allow the men to talk
like that. Besides, it's not safe. You never know who you can
trust.'

Gilbert gave a crack of laughter, which sounded shock-
ingly loud in the quiet room. 'You're a great one to talk of
trust, Rance! I'd trust you no further than I could see you. I
know why you have taken to your bed, and the night people
know it, too. You did not like it when Vale came to Mount
Sweeny, did you? You wanted him dead before he came here;
needed him dead! It would never do for his fine lordship to
look too closely into his affairs at Mount Sweeny, would it?'

Gilbert paused. The agent did certainly look far from well.
There was a patchy look about his highly coloured face, and

139

he did not try to deny Gilbert's accusation. He said soberly, discarding his overbearing manner, 'That's true, Mister Gilbert. So I am relying on you to do what must be done.'

Gilbert stared down at Mr Rance, his earlier suspicions beginning to take shape. He decided to press the matter a little further. 'That's all very well, Rance,' he said, in a gentler tone, 'but even suppose you are rid of Vale, you'll have his heir and successor to contend with. Richard Sweeny, it will be. What makes you think Vale's brother will be easier to dupe? From all accounts, he's a thorough, serious-minded fellow – and, unlike the present Earl, given to staying here in Ireland.'

It was obvious that the agent was nonplussed by this question; obvious to Gilbert, at least, who wondered ruefully how he had failed to see the truth before. Watching Mr Rance as he turned his balding head away – as though by doing so he could evade the awkward matter in hand – Gilbert saw it all. It was laughable, really, that this stout, blustering man should be the Serpent – yet there was nothing to laugh at in some of the deeds he had done.

Mr Rance turned his head once more, and looked at Gilbert. He still seemed to hesitate, to be puzzling what best to say. Gilbert found himself impatient of this playacting. 'I suppose you are about to tell me that the Serpent has some hold over Richard Sweeny – some discreditable secret which will ensure he'll give you no trouble? Is that it?'

'Something of that nature, Mister Gilbert,' the agent admitted. His voice was hoarse. He nodded. 'Yes, that's it . . . ' Then, as Gilbert went on standing there without saying a word, he added, with a return to his lordly manner, 'Now, it's time you were gone. I don't know why you are here, wasting my time, when you ought to be about that other business. As you know, if you fail to kill Lord Vale within the allotted time, you can expect no payment, and no help in leaving the country. If you are wise, you will make no more mistakes. His lordship rides out every day, from all accounts.'

'All very well,' said Gilbert sulkily, 'but he has never once taken the same route.'

'You must contrive something,' said the agent. 'When I take you to see the master tomorrow evening, it will be as well for you, if Lord Vale is already dead.'

But once again, rather to the agent's dismay, the younger man seemed unimpressed by the warning. He gave vent to a short, contemptuous laugh: 'Rance, my poor fellow, has it not occurred to you that you can cry wolf once too often? Particularly when your motheaten sheep's clothing no longer serves to hide your true identity. Aye, man,' Gilbert went on, pitiless and a shade triumphant, for he had seen the agent start, and shake his balding head; 'You might well have called yourself wolf, not serpent, for you have harried and herded and savaged those poor sheep you call the night people – not to mention such blackmailing hold as you seem to have over Richard Sweeny and his like.'

The agent did not speak. Gilbert saw him lick his lips, and witnessed the guilty shifting of his glance from one side to another. Gilbert laughed again, a bitter, savage sound, and moved to the side of Mr Rance's bed and sat himself down upon it. 'You want Lord Vale dead. I can understand your wanting that; and I might even be willing to do the task for you – for a price. But the price will be high, I don't mind telling you, and we'll have no more threats, Rance. And you may save your breath denying that you are the Serpent. Come, man. Admit it! And then we'll get down to making new terms.'

When Gilbert had gone away, the panel in the wall of the agent's bedroom slid back. Mr Rance looked up at his latest visitor and said defensively, 'I had to let him believe that. He'd never have gone away, else.'

'You did well.' The visitor's voice was like the rustle of dead grass. 'Very well. He wanted to believe it. People like having their suspicions confirmed.'

'I wouldn't put it past the boy to back off from killing his lordship,' said Mr Rance, relieved that he had done the right thing, but still uneasy. 'He might decide to approach the authorities, unless we can silence him. He's greedy for gold, though. He'll come to the chapel tomorrow evening, if only to lay his hands on the reward I promised him. But after that . . .'

The answering whisper was barely audible. Rance caught the words, and hardened though he was, he felt a shudder going through him.

'After that,' murmured the Serpent softly, 'young Morrisey may begin to learn that where there is one wolf, there may well be another.'

Another dawn, another ascent of the mist-wreathed hillside, and a laughing breathless gallop over the high ground. At the end of it they took a leisurely route home, stopping to pay one or two calls on outlying farms. Caroline watched Vale as he listened to yet another tenant's tale of woe. This man was more well-to-do than some, with a stone-built cottage on the edge of his few acres of land, and a dozen sheep and some rangy looking cows cropping the rough hill grass. But his tale was much the same as the others; similar to many Vale had heard that week. In a few weeks' time, the lease of this man's farm would be due for renewal. Mr Rance was once more canting the rents, offering the lease to the highest bidder – uncaring, it seemed, that some tenants had worked their land well, improved it, or had lived on it for some years – as this man had. He told Vale, almost tearfully, he'd never yet been behindhand with sending his potatoes down to Mr Rance's yard, or providing the agent with hay in the autumn. Yet, he greatly feared that there would be others offering more than he could afford. If his lordship would put in a word for him?

They rode away at last. Vale made no promises. Nor did his long face give any hint of what he was thinking; but Caroline had felt reassured, all the same. From the look on the farmer's face when they departed, she thought he too had gained some comfort from meeting his landlord face to face.

They skirted some trees, and when they had passed them, Caroline gave a little sigh of relief.

'Safely past another place of peril, Miss Caroline?' murmured the Earl, smiling thinly. 'I wonder who's side you are really on? Mine, or Gilbert's? Or don't you know, yourself?'

She turned her head to look at him, her eyes wide and apprehensive. 'I don't know what you are talking about, my lord.'

'No? Strange, isn't it, how dense you become whenever his name is mentioned? All the odder, really, because on all other matters, you understand me very well. It's time you tried to be a little frank with yourself, Miss Caroline. You prevented your precious Gilbert from killing me the other day. Plainly, you are in dread of him trying again; yet, when I ask you to tell me who Gilbert is, or what these night people he has joined are trying to do, you will not. So, I'm asking you; who's side are you on? You will have to choose, you know.'

She looked away then, shaken that he had perceived so much. She pushed down her bewilderment as to why, if he knew it all, he did not hand her over to the authorities. She said gravely, fearfully: 'You have no proof, my lord, that it was Gilbert who shot at you.'

'No proof?' He looked at her, and there might have been genuine regret in his hooded amber eyes. 'My dear, the proof is in your face. You know, I am tempted to send you away, after all. This game that your Gilbert is playing is no game for you. Yes, it might be better for you to go, before it is too late.'

She found this gentler tone almost impossible to withstand. She said curtly: 'Go? And where would I go, my lord? After the past few days, everyone in your household believes me to be your mistress. I have no reputation left. No respectable lady would employ me as her child's governess now.'

'Just as well,' he said cheerfully. 'You are not cut out to be

143

a governess, my dear. I have told you that before. And you are grown far too pretty in the past few days. Did you not see how my sister Augusta has been staring at you?'

She had indeed seen it, and could have done without that speculative, amused scrutiny. She said in a nettled tone, 'That merely proves my point, my lord. If you say I ought not to earn my living as a governess, perhaps you can suggest some other way?'

'Why doesn't Gilbert support you?' he enquired blandly. He saw her flinch, and added softly, 'You think he will not? My dear, you have made a poor choice. You have a low opinion of me, I know, but even I do not refuse support to my women, when they are in need.'

'No doubt with such an army of them, it proves a heavy charge upon you,' she said crossly. 'And since all the world believes me to be yet another of your women, my lord, perhaps I should apply to you for aid? Shall I do so?'

'That,' he said coldly, 'is a remarkably tasteless remark, Miss Caroline. I am surprised that you should display so little delicacy of mind.'

'Are you, my lord?' she retorted, her tone of voice quite as glacial as his. 'The sad truth is that since coming to Mount Sweeny. I have had to dispense with delicacy of mind or feelings. Only this morning one of your household advised me to ask you for some tangible memento of . . . of our relationship: something to take with me when I cease to amuse you.'

His expression changed. 'Which of my servants dared to say such a thing to you?'

She was startled at his sudden fury. She said, laughing shakily, for it had been Maura who had made this suggestion, 'No need to look so savage, my lord. It was kindly meant. And I don't mean to tell you who it was.'

The fierce gleam died, to be replaced by a warmer look. 'You're loyal to your friends, Miss Caroline, I'll say that for you.'

'Why, yes,' she said, in surprise. 'I try to be. Don't you?'

He smiled crookedly. 'I do: but loyalty is not a common

144

quality in females.' He saw that she was still eyeing him in a startled, puzzled way, and added impatiently: 'We were discussing what you should do, Miss Caroline. I think you should marry Richard.'

'No, I can't do that, my lord. Certainly not.'

'So adamant, Miss Caroline?' He was once more amused and mocking. 'Why do you spurn my poor brother? What has he done to offend you?'

She gave him a very straight look, her gravity masking the pain within. 'Mr Sweeny has always been most kind to me, my lord. But kindness is not enough. I could not enter into marriage without more than that.' She broke off, wanting to make him understand, yet fearing that he would not. 'To my way of thinking, my lord, there must be a meeting of minds, a sharing of laughter. There must also be trust, and . . . and love.'

Vale gave a sharp sniff of disgust. 'Just as I thought! Women always babble about love.' He saw that she was regarding him gravely, even sadly, and he went on: 'My poor Miss Caroline; love is a fantasy, a figment of your youthful imagination. All you females think that it is love you need. You don't. What you want is admiration, adulation, petting and pampering; and when the poor man you have chosen tires of providing this syrup,' he added, looking with a certain grim satisfaction at her suddenly stricken expression, 'when your husband or your lover grows weary, you'll start looking elsewhere. As for marriage; when I marry again, I shall choose a woman who sees things as they really are. She'll know how to strike a bargain with me, and be willing to keep it; but if she starts to talk of love, I'll be off!'

Caroline said quietly, 'No doubt you know more about married love than I, my lord. But married love is not the only kind. There can be bonds of affection between all manner of people.'

'Bonds!' he echoed, derisively. 'Oh, I know all about bonds, Miss Caroline. I've had my share of bonds and shackles and grasping female hands . . . '

145

She shook her head at him, as she might have done at Jemima when she was being contrary. 'You are twisting my words. You know there can be love and caring between brothers and sisters, between parents and their children? Do you set no value at all on Jemima's love for her puppy, for instance?' She saw that he was looking ahead to where Jemima was riding with the groom, Paddy. His face had lost its bitter look. She added, 'I think you are a little fond of Jemima, my lord; only you hate to let people guess how much you care.'

He raised his hand as though acknowledging a hit. Jemima had turned to look back at them, shouting at them to watch her jump a grassy bank into the next field. He waved at the child, and turned to look at Caroline. 'When I first met you, Miss Caroline, you accused me of being an uncaring parent. Don't tell me you've changed your mind?'

She laughed, warmed by a small glow of triumph. They reined in their mounts and watched as Jemima set her pony at the jump, and together they applauded when she arrived safely and triumphantly at the other side.

Fourteen

CAROLINE WAS WEARING one of the late Countess's evening gowns for the first time, and had just finished fastening her long shining hair in a smooth coil, when a small sound at the door made her turn. Gilbert was standing there, watching her. She gave a gasp.

'Oh, Gil! What a fright you gave me!' Then she realized the danger, and added in a low, urgent voice, 'You must not come here!'

'You're a fine one to tell me what to do, Caroline,' he said, breathing fast. He looked, she saw, as if he had been riding hard, or running. His coat was muddy and torn at the sleeve, and there was a livid scratch on one cheek. He came and loomed over her. 'From all I hear, it's high time I took you away. No wonder you didn't want to leave before. Were you too busy setting yourself up as his lordship's doxy?'

She shook her head, hurt that her twin should believe the current gossip. She said gravely, 'It's not so, Gilbert. Lord Vale is not interested in me, not in that way. He's keeping me here as a hostage for your good conduct. He has pressed me several times to tell him about what you and the night people are doing, you see, and I would not say.'

That rocked him. He came closer and grasped her shoulders painfully. 'I hope you've held your tongue about me!'

'Don't Gilbert! You're hurting me.'

'I'll do more than hurt you, if you don't tell me what you're up to, Car.' And when she only stared up at him in a

147

grave way that made him feel both nettled and reproached, he added resentfully: 'Damn you, Caroline! What am I supposed to think? I'm told you've set the whole place by the ears, flaunting yourself in a dead woman's clothes, playing cards with Vale . . . ' He gave her another shake for good measure, and added, 'I used to think that nothing would shake your loyalty, but now—'

She said sadly, 'You weren't very loyal to me, were you, listening to Maura's gossip?'

'Maura? I haven't seen the wench for days. It's Rance who told me . . . ' He broke off, gave vent to a sound that was halfway between a groan and a sob: 'Oh God, Car! That's what I came to tell you. Rance is dead! I've just found him, hanging in the chapel crypt.' Caroline could feel him trembling, and his mouth shook uncontrollably. 'You've got to come away with me, Caroline, while there's still time. They're bound to think I killed him.'

Caroline could not remember a time when she had not felt responsible for Gilbert. It had always seemed natural for her to fight his battles, minister to his wounds, to defend him from her father when he had done some wrong. Gilbert had taken her devotion for granted, and this she looked on as natural, too. He was part of her, her twin, her other, more turbulent, more charming self. But as she stood there, holding him in her arms and listening to his tumbling, hurrying words, she found herself gripped by a spasm of revulsion and dismay.

Gilbert had found out that Mr Rance was the Serpent.

'I accused him of it,' he said, 'and he admitted it. Think of it, Car! I've been going around in deadly fear of the Serpent, and all the time it's been old Rance. He was cornered, and he knew it,' Gilbert added, with a certain relish. 'He offered me twice the original reward for killing Vale, so long as I kept silent about who he was.'

Caroline made a protesting sound, and would have tried to

148

argue, but he cut her short. He told her not to interrupt. She bit her lip, and clasped her hands together, listening with growing terror to the tale he had to tell.

'I was to meet him in the crypt of the chapel – you know the place, on the cliff above Sweeny's Port? He said he'd bring the gold. Well . . . ' Gilbert drew a shaking breath, remembering, and his voice became an unconscious echo of the Serpent's whisper. 'I went down into the crypt. It's a creepy place when it's growing dark, I can tell you, Car. I sensed that something was wrong almost at once. The other time it was silent until the Serpent came; but this time there was a sort of thudding noise, like a door swinging in a draught. I was trying to puzzle out what it could be, when there were men's voices and footsteps overhead in the ruined chapel. So I groped my way to the far end of the crypt – where the Serpent's voice usually seemed to come from – and – ' Gilbert's voice seemed to waver. 'It was horrible! I bumped up against Rance's body as he was hanging there. It was Rance, I tell you! I saw him clearly for an instant as those damned torches came flickering down from the top of the crypt steps. And then I just panicked and ran for it; charged up the steps and through two or three of Mannering's Volunteers, and out into the graveyard. I knew if I could get to the boys who were holding the horses, I'd stand a good chance of getting away. But I never expected to see Mannering . . . '

Caroline gave a gasp, and stared in consternation at her twin's scratched, ashen face. 'Sir Giles? Was he there?'

Gilbert nodded, and said with a groan, 'Ay, I ran right into him. Those men of his in the crypt were shouting after me to stand, and he turned and saw me. Oh, he knew me all right. He even shouted back at the others, telling them not to shoot.' He saw the relief in Caroline's eyes, and shook his head at her. 'Don't you see? When they find Rance – which they must do at once – they're sure to think I killed him. What else should they think?' He gave her arm a shake, and added urgently, 'Come on! There's no time to lose. The others are waiting for me; and they've promised to see us both safely out to the French ship tonight.'

'No.' She stood where she was, looking at him sternly. 'No more running away, Gilbert. You must stay and tell the truth about all this.'

'They'll never believe me,' he said, seething with his need to be gone. 'Come on, now! Get your cloak and a change of clothes. There's no time to lose.' She did not move, and he added in an anguish of impatience, 'There's the run on tomorrow night, which is nothing short of a miracle. They've promised to see us on board the French ship with the outgoing cargo.'

But even as he spoke, the door opened and Jemima walked in. She was neatly brushed and dressed for dinner in the muslin gown that Caroline had made for her. She stopped short at the sight of Gilbert, and favoured him with one of her darkling looks.

'So this is Vale's brat,' he said, his voice jerking with tension. 'Trust a Sweeny to come in when they're not wanted!'

'How should I have known that you were here?' Jemima demanded in her haughtiest manner. 'Who is this man, Miss Caroline?'

Caroline went swiftly over to her, hoping to reassure the child, yet having no idea how she was going to do it. She said with a forced smile, 'This is my brother, Jemima. He's not ill-mannered in the ordinary way, but he's in a little trouble.'

'Oh?' Jemima's eyes had followed Gilbert as he went to the window, and was trying to peer down to ground level. He uttered a sharp oath, and came back to them, seizing Caroline by the upper arm. 'Mannering and his fellows are down there already. Make haste, Caroline! Get a cloak and leave the rest.' He stared down at Jemima, and seemed to make up his mind. 'We'll take the brat with us.'

'No!' Caroline's horrified protest might never have been uttered, however, for two cloaked and masked men came in, one carrying a pistol and the other a stout stick. Jemima

150

stifled a scream of terror, and ran to Caroline for safety.

'Come on, lad, we've got a ladder to the passage window,' said the first of these men. 'The yard's swarming with military, and that's the only way out.' He turned his hooded face towards Caroline and Jemima, who were standing clutching each other by the bed, and added, 'We've no time for women and children, and that's a fact. We'll be done if we don't reach the horses before the military find them.'

'Yes,' said Caroline, much relieved to hear this. 'Go quickly all of you! I'll try to delay them, if they make for that passage.' Gilbert was glaring at her, his eyes narrowed and blazing with inner excitement and fear. She said hastily, imploringly, 'I'll be all right, Gilbert! Truly . . . '

But he had turned his gaze on Jemima, and before Caroline could move, had hoisted the child into his arms. The child gave a gasping shriek of fright. Gilbert clamped his hand over her mouth and was running from the room, followed by his two ruffianly companions.

'Gilbert!' Caroline's agonized cry was cut short, as she realized that none of them would have heard it. It seemed, afterwards, that her brain had been seized by a kind of paralysis. She had no recollection, later, of how she managed to get to the far end of the corridor, with a heavy brass candlestick in her hand. She saw the window, and the men silhouetted against it. One of them had just disappeared down the ladder to the ground below.

Gilbert was holding a wriggling, kicking Jemima under one arm, and as he swung a leg over the window sill, he saw Caroline running towards him. The man with the stick was steadying the top of the ladder, the cudgel on the floor beside him. Caroline knew what she had to do. She raised her candlestick and hit the man on the side of the head with all her might. He made a horrid grunting sound, and slid to the ground at Gilbert's feet.

'Damn you, Car!' he said furiously. 'What have you done to Mick?' He stared despairingly at the man's slumped, groaning form, and called his name: 'Mick! Mick!'

Jemima's mouth was still clamped inside Gilbert's hand. Her eyes, wide and terrified, were fastened on Caroline. 'Put Jemima down, Gilbert!' she ordered him sharply. 'Put her down and take your horrid friend with you!' There were unmistakeable sounds of pursuit, growing nearer every second. She could hear shouts, running feet, doors banging. She said again, 'Give her to me, and for goodness' sake, go!'

Gilbert, a wild-eyed version of her twin she could hardly recognize, said through set teeth, 'Vale's fond of her, isn't he? She's coming with me. You can stay and tell him that it'll go ill with her if he tries to follow.'

'No!'

They stared at each other, both furious, both determined; each the mirror image of the other. Jemima gave a convulsive wriggle, and Gilbert took his free hand and grabbed a handful of the child's hair. He gave it a vicious tweak, saying, 'Keep still, you little devil! Keep still, or I'll scrag you!'

That small act of cruelty gave Caroline the impetus she needed. She swung the candlestick for the second time and struck her twin on the elbow. He uttered a cry of pain, and let Jemima go. Caroline seized hold of her and began to run, bundling the child down the corridor.

But Gilbert caught up with her. She pushed Jemima ahead, turning to face her twin. He tried to lunge past her, but she intercepted him, hanging on to his shoulder, clutching at his coat tails, screaming to Jemima to run.

But she had not reckoned on the second man. She heard him behind her and turned her head. She saw his upraised arm and the cudgel; then the world seemed to explode in a blinding flash, and there was nothing but a roaring darkness.

Consciousness came back, slowly, painfully. There were sounds all around her, exclamations, and she was being carried. Somebody was in pain. She could hear them whimpering. Then, the pain became hers. A blacksmith was hammering inside her skull, an insistent, intolerable rhythm which went on and on, compounding with the tiresome voices, hurting her dreadfully. She wished they would go away. Presently, they did go away, and the darkness reclaimed her.

Down in some deep, dark place, Caroline knew that she must make the effort to bring herself to the surface. There was danger, something to be done.

She opened her eyes, flinching as hot swords of pain pierced them. The room swung round, tilting, then lurching sickeningly. She closed her eyes.

Later on she woke to find someone looking down at her. She tried to focus, and in a little while made out Lady Augusta's face. She wished very much that it had been Vale. She said weakly: 'Jemima . . . '

'Jemima's safe,' said Lady Augusta. 'Safely asleep in my room.'

Caroline gave a little sigh, and shut her eyes again. Her private blacksmith was still hammering away, but more distantly. She tried to focus her mind, but it would not work for her. Gilbert? She must not speak of Gilbert, or ask if he had got safely away. What was it that Gilbert had said about the Serpent? That Mr Rance was the Serpent; and that he had been murdered. She opened her eyes and said faintly, 'He did not kill him, you know. He should have stayed to explain . . . '

'To be sure he should,' said Lady Augusta in the same quiet voice. 'Go back to sleep now.'

Time ceased to have a meaning for Caroline during that long night and the bleak dawn that followed. She woke several times, but had only a blurred recollection of these wakings. Next day she was visited by the doctor and pronounced fit enough to get up; but she did not at once do so. She lay back in her empty room and tried to piece together the fragments of memory. It seemed that Gilbert must have got away; but for how long would he remain free? Then she recalled that he was to go on a French ship that night. She wondered numbly if she would ever see him again.

The housekeeper came into the room. She seemed upset, and instead of replying to Caroline's greeting, she turned her back and locked the door. She took the key out, and fastened it to the chain she wore round her waist.

'Am I a prisoner, then?' demanded Caroline, with a wan attempt at flippancy. 'Or are we defending ourselves from some outer danger?'

'His lordship has left word that you are not to be left alone, Miss Caroline,' said the housekeeper, stiffly. 'Dear knows how he thinks the house can be run, if I stay in here with you.'

Caroline looked at Mrs Datchet in a dazed way. The housekeeper seemed to be in a state of unusual agitation. She was clasping and unclasping her hands as though kneading some invisible object between them, all the while looking uncertainly at Caroline.

She said distractedly, 'They found Mr Rance, Miss Caroline. He'd been hanged . . . ' Mrs Datchet's fingers worked and writhed again, and her face twitched. 'But that's not all.'

Caroline said gently, 'It must have been a terrible shock for you, ma'am.'

But the housekeeper did not seem to have heard Caroline's words. She went on speaking, her eyes with their wrinkled lids fastening upon Caroline's face, beseechingly. She said: 'I always thought there was something queer about Miss Prendergast going off like that. But Mr Rance was so sure that she'd gone to her mother. Come to think of it, Lady Jemima always said Miss Prendergast's mother was dead . . .'

Caroline felt cold. She said, 'What happened to Miss Prendergast?'

The housekeeper answered in a frightened whisper. 'She never went away at all. They found her body, buried in Mr Rance's garden. They say she's been dead a month, or more.'

Fifteen

'NO SIGN OF THEM AT ALL,' said Richard Sweeny wearily. 'Those night people have given us the slip once again, Mannering. What's to be done now?' He fingered his unshaven chin and yawned. 'I confess I'd like nothing better than to go home and tumble into bed. I feel I've been banging on doors and searching hay barns forever. No one knows anything, no one has seen or heard anything at all. They never have, of course.' He sighed a second time, but said, brightening, 'Well, at least we know that it was Rance at the bottom of it. The Serpent and his followers don't quite seem so invincible, now that's come out into the open. Extraordinary to think of old Rance being the leader of the night people all this time, right under our noses. Are you sure of it, Mannering?'

The magistrate was sure. He was feeling his age. Finding that poor little woman's corpse in the agent's garden had been unpleasant enough. It had been much worse sifting through the contents of the leather-bound box in Mr Rance's study. It was in this box that the Serpent – and it seemed it could be none other than Mr Rance – kept a careful record of his villainous transactions. He had documented his evil activities with meticulous and painstaking precision. It was all there in the agent's small, crabbed hand; rows and rows of figures, a tally of months, and in some cases years of blackmail, extortion, smuggling and other crimes of a profitable nature. The worst, Sir Giles thought, was the blackmail.

There had been well-known names among the Serpent's victims – one a close friend, who had killed himself only two months since.

Sir Giles said bitterly again: 'Yes, Sweeny. Rance was our Serpent, I'm afraid. There can be no doubt about it.'

'Then Gilbert Morrisey did the world a service by killing him,' said Richard in his strong, sensible voice. 'There'll be many people who will sleep easier in their beds now that Rance is dead.'

Sir Giles did not deny this; but his dour expression did not lighten. What Richard said was true; but the law took no account of a victim's morals. Murder was murder, and it looked very much as if young Gilbert Morrisey was guilty of this one. It was a pity. By even the most lenient reckoning, Edward Rance deserved to be hanged by the neck until he was dead. The magistrate gave voice to another thing that was confounding him:

'What I cannot understand is why Rance killed the Prendergast woman, and then buried her in his garden in that amateurish way? It doesn't marry with what one knows of the Serpent. Why should he want to kill the poor woman, anyway?'

Vale was writing at his desk, and at this he lifted his head and said bleakly, 'He had to dispose of one governess, didn't he, before engaging another? How else could they have got Miss Caroline Morrisey into the house?'

'You're not being fair to Miss Caroline!' protested Richard vigorously. 'I simply do not believe that she came here from any ulterior motive. It was coincidence which led Rance to engage her.'

Vale laid down his pen and got up in a leisurely way. 'You are welcome to believe anything you choose, dear boy. For my part, I am no longer able to take so sanguine a view.'

'I'll swear she is innocent.'

'Innocent? She came here to help her brother. If we had not been quick to follow last night, the pair of them would have got Jemima out of that window and used her as a

156

weapon to aid their escape; and afterwards . . . ' He paused, and his thin lips took on an ugly twist, 'Afterwards, God alone knows what they would have done with her.'

Richard shook his dark head. 'I don't believe it. It cannot be true, Hugo. How do you explain the fact that Miss Caroline was unconscious when we reached the corridor? She'd been hit on the head. Doctor Garrity has vouched for that. Explain that, if you can?'

'I shall do nothing of the kind,' retorted the Earl coldly. 'Miss Caroline shall explain it herself. I daresay she will give a good performance, as always. Come to think of it, her brother must have struck her to give her an alibi. He had to do that, or take her with him. He'd have stood little chance of making a getaway with a female in tow.'

'Well, at least wait until you have talked with Jemima,' begged Richard. 'She must surely wake before long.'

But Vale would not. He was not going to have Jemima upset with questions, he said. The child had been hysterical, and had been heavily sedated. She was still asleep under the watchful eye of Lady Augusta and her personal maid. Vale said that he meant to take his daughter back to England as fast as he could. If he had his way, she would never learn of what had happened to Miss Prendergast: and the sooner Jemima forgot all about Miss Caroline Morrisey, so much the better.

Sir Giles listened to the brothers wrangling, and found his heart weighing heavy within him. He was growing every minute more resentful of Vale, who had returned from pursuing the night people earlier than the others, and had changed his clothes. He looked cool and composed, as if none of the present trouble had really touched him. Come to think of it, Sir Giles reflected sourly, if Vale had paid better attention to his estates, Mr Rance would never have been in a position to embark upon his villainous enterprises. If Vale had been more caring, young Gilbert Morrisey would not now be on the run from the law, and they would not be faced with the disagreeable task of questioning his sister. Sir Giles had always been fond of Caroline, and he shrank from what lay ahead.

When Caroline came in, the candles had been lit in the bookroom, and she was feeling tolerably composed. She knew that the time for subterfuge was past. The only hope for Gilbert lay in telling the truth, all of it. She began to do so.

She told them of how she had been brought to Mount Sweeny by Mr Rance, how she had hoped to meet with her brother, to persuade him to go abroad. She told them what she knew of Gilbert's dealings with the Serpent, and of the bribe he had been offered to murder the Earl of Vale – carefully looking away from her employer all through this recital. When he interrupted, she was taken by surprise.

She turned and stared at him, shocked. 'Wh . . what did you say, my lord?'

'I said, "Enough!" Do you think we're still as gullible as we were, ma'am?' The look in his hooded eyes made her wince. 'And you may take that innocent expression off your face, my girl. It's too late for simpering looks and appeals to our sympathy. To my mind we are wasting our time listening to this farrago you have made up. No doubt, it would be a good tale by normal standards; but we know too much to be taken in. By your own admission you came here to help your brother, who was pledged to kill me. Very well. I have known as much, and in a way I could understand it. You blame me, don't you, for the loss of Whitefield, for your father's death; and in your case, ma'am, you would wish to aid and abet your twin. But you made a bad mistake, my dear, when you tried to abduct Jemima.'

Caroline gasped, opened her mouth to deny this charge, and then closed it again. Even if she was not guilty, Gilbert had tried to take the child with him. She must accept some share of blame for her twin's actions.

'What, ma'am?' he demanded, with a glint of bitter mockery lighting his ugly features. 'Aren't you going to deny it? Go on! Tell me you had nothing to do with trying to abduct Jemima! Surely you can make a little effort to seem worried about her, to make us believe how much you love my dear little daughter?'

She was very pale, her grey-green eyes dark with distress. She did not think it would do any good to say anything in her defence. In this savage mood he would listen to nothing, believe nothing. She shook her head slightly as he tried once more to goad her into speech. The movement pained her, and she put a hand to the tender swelling on the side of her head.

'Ah!' The Earl's eyes glinted appreciatively. 'You've not yet wholly lost your touch, I see? Not you, consummate actress that you are! You had Jemima and Richard eating out of your hand, as you well know. Even I was beginning to succumb to your spell, my dear. If you had kept your head a little longer, you might have had me believing in your mawkish theories about love and marriage.' He laughed a little, a bitter sound. 'That surprises you, does it? You didn't know how near you were to winning my trust . . . ' He paused, and said with a contemptuous shrug: 'I should have known, of course, that you were no more to be trusted than your father.'

'That's enough, Vale,' said Sir Giles, in the tone of one who has put up with more than he can bear. 'Peter Morrisey was as honest as the day is long.'

The Earl was still watching Caroline. He said softly, 'So I used to believe myself, until I learned otherwise. Morrisey and his daughter have a good deal in common. They shared this ability to inspire trust and affection; and they were both cheats.'

Caroline said, frowning in a puzzled way, 'Papa never cheated in his life, my lord. You played cards with him. You must have known that. What are you trying to say?'

'I'll vouch for that!' put in Sir Giles strongly. 'Morrisey was as straight a man as you could find, and I don't mean to sit by and hear him maligned.'

'Don't you, Mannering?' drawled the Earl. 'Then you had better take yourself off. It's time for things to be said, and

159

nobody is going to stop me. There have been too many secrets, too many confidences kept; and all manner of falsehoods and misconceptions have been given credence. I blame myself for allowing it. I am keeping silent no longer.'

Richard said in a voice of quiet concern, 'Think before you speak, Hugo. You are angry, upset. Wait until you are more yourself, and have had a chance to reflect . . . '

'I have waited far too long already,' said Vale curtly. 'Much of this present trouble – perhaps all of it – might have been avoided if there had been more openness. I am to blame. I admit it.'

His three hearers gazed at him, waiting for him to go on. Only Richard seemed to doubt the wisdom of it, for he laid a warning hand on his brother's arm. Vale shook him off.

He was still looking at Caroline, who could no more have unlocked her gaze from his than she could have denied him the power to hurt her. She felt oddly calm, as though at the centre of a storm.

Vale said quietly, speaking to her alone, it seemed: 'You blame me for your father's death, do you not?' He did not seem to expect an answer, but went on, still in that cold, analytical tone, 'No doubt you are not alone in blaming me. If I had not been half way to Dublin by the time Peter Morrisey shot himself, they'd have tried to pin his death on me, just as they tried to say that I had killed my wife. There were many who thought I'd done that, weren't there, Mannering?'

The magistrate nodded in a bemused way; but he did not speak.

'Quite so.' Vale acknowledged Sir Giles's wordless admission with a twisted smile. Then, in an altered tone, he said: 'You know, Mannering, I've never been able to credit that tale of Morrisey shooting himself. I still cannot believe it.'

'Can you not, indeed?' said Richard acidly, moving over with deliberation and stationing himself behind Caroline's right shoulder, as though hoping to lend her some of his strength while she sustained this bitter onslaught. 'You say you cannot believe it, Hugo, but poor Morrisey undoubtedly

160

did shoot himself. I had the misfortune to find his body.'

Vale's crooked brows were knitted together in a frown. He said, 'I know it looked as if he had; but why would Morrisey do it?'

'My dear Hugo!' protested Richard, outraged at the heartless disinterment of this matter in Caroline's presence. He frowned at his half-brother, but when this had no noticeable deterrent effect, he said hotly, 'Miss Caroline's father had come to realize that he was ruined that morning! He had staked everything he owned, and lost it to you! It cannot have been a happy awakening for him.'

Vale said coolly, 'Morrisey was always on the verge of ruin. I never knew him when he was not.' He looked at Caroline, and said in a musing tone, 'Yet he always believed that his affairs would come about . . . '

Her gaze locked to his, Caroline whispered, 'That was so . . . yes.'

Richard put a hand on her shoulder. 'My dear—'

Sir Giles said suddenly, 'I've often puzzled about Morrisey's suicide myself. You're right, my lord. It was an unlikely thing for him to do. Peter never saw an end to the road he was travelling, for all that his friends tried to warn him . . . ' The magistrate paused, peering into his empty tankard as though expecting to find an answer there. He said at last, with an awkward kind of doggedness, 'Lord Vale, there is only one explanation that fits, for me. Morrisey must have been affected by your own attitude, by the way you behaved during that damnable card game at Whitefield.' He met the Earl's look of cold hauteur without flinching, and went on, 'You acted for all the world as though Morrisey was your enemy that night. It put me in mind of an execution, my lord. You might have come to Whitefield with the express intention of ruining Morrisey. That was how it looked to me at the time.'

'Observant of you, Mannering,' returned the Earl in a dry tone. 'You are perfectly right, as usual. I did mean to do just that.'

'In heaven's name why?' demanded the other. He added on an almost pleading note, 'Morrisey and you were friends. Damn it, Morrisey actually liked you! He was one of the few men round these parts who had a good word to say for you!' Vale's long, ugly face gave nothing away. He said in a baffled tone, 'I shall never understand it . . . '

'Morrisey had wronged me,' said Vale coldly. 'I have never been a believer in turning the other cheek. So I decided to take my revenge.'

Richard was staring at his half-brother as though he suddenly saw him in a new guise. He said slowly: 'Hugo! Was it . . . could it have been because of . . . Sybilla? I . . . I have wondered . . . '

There was a pause, and then Vale said in a lighter, almost flippant tone, 'So you've wondered, have you? How many others have wondered the same thing, I ask myself? Odd, isn't it, that I should have been the last to know what Sybilla and Peter Morrisey were up to?'

'What in the world are you saying?' demanded Sir Giles. Caroline just looked at Vale blankly. She had an odd feeling that she ought to know what Vale was talking about; but it made no sense.

But Vale seemed to notice neither Caroline's blank look, nor the magistrate's interruption. He went on in a musing tone, 'The ironic thing is that I might never have known, if I hadn't come across that journal that Sybilla was always scribbling in. I found it in a locked drawer after she was killed.' He gave vent to a short, mirthless laugh. 'She had written it all down, my lovely, faithless wife! Well, I knew she had a lover. She was pregnant when she was killed, but it never occurred to me that Peter Morrisey was the father.'

Sir Giles was the first to speak. He said in a strangled tone, 'Are you trying to make us believe that old Peter Morrisey and . . . and your wife were lovers, my lord?'

Vale's look would have daunted most men. 'I am not trying to make you believe anything, Mannering. What does it matter now? It all happened four years ago, and it was

162

hardly an extraordinary occurrence, even then. Men are
made cuckolds every day.'

'You misjudged Morrisey, my lord,' said Sir Giles sternly.
'I don't believe a word of it, and nor should you!'

'No,' said Caroline, finding her voice. 'You shall not say
such things, my lord. There must be some mistake.'

'Peter Morrisey was no lady's man,' argued the magistrate, strongly. 'And he must have been fully twenty-five
years older than Lady Vale.'

'He was not the first old fool to be ensnared by Sybilla's
charms,' retorted the Earl, with a contemptuous tightening
of his thin mouth. 'My beautiful wife collected men in the
same way that some people collect china, or pictures.'

'Hugo!' said Richard. 'Don't talk like that. You shall not
sully Sybilla's memory by suggesting she was promiscuous.'

'Her memory?' echoed the Earl, casting a pitying look at
his frowning brother. 'I knew Sybilla better than most,
Richard. Did you not know that enslaving poor witless males
was almost a game with her? I knew. I thought it a harmless
enough hobby, and I condoned it for the most part. I could
not satisfy her insatiable hunger for admiration, so it seemed
only fair to let her seek it from others.' He laughed, and
something inside Caroline shrank at the sound. 'I misjudged
her, though. She was not the ice-maiden I thought her. I only
discovered that when I read her journal. It was most reveal-
ing, I assure you. Funny that old Morrisey should have held
the key to Sybilla's cold little heart.'

They all looked at him, stunned into silence.

Vale said indulgently, 'I had trouble in believing it at first.
I was furious, wounded in my vanity. I would have liked to
kill Sybilla then; but she was already dead.'

'So you stormed over to Whitefield and deliberately used
your skill at cards to ruin Peter Morrisey?' said Sir Giles
accusingly. 'Tell me this, my lord. Did you give Peter a
chance to deny it, to defend himself?'

'As a matter of fact I did not,' said the Earl, drawing his
crooked brows together. 'He never mentioned Sybilla all the
time we were playing.'

'Of course he did not,' said Caroline scornfully. 'There were other people there, were there not?'

Vale looked at her as though he had temporarily forgotten that she was there, and had rediscovered her. 'If your father had tried to explain, if he'd told me why he loved Sybilla, I might not have gone on to the end.'

Sir Giles found that his brain was violently rejecting this whole scenario. He just refused to believe, could not make himself begin to credit, that his friend and neighbour, Peter Morrisey, had been the lover of the flighty and beautiful Countess of Vale. But it was clear that Vale believed it, and had allowed himself to believe it for four years. He said, latching on to Vale's latest remark, 'Why would it have made it better if Morrisey had spoken of it?'

Richard chimed in, 'If it had been my wife, and he'd admitted it, I'd have wanted to kill him.'

Vale smiled at his half-brother, and said in his drawling way, 'Dear boy, I know you would! But we have not all such a high opinion of women, you know. Personally, I've yet to find a female worth losing a night's sleep over, let alone doing a murder for.' He yawned a little, as though these revelations had wearied him, and with a suddenness that made Caroline jump, he grasped her by the shoulders and said: 'Look at Miss Caroline, will you? All innocence and honesty on the surface, so that no one can bring themselves to believe ill of her! Not even Jemima, despite her usual suspicion of paid keepers; and what do we find? She's no better than her father. She came here to help her brother to kill me, no doubt hoping to share in the spoils; and when her plans miscarry, she tries to abduct the child she's been professing to care so deeply for! Like father, like daughter, is what I say!'

'You may say what you like of me, my lord,' said Caroline unsteadily, 'but to say that Papa would do those things is just nonsense; wicked nonsense, my lord! No one who knew my father well could possibly believe it. He would never have hurt anyone – least of all you,' she finished in a biting voice. 'You who he counted on as a friend.'

'It's all down in that damned diary,' said Vale in a voice that had grown wearier and drier. 'If I hadn't been so jealous and angry, it would have sickened me. Sybilla was most explicit about her love for P – that's what she called him. She left few aspects of their loving to the imagination.'

Caroline frowned up at him. 'P? Your . . . your wife might have been romancing, writing of an imaginary love affair, don't you think?'

'No, I do not think it, ma'am,' he retorted, with blighting certainty. 'You claim to have known your father. So did I know my wife. She was not given to imaginary romances. She had no need, when so much more tangible and satisfying ones were at hand. Besides,' he added, remembering, 'there was something that rang true about that journal.'

'May I see it, my lord? There might be some clue.'

'I doubt it,' he said with a contemptuous shrug. 'And I haven't got it. I sent it to your father to read. I left for Dublin directly after that night of cards; and it seemed only just to make him understand that his seduction of my wife had been at the root of his misfortunes.'

She would have struck him then, but he caught her hand and pinioned it brutally, taking the other as well and holding her thus in an iron grip.

'Oh, no, my dear! It might relieve you to strike me, but I don't mean to allow you even that much satisfaction. You shall stand still and listen to what I have to say. Your father and my wife planned to kill me, even as your brother has lately tried to do. They were to be married after my death.' He broke off, struck by a bizarre thought. 'If they'd succeeded, you'd have had Sybilla as a stepmother. I wonder how you would have dealt together?'

Caroline was breathing in a gasping sort of way, for which his bruising grip was partly responsible. She said: 'Why are you so sure that they meant to kill you, my lord? Was that in the journal, too?'

He nodded. 'Sybilla was expecting a baby. She was anxious that her little viscount should be born with a father who would be proud to own him.' He paused, frowning. 'Foolish

165

of her, that. If she'd married Morrisey, the child would have taken Morrisey's name.' He added, after another pause: 'At least she had the sense to realize that I was not likely to own the little bastard.'

Caroline shook her head in a dazed way. 'I just don't believe it. Not Papa.'

'That's right, ma'am. You'll have Richard in tears if you persevere. He's looking pained at my rude treatment of you, already.' Vale seemed to think of something else, for he turned to the magistrate and said in a quite different tone: 'Mannering! I can give you a clue to why Morrisey killed himself, I do believe!' Sir Giles looked blank, and Vale went on, sounding even quite animated. 'If you wanted to kill me, and wanted it to look like an accident, how would you go about it?' Sir Giles just stared, and Vale supplied the answer to his own question. 'You might decide to arrange an accident to my curricle, don't you think? It's easy enough to tamper with a wheel, so that it would be bound to come off after the first mile, or so.'

They all stared at the Earl as though in a trance. Vale went on, thoughtfully, 'Sybilla was squeamish about some things. She might not cavil at her lover killing me, but I doubt if she would want to know details.' Sir Giles made a sudden movement, as though he had suffered an inner jolt of some kind. Vale gave him a comprehending nod. 'You see? No one drives my curricle – except myself or Paddy – and everyone knows that for a fact. Now, suppose that Morrisey had tampered with that wheel on my curricle? Suppose – and it was the case – that Sybilla was greatly enraged with me because I had forbidden her to leave the house? She wanted to leave, and none of the servants would summon her a carriage: and she badly wanted to annoy me. So she took my curricle, which was harnessed at the door, and drove off. Sybilla, I now see, died in the accident which was meant for me.'

'It sounds possible,' said the magistrate doubtfully. 'But how would you prove it, my lord?'

'There'd be little point in it,' said Vale. 'I merely offer you a reason for Morrisey killing himself. It had not occurred to me before. If he'd set a trap for me, and killed the woman he loved, it would have struck him a blow, you'll admit?'

Caroline tried to pull away from Vale's grasp, sobbing out a denial as she did so. 'Never, my lord! Papa would not; nor would he have used horses so.'

'True enough,' agreed the magistrate, swinging the other way in his thoughts again. 'I believe Peter Morrisey would have hit upon some way to kill you that did not harm any of your animals.'

'Yet he shot his dog before shooting himself,' said Vale, remembering this other thing he had been told.

'I tell you,' said Caroline in a low, despairing tone, 'I tell you that my father would not have tried to kill you at all. He was not a murderer; and Gilbert is not either.'

'Come, Miss Caroline,' said Vale in a scoffing tone. 'You've just told us that your brother accepted a bribe to shoot me.'

'But he would not have done it! If he'd really wanted to kill you, he'd have succeeded better. He is not a killer.'

'Then explain to us how your brother came to be alone with Rance's body?'

'If Morrisey killed the Serpent,' said Richard strongly, 'one can only call him a public benefactor, Vale.'

'But he did not,' said Caroline, gazing at Richard with brimming eyes, knowing him for her only true supporter. 'He never killed Mr Rance, believe me.'

'It would take more than a few tears to convince us of that, my girl,' said Vale grimly. 'Here, Mannering! I am weary of her protestations. Take the jade away, and lock her up.'

'Take your hands off my sister, Lord Vale!' said Gilbert Morrisey from the doorway of the bookroom. 'None of you are going anywhere until I say so.'

Sixteen

$\mathcal{F}$OR THE SPACE OF SEVERAL HEARTBEATS, no one moved. Sir Giles and Richard gazed towards the doorway where Gilbert stood. Caroline felt Vale's hard fingers tighten on her shoulders. Then he took his hands away, and said smoothly:

'Ah, Morrisey. How obliging of you to call. We've been looking for you all over the place, you know.'

Gilbert chuckled: 'Not in the right places, my lord.' He waited in silence while four armed and masked figures moved swiftly into strategic places around the room. Each man held a gun of some sort, and their aspect was such that none of the three gentlemen in the bookroom felt it wise to move a muscle.

Gilbert's own pistol was aimed at the Earl's head, and as he walked slowly forward, Caroline said in an agonized whisper: 'No, Gilbert!'

'Stand aside, Caroline. You've interfered enough already. Too much, by Mick's reckoning. You've no idea the trouble I've had persuading him that you'd got to be rescued, after what you did.'

'Oh, so you've come to rescue her, have you?' murmured Vale. His level gaze was fastened on Gilbert's taut face, and he did not seem to be aware of the danger threatening him. He added, in a contemptuous tone, 'Well, you won't either of you get far; not at your present rate of bungling incompetence. A fine mess you've made of things, have you not? How do you expect to get paid for killing me, now that you've murdered Rance, who was your paymaster?'

'Don't—' said Caroline again, though whether she was speaking to Vale or to her twin, it was not quite clear. With her back to Vale she said, 'Don't heed his teasing, Gilbert. Tell him the truth. Tell him about the whispering voice in the chapel crypt, that comes out of the bare wall. Tell his lordship the truth.'

'Move out of the way, Caroline. This is no business of yours.'

'Tell him of how the Serpent gave orders for you to go to the crypt under the chapel, Gilbert; and how you accused Mr Rance of being the Serpent, and he actually admitted it. Tell him how you went to get the gold, and found Mr Rance dead, hanging in the crypt. It's no good running away any more. Lord Vale is perfectly right, Gilbert. You won't get far.'

'Quite so,' murmured Vale derisively, 'the jade is speaking the truth for once.'

'Don't!' said Caroline, for the third time, placing herself between the Earl and Gilbert's dangerously jerking pistol. 'Please, Gilbert!'

'Listen to what that sister of yours is telling you, young Morrisey,' growled Sir Giles from the far end of the book-room. His voice sounded muffled. He and Richard had by this time been herded to one side of the apartment, and were lying face down upon the carpeted floor, having their hands tied behind their backs. The magistrate's stout body heaved as he tried to turn his head to see the group in the middle of the room. He repeated, 'You listen to Caroline, my boy. If you give yourself up now, I'll bring all my influence to bear—' He broke off with a coughing grunt, as the man who was tying his hands dug a knee into his ribs and advised him to hold his tongue. At the same time, a scarf was knotted about Sir Giles's mouth, so he had no choice but to obey.

'Steady, Mick,' said Gilbert, frowning. 'Don't hurt the old boy.'

169

'No time for talking, lad,' said the masked man grimly, securing Richard's gag in a similar fashion. 'We've too much to do before the tide turns.' He got up from his knees, and came over, saying: 'Tie the woman up, too. I've had enough of her tricks. Get the keys, and let's be off!'

'Caroline won't play us false again,' said Gilbert quickly. 'Give us your word you won't, Car,' he beseeched her. And when his sister did not move, but merely looked at him, he added pettishly, 'Don't look at me like that! If you must know, I've no notion to shoot his lordship, not until he's helped us out of our present coil, at any rate.' And when she still made no move, he added, rather despairingly, 'If you don't promise to behave, I'll have to let Mick tie you up and gag you like the others.'

'That'll be a grand treat, entirely,' said Mick, his eyes glinting behind the dark material of his mask. 'Indeed, it will be.'

'It will not be necessary, however,' said the Earl calmly, pulling Caroline aside and dumping her down on to a chair. She gave a gasp of surprise and protest, and he said curtly, 'Your brother is right, ma'am. You're far too given to interfering in what does not concern you. Now, Morrisey?' he added, before Caroline could say anything. 'In what way do you imagine that I will help you?'

Gilbert hesitated. His eyes flicked from Vale's face to Caroline's and back again. The pistol in his hand wavered, and then steadied. He said curtly: 'You have had the locks to the cellars changed, my lord. We need the new keys, and understand that you are the only one to hold them.'

'Ah! So that's it? And if I don't oblige you in this, Morrisey? What then?'

The masked man made an impatient movement, and Gilbert said savagely, 'If you do not hand them over, and quickly, we'll bring all your family down here and shoot them, one by one, until you decide to co-operate.' Caroline would have started out of her chair, but Vale's heavy hand on her shoulder kept her pinned where she was. Gilbert laughed, a high excited sound which made her wonder if he had been drinking to give himself courage. 'Don't think I am bluffing, my lord, or that I would put a child's safety before my own. I did not kill your agent, as it happens; but I'd have done so, if it had suited my purpose. I'll kill your little daughter if I have to, or anyone else who seeks to stand in my way. Thanks to you, Lord Vale, I have spent four long years in America, as near starvation as made little odds. I've no liking or sympathy for you and your kind. You are no better than parasites, living at your ease while others labour to earn your comforts. Well, today you are going to be useful for the first time in your life.'

'Dear me,' murmured the Earl, 'I only hope I prove as useful as you hope. Would it be too much to ask what you want with my cellar keys?'

The man next to Gilbert made an impatient movement. Gilbert cast him a sidelong glance and said defensively, 'It can't hurt to tell his lordship, can it? After all, he might as well know how we mean to put him to good use.' This aside won only a grunt, so he went on: 'There's a run due tonight, my lord. The night people judge the tide and the wind to be right, and they have most of their cargo stored below in your cellars. If you had not seen fit to change the locks, we might have spared you all this bother.' He grinned suddenly, more of a nervous grimace than a real smile, and added triumphantly, 'You said we would not get far! You're wrong, you know. Caroline and I are going on board a French sloop this very night, part of the outgoing cargo. And you, Lord Vale, are going to help us to get there. First, you are going to hand over your keys, and funds to help Caroline and myself in our new life. Secondly, you are going to be our safe conduct out to that ship. If the excisemen know you are aboard, my lord, they'll hardly dare to attack us.'

Vale seemed to be considering this. Caroline tried to catch Gilbert's eye. Then she heard Vale say calmly, 'And then where will you both go?'

Gilbert shrugged and said, 'Somewhere we won't be found.'

171

Caroline said gravely, 'They already think you have killed Mr Rance, Gilbert. If you run off, they'll reckon their suspicions are confirmed.'

'Let them think what they like,' he retorted recklessly. 'I'll not be here for them to catch. I'll be at the other end of the world by then.'

'You'll be a hunted man all your life, Morrisey,' said Vale evenly. 'If you did not kill Rance, someone else did. Your evidence might lead to finding his murderer. You ought to stay and give that evidence.'

'Why should I want Rance's killer brought to justice? He deserved to die ten times over.'

'Very likely; but don't you want to establish your own innocence? Would you not wish to be cleared, to be able to walk about Ireland as a free man again, to hold up your head in this district?'

'How should I ever do that?' said Gilbert resentfully. 'There's nothing to stay here for. Nothing for me.'

'I wouldn't be so sure of that,' said the Earl quietly. 'As Mannering tried to tell you, before your friend here – er – interrupted him, you would get help and sympathy from many quarters.' And when Gilbert seemed unimpressed by this, Vale added, 'And though it goes against the grain, after the way you and Miss Caroline tried to abduct my daughter, I might even decide to help you, myself.'

'After what?' Gilbert's ejaculation was full of pure consternation; but only for a moment. After that, he cast a mocking look at Caroline, and said: 'If that don't just serve you right, Caroline. You'd have been better to have helped me!' Then he returned to the matter in hand. He said sourly, 'You say you might help me, Lord Vale. It's easy to make promises, though, when you've a gun at your head, and to forget them afterwards.' He met a look of haughty disdain from the Earl's eyes, and added sullenly: 'Well, how should I believe you, my lord? You did nothing to help us four years ago.'

'I know it,' replied Vale gravely. 'And I make no excuse for myself. It was unpardonable. But I'll tell you this. Four years ago I was as desperate and as bitterly angry as you are now, Morrisey. Like you, I was suspected of murder, a murder I did not do. My wife died driving my curricle, and they thought I had contrived it. And there were other things. Like you, I thought it best to run away from it all. But I was wrong.' He paused, and said slowly and pensively, as though he was thinking out a complicated conundrum while he yet spoke, 'It was not a better way, as I am only starting to see.'

To Caroline's ear he sounded burdened, weighed down by some unwelcome consciousness. He went on, seriously: 'Things don't stay quiet and buried, however much one might cover them over and wish to forget. They breed and fester in the darkness where they lie hidden.'

'I don't know what in the world you are talking about,' said Gilbert sullenly.

Vale smiled crookedly, 'Of course you do not. How should you, when I hardly know what I am talking about myself? But you must believe this. If I had not been so hell-bent on getting out of this countryside four years ago, you and your sister would not now be in this awkward case. I don't blame either of you for hating me. You have suffered more at my hands than ever your father did: and through no fault of your own.' The masked man was by this time fidgeting and clearing his throat in an impatient fashion. Vale said quietly, 'If you will stay and help untangle the facts of Rance's death, Morrisey, I'll do all I can to help you. I give you my word on it.'

Gilbert hesitated. He looked to see how Caroline was feeling about this. This time it was she who failed to meet his eye. She was gazing at the Earl with a look on her face which gave Gilbert an uneasy, bereft feeling.

He frowned at Vale, suspicion and hostility welling up in him. 'Why should I believe anything you say, my lord? I'm not a gullible female, to be seduced as my sister seems to be. We've wasted too much time. Hand over your keys, Lord Vale; and I shall want money for our journey. If you prove fine and generous, we will not need to send for your little daughter.'

Seventeen

*I*T WAS VERY COLD IN THE CELLAR where the night people had left them. Gilbert had prevailed on Mick to spare Caroline the stifling indignity of a gag in her mouth and a sack tied over her head; but her hands had been roped behind her, and her ankles were secured in the same way. Before long, the cold of the cellar seemed to seep into her very bones.

Still, she knew herself to be in a better case than any of the three gentlemen, who lay at the far end of the dark, freezing cellar, prostrate upon the stone floor. They were roped hand and foot as she was, and also blindfolded and gagged. Occasional gleams of lantern light from the passing night people showed their three pairs of legs jutting from behind a stack of casks. They looked like three well-tied parcels. Caroline, trying to ignore her own discomforts, knew at least that she was more fortunate than Vale, or than Richard and Sir Giles Mannering.

It took all her resolution to sustain a cheerful view as the hours dragged by. At first she had hoped against hope that Gilbert would come and release her; but he did not. On one occasion some of the night people came into their cellar, two of them carrying lanterns. The gleam lit their masked faces, and sent shadows chasing along the vaulted ceiling of the cellar where she lay. One of these men came over and checked Caroline's bonds, but he did not speak and neither did she. Others counted the row of casks. And before

174

Caroline could summon up courage to ask them what their intentions were, they were gone again, and the cellar was once more in darkness.

All the time there were sounds of coming and going outside the mouth of their cellar. Intermittent gleams of lantern light licked the walls and roof of their prison, distorted shadows sailed within range of Caroline's vision, but were mostly gone again before she could make out what they reflected. There were continuous sounds of lapping water, of muttering voices and heavy objects being moved about, things being rolled and dragged and an occasional clang of iron. Then, a second group of men came into their cellar and bore the casks away. Plainly, the night people were loading up for the outward run. Caroline became less painfully conscious of the cold, and a tight, painful knot of fright and dread began to form inside her.

She wondered what the night people meant to do with them, once their work in the Mount Sweeny cellars was done. Had Gilbert been serious when he spoke of taking her with him on the French ship? She felt a deep reluctance to be so transported: yet she did not think she could stay any longer in Vale's house – not after the things he had said about her father. Her thoughts veered away from Vale. Better not to think of him at all. Better for her if she had never met him.

She tried to concentrate her thoughts upon Gilbert, willing him to come to her, praying that there would be time to argue with him before he tried to bundle her aboard a French ship.

All at once, the place was full of men and lights. Gilbert came over to where Caroline was lying, propped against the dank stone wall. He said in a low, shaking voice: 'You were right, Caroline. They're all robbers. Oh God, you were right.' And in a loud voice, meant for others to hear, he declared with false heartiness, 'We won't be long now. The Frenchmen want to cast off in a few minutes.'

There was a delay while the night people argued about

175

what to do with their prisoners. The Earl was to be used as a hostage. They were intending to take him in the cutter as far as the French ship, in case the Preventives came in pursuit of them. The excisemen would never risk harming his lordship. There was a divergence of views about what to do with the other two. Some wanted to leave Sir Giles and Richard where they were. They would be found in due course by the Mount Sweeny servants. The second and more vocal contingent wanted to kill them, shoot them while they lay there, bound and gagged. It was the Serpent's way to leave no witnesses. It was better to go by the rules.

'And who is to say what the rules are now?' demanded Gilbert, going over to join the knot of arguing men. 'The Serpent is dead. Rance was found hanging in the crypt last night. I know, because I found him. So I say we have no need to go by the Serpent's rules any more. Let's leave those two gentlemen here.'

There had been a stir of astonishment as Gilbert made this declaration, and something almost like a cheer from some quarters. The man called Mick, however, said scornfully:

'Mr Rance was never the Serpent! Never!'

'He was, you know,' said Gilbert, sounding confident. 'I accused him, and he actually admitted it to me.'

'He was not, then!' The other man sounded every bit as sure of his ground. 'I've been in the same place with the two of them – so how could Mister Rance be two people?'

But before the argument could be taken further, someone hurried up to say that the tide was on the turn, and they must cast off. The argument about what to do with their prisoners was resumed with renewed urgency, and it was decided to leave Richard Sweeny and Sir Giles where they were. Mick was disgruntled at being overruled by the majority opinion of the others, and he came to look at Caroline, and said:

'And what about this one? She's been a trouble from the start; always in the way, always there. She'll bring us bad luck, I'm thinking.'

176

'She's coming with me on the French ship,' said Gilbert quickly. 'You promised, remember?'

'Gilbert,' Caroline began. 'Gilbert, please.'

Someone laughed, and suggested they ought to send her out to sea with his lordship. 'Let the poor man go to the bottom with his doxy to keep him company,' said the joker. ' 'Tis fair enough to give him what he wants, before he drowns.'

'Drowns?' said Caroline, glancing in horror at the masked man who had made this jovial pronouncement. 'You cannot mean to let Lord Vale drown?'

But the man called Mick growled at her to shut her mouth, telling Gilbert if he could not keep the wench quiet, he'd better gag her. 'Get the lord to his feet,' he ordered, once more taking command. 'Him and the woman, both. Hurry, now, or we'll miss the tide.'

'Better take the sack off the lord's face,' said another voice. 'How will the Preventives know him, if he's hidden under that?'

'They'll not know him anyways,' said another derisively. 'His is not a face that many of us have seen. Better to take Mister Richard, come to that.'

'It's the lord the Serpent wants rid of.'

At this point in the argument, Caroline lost track of what they were saying, because Gilbert was whispering in her ear. And he had come behind her as she stood swaying weakly on her numbed and newly released legs, and was sawing away at the ropes that tied her hands.

They all left the cellar, and began to descend some uneven stone steps. Gilbert propelled Caroline in front of him, half carrying her when she stumbled, and presently she felt him closing her fingers over something slender and hard. It was a knife. 'Hold on tight to that, Caroline. You're going to need it. They mean to cast Vale adrift and the two of us with him. Only we'll be dead when they put us in the boat. Our only hope is to reach that boat first, and cast off. I heard them planning it.'

177

Caroline was thrust down upon some bales of wool in the stern of the cutter, and a moment later Vale was thrown more roughly across her outstretched legs.

He was lying where they had thrown him, his roped arms uppermost, and his face hidden between one bale and another. He did not move at first, and she thought he must be unconscious. However, a hand came over and seized his hair, dragging him into an upright position like a broken rag doll, forcing him to sit in front of Caroline in the laden boat. Someone threw a frieze cloak over them both, and a rough voice told them to keep down and keep quiet if they did not want a knife in their guts. A few seconds more, and the boat was sliding along the cave mouth towards the cove and the open sea.

After the dankness of the cellar, the blast of a stiff sea breeze almost took Caroline's breath away. She drew several gasping, grateful breaths, and her head began to clear. She glanced astern, and saw, against the darkness of the water, the outline of a small craft bobbing crazily behind them on the end of a long rope. Was this the craft that was to take their bodies out to sea? She looked away, trying to grasp what Gilbert had whispered to her on the way down the last flight of cellar steps. It seemed a hopeless plan, unlikely to succeed; and yet, it was better to fight than to accept.

One of the night people was crouching by her side, clutching the tiller, his mask-muffled profile averted as he gazed into the blackness ahead. A rocky cliff loomed almost overhead as they came out of the cove into the open sea. The oarsmen bent to their work, the craft lurched and tilted as the man at Caroline's side swung the tiller.

On Caroline's other side, pressed up against her by the latest swing of the boat, another of the night people – masked as they all were – was audibly praying. His hands clutched the side of the boat. His whole attitude was expressive of tension and terror. Somehow, the sound of his praying gave

178

Caroline fresh heart and encouraged her to begin groping under the frieze cloak, feeling her way towards the ropes that bound Vale's arms. A shower of spray doused them all, and everybody ducked. Under the cloak, Caroline's fumbling fingers found what they sought. She brought the knife forward in the other hand, and began to work the blade against the stiff ropes. The wind and the rain battered them in squally bursts. The boat pitched, rose and fell with the heavy swell, and those night people who were not rowing craned forward in the darkness, looking for the lantern signal which would lead them to the French sloop.

The masked man at Caroline's side continued to pray for deliverance. Caroline prayed too, but silently; and when the first of the ropes which bound Vale's arms gave way, she almost began to believe that their prayers would be answered.

Once out beyond Sweeny's Head, the last long promontory before the open sea, the squall died and the sea grew calmer. Straining eyes in the darkness showed the anxious night people that the coast was clear. A light flashed once ahead; then flashed twice again. The rowers took up a steady rhythm, and within twenty minutes the heavily laden cutter was lashed to the side of the French ship.

All hands were put to unloading the cargo, passing the crates and bales from man to man, before being hooked up the side of the larger vessel. It was done quietly, with the ease of practice. The leader of the night people went aboard the French ship and was standing with his French counterpart, both of them making a tally of the goods which came aboard. It was only when this task was finished that Mick looked down and saw that something odd was going on below.

The small rowing boat was drawn right up to the stern of the cutter. Mick saw the woman climb into it, crouching down beside a longer, prostrate form. Gilbert's fair head was clearly to be seen, even in the subdued light and it looked as

179

if he were about to jump into the smaller craft. Mick realized that Gilbert had taken matters into his hands, and was trying to escape.

He lunged forward with a muted cry of warning. One of the night people in the cutter turned and saw what was going on. He gave a shout, and started to make his way over the shipped oars to the stern of the cutter. He was too late. Gilbert had seized one oar from the larger craft and was springing into the rowing boat, straddling the prone forms of his sister and Vale. As he did so, he cast off. The impatient current took the little craft, sucking it along the side of the tall French sloop, swirling it, making it swing crazily like a leaf in a whirlpool.

Mick knew what he must do. He raised his musket and fired at Gilbert's dark form. He saw the pale head go down, and Gilbert's body slump out of sight, just seconds before the little rowing boat was swallowed by the gusty darkness.

There was a hubbub of dismay and angry fear among the night people. Mick took no heed of it. He knew there was no need to give chase, as some of the men wanted to do. He had hit Gilbert Morrisey. He was sure of it. With Gilbert wounded and the lord trussed up, there was no danger of any of them surviving. The leaking tub they were in would not get far. And if it did stay afloat for longer than was likely, the current was strong, and the rocks on Sweeny's Head were waiting for them. Mick gave a grunt of satisfaction, and began to climb down into the cutter, content in the knowledge that the Serpent's commands had been carried out.

Caroline lay as she had fallen, pinned under Gilbert. Vale struggled upright, and nudged her shoulder.

'I think your brother's been hit,' he said. 'Try to rouse him.'

The true state of things began to dawn. A warm sticky wetness seeped between Caroline's probing fingers as she felt for Gilbert's heart. She said, 'He's bleeding . . . bleeding dreadfully.'

'Then, you'll have to bail, ma'am. Here—'

He put something in her hand. It was Gilbert's hat. She peered up at the shadowy form that was Vale and said more loudly: 'Gilbert's bleeding. He'll die if we don't do something for him.'

'We shall all die, if this holed bucket sinks under us,' he said curtly. 'Get up, girl, and start bailing.'

Furious, she knelt upright, meaning to tell him what she thought of his callous behaviour. Her reproaches were never uttered. A rock hovered over them like a great moving bird of prey, then swirled past within inches of the boat. Another, lower, but just as jagged and menacing went by at the other side. Caroline stifled a squeak of terror, and tried to steady herself in the small, rocking craft. Vale was wielding the single oar, staring intently ahead into the thick darkness. Even as she watched him, another rock loomed up, and the boat swung as Vale dipped the oar and pulled it gently.

Caroline began to bail, scooping water from the bottom of the boat – it had risen half way to her waist – and tipping it over the side with desperate urgency. She knew about the rocks around Sweeny's Head, and that their chances of survival must be slim, indeed. She pushed that thought away, and bailed for all she was worth, mindlessly, panting with exertion and the extremity of her fear; never looking up, for fear of what she would see.

When the collision came, she had only a moment of warning. She heard Vale cry out, thought she heard the crash of surf nearby. Then a terrible rending sound surrounded them, and an avalanche of water engulfed them. Caroline found herself being swept down, down, down into the choking depths of the dark sea.

Eighteen

*J*EMIMA KNEW THAT THINGS WERE WRONG from the moment she first woke. Mrs Datchet and Lady Augusta's maid were exclaiming in urgent whispers outside her door. When she called out to them, their talk was cut off as though by a knife.

It was a weird and frightening day. Nobody would tell Jemima anything. She missed Miss Caroline, and her papa; but when she asked for them her Aunt Augusta said they had gone off for the day together, and grew sharp and irritable if pressed for further information.

And there was another odd thing. Her Uncle Richard's face was bruised about the mouth, so swollen that he could only speak with care, and his wrists were bandaged. She stared at him, wondering why he looked like that. He patted her head, and told her not to worry. She played with Ferdy at one end of the bookroom, and grew more and more uneasy as the day went by.

She was not allowed to go out. She and her Aunt Augusta stayed closeted in the bookroom while the servants came and went with stiff, closed-in faces, refusing to meet Jemima's enquiring gaze. There were sounds of men coming and going in the hall outside, tramping feet, and muttered conversations. Richard and Sir Giles Mannering came in looking tired and frowning a lot. They quaffed their beer and ate hasty meals in company with some other Volunteer officers, but they did not stay long. Richard once more patted

182

Jemima's head, and told her not to worry for the second time; which advice made the qualms of anxiety grow worse than ever.

It was only when Richard came in once more, and her Aunt Augusta sent her up to bed, that Jemima was able to lurk outside the bookroom door, and learn what the trouble was.

'Is there any sign of Hugo?' demanded Lady Augusta, once she was sure that her niece had gone. 'Any sign at all?'

'No sign yet, Gussie,' said Richard, sounding weary. 'Mannering's spies have reported that Hugo and the Morriseys were put in a small boat off Sweeny's Head. It doesn't look hopeful.'

Lady Augusta said painfully, 'Those rocks, Richard! They'd have stood no chance, surely, in the darkness.'

'Mannering thinks they must have drowned. But, as you know, Hugo knows those rocks. If anyone would stand a chance, it would be he. Remember how he used to go with O'Grady's lot?'

Lady Augusta nodded. She said, as another thought struck her, 'Why did the night people put young Gilbert Morrisey in that boat with Hugo? I thought he was one of them?'

'Apparently,' said Richard evenly, 'Gilbert Morrisey had offended the Serpent, and was under sentence of death.' And when Lady Augusta protested that surely with Mr Rance dead, the Serpent's orders would have no longer been paramount, he gave a grunt and said grimly, 'Rance may be dead, Gussie, but the fear that the Serpent inspires in these people will not easily be got rid of. They have lived with it, been ruled by it for so long, you see.'

Lady Augusta shivered, and looked out of the bookroom window at the grey, tumbling sea. 'They'll have been torn to pieces on those rocks, Richard. What a horrible way to die!'

'I don't mean to give up hope until we find their bodies,' said Richard firmly. He, too, looked out at the sea. 'It might

183

be some time before we do, however. Gussie, I hate to ask it of you; but . . . but do you think you could bring yourself to take Jemima back with you to England? She'd be better away from here, as soon as may be.' He won no response, so he added insistently, 'I believe that it would have been Vale's wish.'

His sister was frowning down at her hands. She said in a low, uncertain voice, 'What in the world am I to say to Jemima? I might take her away with me, perhaps, but she will ask why. She's so like Hugo when she eyes one with that suspicious, doubting look. I have endured that look several times today. We shall have to tell her something.'

'Tell her that it's Vale's wish that she goes with you. She's used to being bundled here and there at his whim. Used to him going off without a word, I shouldn't wonder.'

'What about that abominable dog, then? You need not ask me to take that little brute up in my carriage, for I shall not. He ate one of my best lace kerchiefs this morning.'

'Very well, Gussie,' said Richard, relieved that his sister had at least not refused to take Jemima with her. 'You take the child, and I'll dispose of the puppy. That's a bargain.'

Jemima began to creep away. She did not want to hear any more. She slipped like a shadow across the marble floor of the hall, and went to find Ferdy. She did not take time to think that it would soon be dark, or that she might need a cloak, or provisions for her flight. Only one thing seemed important. She must get away. That way she might hope to save the only being left in her world that mattered.

They might have missed Jemima sooner if Sir Giles had not come riding back. He gave his cloak to a footman, and trod heavily and reluctantly to where Richard and his sister were waiting for him.

He stood before them, his grizzled head erect. His eyes were sombre. He said bluntly, 'I've bad news for you. We've found Vale.'

184

Neither of his hearers spoke for a long moment. There seemed to be a spell on them. Lady Augusta put out a hand and groped rather blindly for the mantelshelf, seeking its support. Richard said in a voice which sounded hoarse, 'Tell us, Mannering. Where did you find him?'

Sir Giles said stiffly, 'On the rocks near Sweeny's Head.' He went forward and took Lady Augusta's hand in his and said simply, 'I'm sorry. We'll find those fellows who killed him. I pledge myself to bring them to justice if it's the last thing I do.' He turned back to Richard, and said with a grim twitch of his lips, 'I've said some harsh things about your brother in my time; but I could have grown to like and respect him, had he lived.'

Richard had grown noticeably paler, despite his tan. He said evenly, 'Thank you, Mannering. We've all said unflattering things about Hugo; I, more than most . . . ' He paused, and then said, 'I should like to see him.'

'I hoped you wouldn't ask that, Sweeny,' returned the older man. 'Those rocks are as sharp as razors, and in that sea . . . You would not know him, not as we found him.'

'And the girl . . . and her brother?' Lady Augusta's voice was almost steady, though her eyes were blank with shock. 'Did you . . . was there any sign?'

'Not so far, ma'am,' he told her soberly. 'Frankly, I cannot hold out much hope for them. The boat they were put in was smashed to splinters. That was what led us to find . . . Vale's body.'

Richard, in the manner of people who have sustained a stunning blow, was holding to a single line of thought. 'You say I would not recognize my brother, Mannering. How did you do so yourself?'

Sir Giles made a sudden sound in his throat, and said: 'My wits are wandering, my boy. There was one thing that made it possible to know him, and I have it here.' He dropped something small and gleaming into Richard's hand. 'This is your proof. This is now yours . . . my lord.'

Richard stood with his dark head bowed, gazing at the

185

Sweeny ring in his palm. He seemed to find it difficult to speak, for he cleared his throat twice, but said nothing. Then he slid the serpent ring onto one of his fingers. It fitted. He went on staring down at it.

Sir Giles watched him, his grizzled brows drawn together; but at length he said with some awkwardness, 'There's just one more thing, Sweeny. It concerns one of your people, so I feel bound to mention it.'

Richard raised his head. 'One of my people?'

'Your man, Slattery,' said the magistrate, nodding. 'He claims that Peter Morrisey knew the identity of the Serpent, and that he went to meet him on the morning he died.'

'Slattery!' exclaimed Lady Augusta scornfully, 'That drunkard! The poor man's wits must've been wandering, Sir Giles. I hope you sent him about his business.'

Richard held up his hand. 'Hush, Gussie! Let's hear what Mannering has to say.'

Sir Giles said in a worried way, 'He'd taken a drink or two when I saw him, I'll grant; but he seemed sensible enough, for all that.' He sighed in an exasperated way, and went on, 'According to Slattery, Morrisey wrote a long letter before he went out, and gave instructions to Slattery that no one was to read it but Gilbert. Well, as you know, Gilbert went off to America, and has only lately returned.'

'What a perfectly preposterous story!' said Lady Augusta who felt that Sir Giles might have had the good feeling to spare them this farrago at such a time. 'Why, Colonel Morrisey killed himself four years ago. What if he did write a letter, and what if he did go to meet Rance over some business? It can hardly be of interest to any of us now.'

'I believe it could be of very material interest, ma'am,' said Sir Giles apologetically, 'if it sheds some light on the Serpent's identity. You see, there seems to be some doubt as to whether Rance really was what he was made to seem.'

Richard's blue gaze fastened upon Sir Giles's face, comprehending but doubtful. 'You think all those documents might have been placed in Rance's house to mislead us? Surely not?'

'I don't know what to think,' replied the magistrate, sounding beleaguered, and looking utterly weary. 'Believe me, Sweeny, I don't at all like troubling you with this when you have this tragedy to contend with. But Slattery was in such deadly earnest. I said I'd meet him at Whitefield in the morning, so that he can show me where Morrisey hid this document. Slattery assured me it was in the muniment room. There's some place of concealment there, where the family used to leave each other messages.'

'Why wait until tomorrow?' demanded Lady Augusta with asperity. 'Better to get it over with.'

'Slattery was in no state to find anything when I left him,' retorted Sir Giles drily. 'I had one of my fellows take him home to his bed, which was all he was fit for.' Lady Augusta said that only proved how unreliable the old man was, but Sir Giles had his gaze fixed upon Richard Sweeny. He said quietly, but with unmistakeable insistence, 'Now, Sweeny, what do you say? Slattery is your man. Will you come with me when I question him tomorrow? Or would you prefer to talk with him tonight – always assuming you can sober him up enough to make head or tail of what he's saying?'

Richard shook his dark head. 'I'll wait 'til tomorrow.' He shook his head again, and said wearily, 'Let's hope that Slattery knows where to look in the muniment room. The place is positively packed with books and estate papers from floor to ceiling. I doubt if Morrisey ever threw away a paper in his life.' Then he seemed to put this wearisome matter to one side, for he added practically, 'What time shall we meet at Whitefield, Mannering? You'll have to forgive a degree of muddle when you come there. All my people have been out searching the shore today, and there's no one lodging at Whitefield but the housekeeper and Slattery, I fancy. But I daresay you'll make allowances . . . '

'I know this must be an imposition, Sweeny. I'll try not to keep you too long.'

'You'll be welcome at Whitefield at any time,' said Richard, with his easy courtesy.

He might have said more, had not Mrs Datchet come into the room. She sketched a hurried curtsey, and announced that Lady Jemima was missing. 'The bootboy saw her going across the orchard more than an hour ago, milady,' she said, as Lady Augusta gave a small horrified exclamation. 'Dear knows where she was going, for she took that animal with her.'

Nineteen

CAROLINE LAY STARING UP at a low, raftered ceiling, wondering dreamily where she was. This drifting condition did not last long. Too soon, recollection and anxiety came rushing back in a familiar and irresistible tide. She wished she could have stayed asleep. She was lying on a straw-filled pallet in Miss O'Grady's attic, where she had promised faithfully to stay until she was sent for: until Vale came.

'It's better that you know nothing; better still for you to keep out of the way until this is finished,' Vale had told her. 'Promise me that you will stay with Miss O'Grady until you hear? Promise?'

She would have promised him anything, of course. Besides it had been too cold to argue. She said through lips that were stiff, 'Until I hear what, my lord?'

Afterwards, she remembered that he had hesitated. At the time she had only been conscious of his finger on her lips, and his voice that said: 'Don't ask me to explain. I know what I have to do, and it should not take long. And if I cannot come myself, I want you to look after Jemima.'

So, mindlessly, she had given him her word, with no real comprehension of what she was agreeing to, or of what the future would hold. There had been no thought of future or past for Caroline during that freezing vigil on the rocks. With Gilbert lying between them in a half-conscious state, they had talked and talked, and waited for the dawn. There had been an urgency about Vale's questions. He must have

189

known, even then, that their time was limited. She had answered him to the best of her ability, half-frozen in her sodden clothes, and more conscious of Vale's arm around her shoulders than the meaning of his inquisition.

As soon as it was light enough, Vale had gone clambering off over the black rocks. It seemed hours before Joey's flimsy coracle had rounded the point, and together she and Joey had helped her groaning brother into the little boat. Miss O'Grady came to meet them when they had beached beside the ruined jetty of Sweeny's Port.

Caroline was disappointed that Vale was not there; but, mindful of her promise, she stood unresisting while Miss O'Grady stripped her sodden clothes from her, wrapped her in a rough blanket, and directed her clumsy progress up the ladder to the attic. Gilbert was driven off in the O'Grady's cart, and Miss O'Grady called up to Caroline later in the day, to tell her that Gilbert was safely hidden with good sisters, and was going on as well as could be expected. Caroline roused herself to make suitably rejoicing noises, and sank back once more into an exhausted sleep. It was only when she woke again to find the rafters glowing pink with the reflection of the setting sun, that she wondered why Vale was still away on his mysterious errand. He had told her that it would not take long, yet he had been gone for a whole day. Why had he not come?

His voice seemed to haunt her as the light faded and the loft became a pool of darkness. 'It's time you tried to be a little frank with yourself, Miss Caroline. Whose side are you on? You will have to choose, you know.'

Well, she had chosen. There was no doubt in her mind that she loved him. How ironic it would be, if she could never tell him so. Vale had saved her life, and Gilbert's. She ought to be pleased and grateful. His had been a feat of fearless judgement and skill that had landed them within yards of the only strip of shingle on that cruel promontory of rock. But as she lay in the newly gathered darkness, she could think of nothing but her gnawing anxiety for Vale. She remembered

190

his patient questioning about the night people and their leader, recalled his reluctance to tell her where he was going, or what he meant to do. And with every minute that passed, Caroline's anxiety grew. If he was alive, surely he would have come?

It no longer seemed bearable to lie meekly in the darkness. She called down to Miss O'Grady, asking for her clothes. She dressed quickly, fumbling in the gloom, and clambered awkwardly down the ladder and went out. Miss O'Grady did not fret her with protests or questions, and Joey was asleep in his bunk beside the driftwood fire. Caroline walked along the ruined quay, and the sightless cottages looked back at her in the gloom, ghostly reflections of her dark thoughts.

There came a scuffling and a snuffling at the hem of her skirts. She bent down, and found, with a feeling of disbelief, that Jemima's puppy was there at her feet. She knelt on the cobbled way, letting him lick her face, and assuring herself that it was indeed Ferdy. She was beginning to wonder what he was doing there, when other sounds made her stiffen.

Something was going on at the far side of the stone wall. She got to her feet and started towards these sounds, all promises forgotten in her sudden conviction that Jemima was nearby. As she rounded the end of the wall, she saw two dark figures bending over a smaller shape on the ground. Caroline called out Jemima's name sharply, on a note of fear.

The taller of the figures turned. Caroline heard Richard Sweeny's deep voice exclaim: 'Miss Caroline! Can it be?'

Her relief at finding that it was only Richard was almost overwhelming, so Caroline found nothing to wonder at when Richard's voice sounded shaken, too. He held both her hands tightly, and said, 'Oh, my dear! We feared you were lost. You don't know what this means, to find you.'

But she was peering past him. 'That's Jemima, isn't it? What is she doing there? Is she hurt?'

Richard released her, though he seemed reluctant to do so.

Together they went over and knelt on the grass, with the puppy joining them, impeding Caroline's efforts to find out what was the matter with the child. Jemima lay frighteningly still, and as Caroline groped past the puppy for the child's wrist, she heard Richard say, 'We found her lying here. She must have fallen and stunned herself. Silly child, she bolted from Mount Sweeny, and we only missed her as it was getting dark.'

'We could take her to Miss O'Grady,' she suggested, a little reassured by his matter-of-fact tone. 'It's the nearest place.'

'She'll be better at Whitefield,' he returned quietly. He told the man who was with him to go and turn the carriage around. 'You'll come with us, Miss Caroline?' he added, as the man went off to do his bidding. 'Jemima will need you when she wakes.'

He seemed to take her acquiescence for granted. She watched him lift Jemima's small, still person in his arms, and followed him wordlessly as he began to make his way along the grassy track that led to the road. He strode out, surefooted, hastening towards the dark shape of the carriage. Caroline, hampered by her skirts and stumbling on the uneven ground, was hard put to it to keep up. There was no time to argue.

She caught up with him as he reached the waiting carriage. She wondered why he was in such a hurry, almost bundling her into the vehicle, and thrusting Jemima down upon her lap. The puppy scrabbled his way onto the seat beside them, and Richard got in, pulling the door shut and fastening the stiff leather blind so that there was no way of seeing out. She felt the urgency and fear in him as though they were tangible things, and wondered what was the matter.

But there was no chance to talk. The road was rough, and no sooner were they on board than the carriage set off at what seemed like breakneck speed. At one time there were flickering lights and shouts, but the carriage did not pause

192

nor its speed slacken until they were scrunching round the gravel sweep at the front of Whitefield.

The door of the carriage was pulled open from the outside, and Caroline saw a woman's face peering up at them. She recognized the face as belonging to Slattery's new wife, and she greeted her with a friendly smile, which won her a darkling look, very different from the smiles and curtseys of the other day. But Jemima was beginning to stir, and Caroline had no time to wonder at this strange surliness on the part of Mrs Slattery. She gave the child into Richard's outstretched arms, and followed him into the front hall of Whitefield. Mrs Slattery shut the heavy door, but not before Caroline had heard the carriage wheels turning once more.

With the exception of the single lantern in Mrs Slattery's hand, there were no lights showing in the front hall. They followed the woman down a long corridor to the room where Caroline's father used to carry out his estate business – known as the muniment room. Richard laid Jemima down on a cushioned settle at the far end of the room. Ferdy jumped up and lay on the end of it.

'My head hurts,' said Jemima fretfully, staring at Caroline in a bemused way. 'It hurts dreadfully, Miss Caroline.'

Caroline knelt beside her, and held her in her arms. 'You fell and hit it, dearest. Lie down, and shut your eyes.'

'A man hit me.'

'What man?' Caroline pulled away a little so that she could watch Jemima's face. 'Did you see him?'

Jemima squinted up as though she had trouble focussing. 'It was dark, and I wanted you, Miss Caroline,' she said tearfully. 'Aunt Augusta said she was going to take me away, but she wasn't going to have Ferdy. Don't let her . . . '

Caroline held the child closer. 'I won't let them take you away from me, at all events, wherever we may go. Is that why you ran away?'

'I had to save Ferdy.' Then the greater horror surfaced in her mind. 'They said that you and Papa were drowned in the sea, Miss Caroline.'

'Well, what nonsense,' said Caroline, aware that Richard was standing by and watching her gravely. 'Here I am, safe and sound. We'll stay together, and no doubt it won't be long before your papa comes to join us. And look, Jemima, here is Mrs Slattery with a hot drink for you, and we'll ask her if she would find some dinner for Ferdy. Drink up, and we'll talk things over in the morning.'

'It's got a funny taste,' said Jemima, sipping it.

'That'll be the honey in it,' said Mrs Slattery from the shadows. ' 'Twill help her little ladyship to sleep.'

'I don't want to go to sleep,' said Jemima, turning her head as though it hurt to move, and staring fearfully into the shadowy corners of the book-lined muniment room. 'Where is this place?'

'This is my own papa's room at Whitefield, Jemima. There's nothing to be afraid of here,' said Caroline gently. She smiled at the child, who had gulped down the rest of her drink and was now lying back against the cushions, her eyelids already drooping: 'You know, many's the time I've fallen asleep on that settle, waiting for my naughty brother to come home in the small hours. He used to come in by the secret door in the panelling. It's full of secrets this room, Jemima. It's got a desk with a secret drawer, and a staircase leading up to the tower. I'll show you all these things in the morning.' She glanced up, and met Richard's thoughtful glance; but he said nothing, and neither of them moved as she went on talking softly to Jemima, and presently fell silent when the child's breathing had grown deeper and her eyes were fully closed.

Only then did Richard come and help Caroline to her feet. She was stiff from kneeling so long, and staggered a little as she stood upright. He held her against him for a moment, before taking Jemima's cup from her and leading her to the fire at the other end of the room.

'She won't wake before morning,' he assured her, as she looked back towards the sleeping child. 'Mary Slattery's an expert with herbs and potions, you know. We won't have to

194

tell her the news before morning, I'm glad to say.' And when Caroline stared at him in a startled way, he smiled at her tenderly, and said, 'Does it worry you that she should have drunk one of Mary's potions? They're harmless, you know. I was reared on them, almost, for Mary was my nurse 'til I was sent away to school.'

It had not been the thought of Mrs Slattery's potions that had startled her, of course, but what he had said about telling Jemima the news. What news, she wondered, as he took her hand and led her to a chair by the fire. She sank into it weakly, and as he turned aside to pour her a glass of wine she saw the serpent ring upon his hand. Then, she knew.

He brought the glass over, but at the sight of her face, he checked. He put the glass on a small table, and knelt beside her, taking her cold hands in his warm ones. 'My dear Miss Caroline,' he said in his deep, concerned voice. 'My dear, I thought you must have known already. Forgive me.'

She felt him chafing her hands, saw the ring which had so recently been on other, far colder hands during that dark vigil on the rocks, and said in a voice which seemed to come from a long way off: 'I think I have known all day, sir. But not for sure, until now . . . ' She shut her eyes for a moment, and then asked him to tell her what had happened. 'I'd like to know, sir, so don't try to spare me.'

So Richard Sweeny told her how Vale's body had been found upon the rocks that evening, and how the magistrate had brought him the serpent ring. She was silent for a little while, trying to work out what had brought about this disaster, and Richard must have grown alarmed at her stillness, for he brought the wine glass to her and begged her to drink.

She sipped a little, obedient, feeling nothing but a sort of tired bewilderment. Then he took the glass from her, and held her hands again: 'Don't look so stricken, Miss Caroline. I'll take care of you. You know that it is my dearest wish to do just that.'

But she did not answer him, and in a moment or two she tried to free her hands from his enfolding grasp. He released

195

her instantly, and she turned away from him, sensing his disappointment, yet unable to help it. She had this odd dislike of him touching her, and the sight of the serpent ring on his square brown hands somehow increased her feeling of revulsion. 'Forgive me, sir,' she said, 'but I . . . I am a little tired, and I find all this difficult to . . . to take in.'

'And no wonder,' he said, as always full of consideration. 'You must be worn out, and I'll not keep you much longer from your rest. Mary Slattery will bring you one of her possets, if you will trust yourself to drink it.'

But she was still struggling to understand the things which did not seem to add up. She murmured that she would be happy to sample Mrs Slattery's posset. 'It's kind of her to go to so much trouble, sir. But where are all the other servants?'

'At Mount Sweeny,' he told her, still watching her with that grave, concerned look. 'They have been searching for you and Vale all day, and then Jemima went off.' Then he added, in a lowered voice, 'To tell you the truth, Miss Caroline, I'm glad they are still away. I don't want anyone to know that you are here. Not for the moment.'

She thought of the promise she had given to Vale, and said curiously, still with this feeling that there was something she ought to be able to understand, yet could not: 'What do you fear, sir?' And when he did not give her an answer, she thought of another thing that she and Vale had talked of in the freezing darkness of Sweeny's Head. She looked at Richard very directly, and said, 'It's the Serpent you fear, is it not?'

He did not move, but she thought she had succeeded in startling him. His voice was as calm as ever, however. 'Now, what makes you think that, Miss Caroline? Mannering was sure that Rance was the Serpent, and Rance is dead.'

She wrinkled her brow, considering, puzzling, groping for reasons. She said slowly, 'I don't think Mr Rance could have been the Serpent. Not really. You see, it was he who first told me about the Serpent, and gave me a little gold medallion to keep in case I met one of the night people. And although he may have been closer to the Serpent than the others, I don't think it was he. For one thing, sir, I think he was frightened himself . . . '

'Interesting, Miss Caroline,' he murmured. 'Go on.'

She looked at him in surprise, for she somehow thought she had said enough. But after a little pause, she went on talking, thinking aloud about this sinister figure who had influenced Gilbert so strongly. She said in her gentle way, 'Gilbert used to talk about this Serpent creature, you know. The night people fear him greatly, and credit him with supernatural powers. The Serpent is everywhere, knows everything. He speaks, but is not there; strikes when nobody can see him. The night people cross themselves when they utter his name, and look on him as a sorcerer.' She glanced past Richard to where the puppy, Ferdinand, lay sleeping off his dinner, and found the allusion that seemed to fit. 'To their minds, sir, the Serpent is Prospero.'

'Yes.'

She looked up at him. His eyes were level, blue and faintly smiling.

'You see?' she asked him. 'That is not like poor Mr Rance. Mr Rance was no Prospero, sir.'

His smile deepened, as though she had said something clever.

'Prospero. That's what Sybilla used to call me.' He stared down at Caroline as though he had suddenly found something quite novel and pleasing about her. 'Strange. You have the same quickness. There really is a likeness. I felt it first when I saw you tricked out in Sybilla's green dress. I could have strangled you for your presumption, yet at the same time, I wanted you.' He laughed, a barely audible expelling of breath. 'Vale little knew what he was setting in train when he first saw fit to make you the object of his newest flirtation. But then, poor Hugo never knew about women, or how to treat them.'

Caroline had not felt wholly warm since her freezing vigil on Sweeny's Head. But she found, suddenly, that there are

197

other kinds of coldness. She gazed at Richard, spellbound.

He smiled at her again, a quick baring of white teeth in the dark, handsome face. 'My dear, don't tell me you took Vale's flirtation for anything else? My dear brother . . . my dear, late brother, I should say, never took anything seriously.' Another spasm of silent laughter shook him. 'Sybilla found him a cold fish, you know. He'll find a more fitting mate for himself, now that he's suffered that long-awaited sea change.'

Caroline felt oddly calm, and a little surprised that she had not seen the truth before. She said in a dreaming tone, 'Prospero? So that's it? You were Prospero in that play with Lady Vale. You were her lover . . . and . . . the Serpent!'

'I wondered how long it would take you to see the truth, my dear,' murmured Richard, sounding for all the world like a benevolent schoolmaster whose pupil had given him the right answer. 'I was sure you would stumble on it before long. How fortunate that I found you and brought you here. It would never have done for you to blurt it out before we had a chance to talk it over. You Morriseys are so impetuous. You really will have to guard against that fault once you are married to me, my dear.'

Caroline stared at him, and said with quiet scorn: 'I would die rather than marry you, sir.'

He sighed, and another breath of a laugh escaped him. 'So impetuous, Miss Caroline! And in this case, so very right. You may count yourself lucky, however, that I am able to give you this choice – to die, or to marry me.'

She stared at him, suddenly very frightened indeed. Then Mrs Slattery came back into the room carrying a steaming jug and a goblet on a tray, and said without ceremony: 'Dan's gone, sir. He'd been drinking, and I thought him safe enough in his bed. But he's gone out of the back door.'

'How long ago?' demanded Richard.

'Twenty minutes since, I'm thinking.'

Richard frowned. 'Likely he'll break his worthless neck, wandering about in the dark in the state he's in.'

'Come with me now, sir,' she pleaded distractedly, 'and we'll be after finding him.' Caroline could see that the woman's face was working with some powerful emotion. She slid her eyes towards Caroline, and added; 'What's to be done with this one, sir? The child won't stir, that's for certain. Will you tie this one up, and come to find my poor Dan? I'll give her one of my possets to keep her quiet. All's been made ready in the crypt above, sir. There's nothing to be done, now, but light the fire.'

They both turned to look at Caroline. She stared back at them, unable to speak or even to move. Mrs Slattery said with feeling: 'You'll need to get her out before Dan sees her, sir. It'd likely turn Dan's mind if he knew the Colonel's daughter was in the crypt with the rest of them.'

'She may not have to be there, after all,' said Richard calmly. 'If Miss Caroline is sensible, there will be no need for such drastic measures. She is going to marry me.'

'Never!' said Caroline quietly in a voice that shook.

'Not even to save Jemima being blown to perdition, Miss Caroline? I thought you were fond of her.'

She gaped at him; but before she could answer, or ask him what he meant, Mrs Slattery had turned to Richard and was putting her work-roughened hands on his arm, as though trying to restrain him physically.

'Don't! Don't do it, Master! You've come by your rights at last! Dear knows, you've waited long enough, and suffered enough to get you where you are! You could look to the highest in the land for a wife, now; but don't take the Colonel's daughter, sir! Dan's not been himself since that Gilbert and his sister have come back into the County.'

Richard did not answer the woman for a moment. Then, with a glance at Caroline, who was still sitting rigidly in her chair, he said gently: 'Mary, you are right. You've always had my best interests at heart, I know that. Well, give your posset to Miss Caroline. She'll drink it for us, I believe. I'm sure we can rely upon her not to put us to the trouble of tipping it down her throat.'

199

Mrs Slattery gave a grunt of satisfaction, and moved towards Caroline with a steaming silver goblet. Caroline shrank against the stiff, high back of the chair, an instinctive movement. The woman came nearer, smiling a little. Then she jerked, and her expression changed to one of blank, wide-eyed surprise. Her tight mouth fell open with a horrid gurgling sound. Richard took the silver goblet from Mrs Slattery's hand and held it carefully out of the way while she slumped past Caroline's chair onto the ground.

Caroline sat where she was, rigid with shock, her mind rejecting what her eyes had just seen. Richard leaned down, and gently extracted a wicked-looking knife from Mrs Slattery's still twitching back. His face was grave, and even a little sad.

'A pity,' he murmured. 'But poor Mary's devotion to that drunken husband of hers was really becoming too much of a liability.'

Twenty

HE THING I LIKE TO DO,' said Richard conversationally, wiping the slender knife upon the dead woman's shawl and sliding it neatly into a sheath in his coat cuff, 'is to keep things simple. Leave things as they are, and let people draw their conclusions. When Dan Slattery comes in from his drunken meanderings in the dark, he'll likely as not pass clean out, and the two of them will be found in the morning. Mannering was saying only the other day that he wouldn't trust Slattery when he was in his cups. He's well known for his quickness with a knife, you know. They'll think he's killed his wife in a fit of drunken rage. You see, Miss Caroline?'

She nodded, feeling sick, and too terrified to speak.

He seemed to take her silence as some kind of tribute, for he said approvingly: 'Good girl. As I say, so long as one takes the trouble to set the scene, there's really no difficulty. So many criminals go wrong by trying to be too clever. No. Simplicity is the key.'

He came round and sat down at Caroline's side, his manner as precise and sensible as ever. Once again she was reminded of a schoolmaster, as he began to speak. 'They credit the Serpent with supernatural powers, Miss Caroline. You and I know there is no such thing, of course. But I found out some years ago that all manner of magical effects can be contrived, just so long as one has a basic understanding of human nature. This is the gift, the magic, and it's there for anyone to take. Merlin, Prospero, all the great magicians knew it. They learned to harness the convenient and recurring stupidity of the common man – and to use their guilts and frailties . . . '

It came to her that while he was talking thus – and it seemed to give him a certain satisfaction – there was at least a likelihood that he would refrain from further violence. She kept her eyes on his face and willed him to keep talking.

'It took me a little time to realize it,' he said quietly, his blue eyes very bright in the tanned darkness of his face. 'That Rance was to be the richest vein in this human goldmine. I came upon him cheating the Mount Sweeny estates, extorting tribute from the night people. But it took me longer to realize that all this would prove such a valuable source of revenue and such an absorbing occupation. Rance was such a useful servant. He kept all the accounts, made arrangements with the night people, saw to all the other collections. But of course that meant that he knew too much; and had to be the first to go.' He smiled at Caroline suddenly, and said in a surprised tone, 'You know, I'm glad you understand how things are. It's not often I get a chance to talk about it.'

She said softly, in hopes of encouraging this horrifying soliloquy, 'We must all have seemed amazingly stupid, sir. What will you do, now that you have killed your two most faithful servants? Who will run your errands now?'

He looked surprised by her denseness. 'No need now. Not any more. It's been a diversion, Miss Caroline, a most profitable one – but it's all finished. Like Prospero in *The Tempest*, my schemes are all knit up. As they should have been long since, if only Sybilla had not been so impetuous and driven off in Hugo's curricle.' He looked at her then, and added thoughtfully, 'Yes, the likeness persists in so many ways – even though you lack her beauty . . . ' His mouth twisted. 'Poor, lovely Sybilla. It was my child she was carrying when she was killed. If only she had waited, I would have been Earl of Vale four years ago, with a son and heir to carry on the Sweeny name. Such a waste. Such a wicked waste.'

She thought of the lives lost, the anguish and the terrors

202

caused by this one man's thwarted ambition, which she was only dimly beginning to fathom. She said softly and sadly, 'A wicked waste, indeed.'

His blue gaze was approving. 'You see? I thought you would, once the matter was made clear to you. You have more intelligence than Sybilla, more understanding of the realities.' A thought seemed to strike him, and he said softly: 'Very different from your twin, you are, for all that you look so like him. I believe that we might deal well together, for you have more sense in your little finger than your twin had in his whole body. It was the same in our family. Hugo never knew what to do with his advantages, unless it was to squander them.'

Caroline said nothing. He looked down at the ring upon his hand, and said grimly, 'Well, it's all mine now, as it ought to have been long since.' She must have made a faint, protesting sound, for he looked at her reproachfully. 'It's true, you know. My father would have given it all to me, if he could. Hugo was the greatest disappointment to him. He looked on me as his true heir, particularly since Hugo was a sickly child, and nobody expected him to live. He was seldom here, always away in England being pampered by his mother's family. Why, you only have to look at the portraits at Mount Sweeny to realize that Hugo is no true Sweeny, Miss Caroline. My mother used to call him the changeling.'

'Did she so?' said Caroline very quietly. 'Then no wonder he stayed away so much, sir.'

Richard frowned. 'You need not think he was ill treated by my mother, Miss Caroline. It was very much the other way round. To begin with, she was all over him, trying to make him like her; but Hugo scarcely ever had a civil word for her, which incensed my father greatly. Hugo did not care. He'd go off without a word, sometimes staying away for days and nights together. My father feared that he'd be drowned, or shot by an exciseman, but he seemed to bear a charmed life. Yes, I've waited a long time, Miss Caroline, for what should have been mine long since. I was groomed for it, trained up

203

in estate management, while Hugo frittered his time away, and brought disgrace to the Sweeny name. I know every field and tree and hillside on the Mount Sweeny estates – and now, at long last, those acres are mine, and the money and the title is mine.'

'And that's what you have worked and schemed for – done murder for?' said Caroline incredulously. 'Do you really think it will have been worth it?'

'Of course,' he said simply. 'This is only the beginning. I mean to make my mark upon the world, to bring glory and fame to the Sweeny name. You shall see, Miss Caroline. You'll be a Marchioness, at the very least, before we're done – perhaps even a Duchess. Our children will thank us for it.'

'And how proud will they be of the Serpent and his works?' she asked him. 'Will they take pride in blackmail and terror, too?'

He said dismissively, 'That's all done with now – finished.' And when she continued to look at him, her grey-green eyes steady and scornful, he added impatiently: 'Must I spell it out for you, after all? Tonight is the close of a chapter. For the night people and some others – even for Jemima and yourself, if I decide we are not suited – it is the end of the road. It stands to reason that I can't afford to leave the night people alive, once I start my new life. Even Mary Slattery had to go, she who loved and served me.'

Caroline gripped her hands together to stop them shaking. She waited for him to go on. She could not imagine how he meant to kill all those people, but she was already able to believe that he would find a way.

He nodded approvingly. 'You begin to see, Miss Caroline? I thought you would. It's easy enough. The night people will be assembled in the crypt after midnight. They will not fail. All of them have been promised their share of the spoils, so there'll be no absentees.'

'And then?' Her voice was a mere thread of sound. 'Then?'

'Then there will be a dreadful explosion, my dear. It so happens that there is a great load of gunpowder stored under

204

the crypt. Gunpowder is dangerous stuff, you know, and in an enclosed space, all huddled together awaiting word from the Serpent, I'm afraid the night people won't stand a chance.' He smiled at her horrified expression, and said thoughtfully, 'And another thing, you know. The explosion will serve a two-fold purpose. There is a secret stair behind the crypt. It is known to no one but myself – it's one of those secrets which is handed down in the family, which my father confided to me before he died. It has interesting acoustics, that stairway, and is known to us as the whispering stair. But like the night people – and indeed the Serpent – that stair has outlived its usefulness. There are bound to be investigations after the explosion, and I promised faithfully that I would guard the secret of that stairway. I feel in honour bound to have it destroyed, rather than allow strangers to find out about it.'

She stared at him curiously. He spoke perfectly seriously about fulfilling this inherited commitment, in almost the same breath as he talked of murdering a dozen unsuspecting people in a horrible way. He probably just as sincerely believed that his new, virtuous, respectable life could be built on such a foundation. He even seemed quite serious about wanting to marry her. She said carefully, 'Why do you need to kill Jemima? She is no threat to you, sir.'

'No,' he conceded, frowning, 'but she's too damnably like Hugo for my liking. Besides . . . ' His frown deepened, as a thought seemed to dawn. 'Mary was right.' He looked down at Mrs Slattery's slumped form, which lay within feet of where Caroline was sitting. A dark stain had spread out upon the rug. 'Mary knew only too well the trouble you Morriseys have been to me. Your father found out about Sybilla and me, you know, and had the effrontery to preach me a sermon about it. I thought it an impertinence. Only, when I told Sybilla that he knew, she chose to make a joke of it, and had the notion to fantasize about him in her journal. It became a game we played. We used to read the journal aloud, making this P into a composite figure, a blend of Peter

Morrisey and Prospero – which was what Sybilla called me. So much of what she wrote was true, a true account of our loving; and she would laugh and tell me that it was quite safe to write it all down. If Vale should come upon it, he'd be bound to think it was all about Morrisey.'

'Which he did,' said Caroline quietly. 'To my father's cost.'

'Which he undoubtedly did,' said Richard grimly; 'but the damage was done by then. I'd have been better to have eliminated your father when he first surprised Sybilla and myself together. It would have saved a lot of trouble. You Morriseys seem to make a habit of meddling in what does not concern you. Mary was right. You have brought me trouble and ill fortune all along.' He looked at Caroline and said softly: 'Tell me, Miss Caroline. If your father had hidden a letter which he meant no one but your brother to find, where would he have put it?'

She dragged her thoughts back from ground which would have been more profitably explored four years before, and blinked at Richard. 'A . . . a letter?'

'That secret drawer you told Jemima about?' he insisted, grasping her by the arm. She sensed the throbbing impatience in him. 'Where is it?'

She said, 'You should ask Slattery when he comes in.'

But even this feeble attempt at delaying him cost her dearly. He pulled her to her feet, twisting her arms behind her as he did so. She gave a gasp of pain. 'Show me that drawer. Now!'

He propelled her across the room to the walnut desk by the curtained window. 'Now, Miss Caroline . . . '

She said painfully, 'Please let me go, sir, and I'll open the drawer for you.'

To her immeasurable relief, he released her arms. But she had learned her lesson. She lost no time in opening the desk and running her finger gently along the panel which concealed the hidden compartment. No sooner had the partition clicked open than Richard elbowed her aside, and was reaching inside it for the papers that lay exposed.

206

There seemed to be quite a bundle of them; heavy parchments folded and refolded – nothing that looked like a letter from her father. Richard gave vent to a small, impatient grunt, and sat himself down before the desk, before beginning to go through these papers systematically. He unfolded the first heavy document, and leafed through it, page by page. He laid it on one side, and started on the next.

'Is this what you are looking for, dear boy?' said Vale's voice. As he spoke, he came out from behind the curtain, with a folded paper in one hand and a pistol in the other. 'I feel sure it must be. I took the precaution of reading it first – so you may save yourself the trouble.'

Within seconds, it seemed, the muniment room was full of people. Sir Giles Mannering, one of these, was not sure what he had expected to find. The events of the past day and night had made him feel that nothing would ever run true to form again. But he certainly had not expected Richard Sweeny to be sitting there at Peter Morrisey's desk, unmoving, completely at his ease. Of the two brothers, it was Richard who might have been the accuser.

His dark, good-looking face wore a stern expression. He said: 'Hugo? Mannering? What's this? Do you mean to tell me that you've been hoaxing us all day?'

Vale's long, ugly face might have been a mask. Only his eyes, narrowed and intent, showed signs of the turmoil within. He said quietly, 'Yes, I've tried to hoax you, Richard.' And then, without turning his head, the Earl said, 'Leave us, Miss Caroline, if you please. Mannering, get someone to escort Miss Caroline to Mount Sweeny.'

Sir Giles looked at Caroline, and then away again. She was gazing at Vale with a look on her face which made the magistrate feel that he was intruding. He said gruffly, 'Ay, Grimshaw'll take you, ma'am. He's outside in the hall.'

But Caroline was not listening. She said to Vale in a low,

207

urgent tone: 'Don't trust him, my lord. He ... he is the Serpent. He told me so, and he'll kill you, if you give him a chance.'

'Don't excite yourself, Miss Caroline,' said Richard gently. He turned his head to look at her. 'You've been so brave and strong, forgetful of yourself, caring for Jemima.'

'Jemima?' Vale's head turned, and his eyes searched in the dim recesses of the muniment room, lighting at last on the small unmoving figure on the settle. 'Jemima?'

'Mrs Slattery gave her something to make her sleep,' said Caroline. 'But she's all right.'

By this time someone had come upon Mrs Slattery's body, and there was a huddle of people round her. Most of these fell back sheepishly as Dan Slattery stumbled into the room, a bottle in one hand and a tankard in the other. At the sight of his wife, dead upon the ground – someone had turned her onto her back and closed her staring eyes – Dan gave vent to a sound which was half hiccup and half sob, and fell on his knees beside her.

Caroline had been watching Vale, who had gone to assure himself that Jemima was sleeping peacefully through all this drama. But she turned to Sir Giles, after Slattery had come in, and said tautly, 'Mr Sweeny killed Mrs Slattery. I saw him do it.' She suddenly felt very sick, and groped her way to a chair, closing her eyes until the threat of nausea should pass off. Dimly, she heard the magistrate charging Richard with murder, using long words that somehow made the whole thing more unreal than ever.

Sir Giles told Richard to stand up. He did so, still looking so like his normal and everyday self that the magistrate found himself even now unable to believe that he was anything but what he seemed – the quiet, likeable young man whom he had come to look on as a son. Well, if a son of his had been in trouble, the magistrate thought, he would have taken pride in his behaviour in this moment of defeat. There was a dignity about Richard Sweeny as he stood up between two sturdy Volunteers, waiting to be led away. There was no bluster, no attempt at protesting his innocence. His dark head was bowed, and he wore a look of quiet acceptance.

The magistrate watched him go, his heart heavy. Caroline opened her eyes to find Richard standing before her. He smiled down at her, his air of concern lifting when he saw that she was able to return his gaze. She blinked at him dazedly, no longer afraid, and visited by a deep sadness. He seemed to share that feeling, for he said gently, 'We could have made a good life together, Miss Caroline. Don't remember me too harshly, I beg.'

Caroline could not think what to say, so she tried to smile at him, to give him some small reassurance. He was struggling to remove the serpent ring, trying to slide it off his finger. 'This is for you to take, to do with as you will,' he said, still trying vainly to ease the heavy gold circle off. 'I want you to have it. Help me, please.'

Unthinkingly, she stood, reaching out a hand to help him, and the escorting soldiers stood back to give her room. And then she gasped, realizing the trap she had walked into.

'Drop your weapons!' She heard Richard's voice ring out, felt his arm across her collarbone like a steel band, and the cold edge of his knife at her throat. She shrank back against Richard's chest, trying to escape that razor like blade, and saw Vale lay down his pistol on the table in front of him. 'That's right,' said Richard, and Caroline, clamped back against him so that she could not see his face, was all the same in no doubt that he was smiling. 'No doubt you realize, Hugo, that it would give me great pleasure to slit the lady's throat before your eyes. You thought you had succeeded in hoaxing me, did you? Well, now we shall see who has the last laugh.'

It did not take long for all the occupants of the muniment room to lay down their assorted arms and move together into an obedient herd. In the centre of this stunned group, Vale stood taller than all the rest, his eyes never moving from

Richard's face. 'Let her go, Richard,' he said, at last. 'You've come to the end of the road, and you know it. You'll not help yourself by harming Miss Caroline.'

Caroline felt the tremor of Richard's laughter. 'You think not, Hugo? You're wrong, as always. Miss Caroline has meddled once too often, but now she is going to prove useful. She is coming with me. If anyone tries to follow us, I shall undoubtedly give way to my desire to punish her for interfering with my concerns. But first, there is one more thing for me to do.'

All the time he was speaking, Richard had been nudging Caroline forward towards the table, where a score of pistols and several muskets now lay. As they came up against the edge of the table, he deftly transferred the knife to the hand which held her, and reached over to grasp the Earl's distinctive, gold-embossed pistol. Caroline gasped audibly, as she realized what he meant to do. Helplessly, she watched the pistol come up level with Vale's head.

'No!' she said sharply. 'Don't shoot him. I'll go with you. I'll do anything you ask, Mr Sweeny. But don't—'

'It's too late, Miss Caroline,' said Richard, keeping the pistol steadily on target. Caroline felt his body tense, saw the muscles of his hand tauten – and forgetting even the knife at her throat in the extremity of her fear, she cast herself backwards and screamed out in protest.

It was Caroline's scream, they said, that saved Vale's life. For a split second Richard's hand shook and his aim wavered; and at that moment, too, Dan Slattery hurled his knife straight and true at a spot between Richard's shoulder blades.

Twenty-One

*J*F THERE IS ANY LEVELLER more devastating than a cold in the head,' said Caroline ruefully, 'I hope I shall never find out what it is. All very well to be sent all those flowers, and be treated like a heroine. With a face like a green cheese, and puffed up eyes, I don't look the part.'

'Then you should take care not to fall into the sea at this time of year,' said the doctor, smiling over his patient's head at Mrs Datchet. 'Besides, it has been a little more than a head cold, in your case, Miss Caroline. You gave us quite a fright, you know, running so high a fever. And you'll have to go slowly for a while yet.'

'I've been in my bed for more than a week,' she protested. 'And it's time I was back on my feet, taking charge of Jemima, doctor. I'm paid to do that, you know; not for skulking in bed, being waited on.'

'You may get up tomorrow, so long as you stay in your room,' said the doctor. 'And as for the rest of what you say, his lordship has given orders that you are to be given all the time you need to make a full recovery. Like everyone else, Lord Vale is most concerned about you, and conscious of how lucky you both are to be alive.'

'Is he, indeed?' said Caroline crossly, looking round at the bowls of flowers and the little stack of letters from well-wishers. There was even a note from Gilbert among them, written in his scrawling hand. He was on the mend, but not yet well enough to come and see her. But Vale had sent

211

nothing. 'If he's so concerned, as you say, he might have taken the trouble to visit me while I was ill.'

'No doubt he thought it not quite proper to do so,' said the doctor, closing his bag of medicines and fastening the straps. 'Besides, his lordship has had a great many other things on his mind this week. He has called a meeting of all his tenants. He wishes to bring them all together and to learn from their own lips how matters stand.'

Caroline thought of saying that considerations of propriety had never stopped his lordship marching in on her in the past. But she felt too listless to embark on an argument, or to do more than feel dimly pleased to hear that Vale was taking his estates in hand. She said rather dismally that she supposed Lord Vale must have been busy indeed. 'But, as for staying in my room,' she added, 'I'd rather go downstairs. All I need to make me quite better now, is a little company. You shall not physic me into a decline this time, doctor.'

Though she made a jest of it, it certainly did feel ridiculous to be so totally overthrown by a feverish cold, after coming through so many dangers and tribulations. But it was so. Caroline's recollection of some of the past nights and days was decidedly hazy, and she found she was not as fully recovered as she declared herself to be.

Next day she got up. But when she put her legs to the ground they felt weak and barely fit to take her across the room; and after fifteen minutes in an easy chair by her bedroom fire, it seemed like heaven to be tucked back into bed again. Nor was the next day much better. The smallest exertion left her feeling weak enough to weep – which she did when she was alone. She asked to be allowed visitors on the day after that, but when they came she found herself counting the minutes until they would take their leave. Food tasted grey, and it was hard to swallow more than a few mouthfuls of the dishes they brought her. Caroline had never felt so dragged down before, and found it depressing and bewildering.

'I am beginning to wonder whether I shall ever feel like an

ordinary human being again,' she told Lady Augusta. 'I don't have any energy left – not even to read.'

'I wouldn't be in too much of a hurry to get better if I were you,' said Lady Augusta, who had taken to bringing her sewing into Caroline's room in the early evenings. She was, surprisingly, a peaceful companion. She looked elegant but somehow older and calmer in her black mourning clothes; and she shared none of Mrs Datchet's urgent desire to plague Caroline with admiring questions, or to impart the latest news. Rather, Lady Augusta seemed content to stitch away quietly until the light from the window faded, only answering questions when asked them. She was smiling when she answered Caroline's rueful complaint. 'No, my dear. I would not be in too much of a fret to be back in harness. Vale's gone to fetch Jemima. She's being sent back to us in disgrace, no doubt with Ferdinand in tow; and it would seem, from an impassioned plea we received from the rectory, that she is no longer welcome under that saintly roof.'

'Oh, dear,' murmured Caroline, sitting bolt upright in her fireside chair, her eyes widening. 'What in the world has Jemima done?'

'Merely poured a jug of cold water over Mrs Andrews from the first floor landing,' replied her ladyship blandly. She smiled at Caroline's not very successful attempt to control her laughter, and added: 'But I am led to believe that this may have been the last of several regrettable actions. Mrs Andrews found it especially tiresome, as she was wearing her Sunday hat at the time. I told Hugo that he ought to beat Jemima, but I daresay he will not.'

'No.' Caroline put her fingers to her shaking mouth. 'Poor Mrs Andrews! What an unfair reward for so nobly coming to the rescue. It was truly noble, too, because she knew Jemima well enough to know she'd be bound to cause havoc in her well-ordered nursery.'

'No doubt the Reverend Andrews will restore order, now that he and his good wife are rid of the Sweeny pest,' said her ladyship drily. 'After a little while, at all events. Thank

213

goodness they bore with her for just long enough to see us finished with Richard's funeral, not to mention Mr Rance's and Mrs Slattery's, and discovering all that explosive in the crypt. It's been a dreadful few days, Miss Caroline.'

Jemima appeared at the door of Caroline's room, with a look of mischievous entreaty on her thin face. 'Papa says I must not tire you, Miss Caroline. May I come in, if I promise not to say a word?'

'Do you think you could manage that?' said Caroline, and when Jemima promised faithfully that she could, she added, 'For how long, I wonder?'

In the event, Jemima kept her promise for fully two minutes, but although she was chattering away for nearly half an hour after that, strangely Caroline did not glance once at the clock, nor remember that she was feeling worn down. She was even quite sorry when Lady Augusta came and shooed the child away.

So gradually there came to be more strength in Caroline's legs, and she was no longer kept awake at night by exhausting and painful bouts of coughing. She bestirred herself to write answers to some of the kind letters, and her visitors no longer tired her quite so much.

Gilbert came. He seemed taller, somehow, and moved carefully as though he feared he might break. But he was mightily amused to find his sister lying back upon a day bed in the bookroom, with a light rug over her knees.

'So this is how you earn your living, Car?' he said, chuckling. 'You've been in a fever over this shocking affair, I hear? You certainly look peaked. Vale drove me over. He thought a visit from me might cheer you up.'

'Oh?' Caroline had not seen the Earl. Even though she had been downstairs for a whole day, she had only heard his voice outside in the hall. She said stiffly: 'That was good of him.'

'Yes,' said Gilbert seriously. 'You know, Caroline, I'm

214

beginning to think Vale is quite a decent sort of fellow, after all. He's visited me almost every day this week, and he even had the notion to bring old Slattery over to look after me. I've taken my old rooms in the town, and Slattery has moved in.'

'Is Slattery . . . all right, Gilbert?'

'Pleased as punch, he is,' said Gilbert easily, and then he saw her face, and added as an afterthought: 'Oh, I see. Of course, Slattery was pretty shook up about his wife's death, and what came after. But Mannering has assured him that there'll be no action taken against him for knifing Richard Sweeny. After all, if he hadn't, Vale would have been a dead man.' Gilbert saw that Caroline was looking sick, and he said with a little impatience: 'Come, Caroline! You never used to be so poor spirited. I'd have thought it capital sport to have been in the midst of all the excitement, as you were. To think that you actually had the luck to find out the Serpent's true identity. What made you guess it was Richard Sweeny?'

'I think he wanted me to know it,' she said soberly. 'I . . . I think, from something he said, that he was lonely, that he needed to tell someone.'

'Lonely? I daresay, but why choose you to confide in?' He looked his sister over, noting her pale face and shadowed eyes, and said with a teasing gleam in his eyes, 'Don't ask me to believe that he took a fancy to a plain Joan like you, Caroline?'

She smiled at him, and said she would not ask him to believe any such thing. The thought crossed her mind that Gilbert, who had been ill too, looked almost ethereally handsome. It was most unfair. 'I just happened to be at hand, that was all. And perhaps living at Whitefield had given him a notion to ally himself with one of our family.'

Gilbert frowned. 'Well, it would not have done. You know, do you not, that Father never took his own life? Mannering came and explained it all to me. It was Richard killed him, and poor old Flivver, and he somehow managed to make it look like suicide. Mannering thinks that there's even a chance that Vale will want to hand Whitefield back to us, you know . . . ' He paused, and then added doubtfully, 'But I'm not sure that I'd want it now. Does that shock you, Caroline? At all events, I gave my word to Clemency that I'd go back and that we'd be wed.'

Caroline listened to her twin as he enthused about his Clemency and that friend and benefactor, her father. It seemed that both father and daughter were possessed of every virtue. Caroline was pleased that Gilbert should have found love and a new direction in his life, but she was not sorry when Jemima came in, and Gilbert suddenly remembered that Vale had promised to show him round the stables before he started back to town.

Jemima was in an ebullient mood. Vale had given her a severe dressing for her behaviour at the rectory, and had forbidden her to ride for two whole days. However, the ban had been lifted, and Jemima seemed to have regained her spirits. She had just finished giving Caroline a spirited rendering of the Reverend Andrews lecturing his children about their table manners, when the door of the bookroom opened and Vale walked in.

He glanced at his daughter, and said: 'Out, Jemima.'

'There's no need to send her away, my lord,' said Caroline, as Jemima got up quickly, and started towards the door. 'I was enjoying her company.'

Vale merely held the door open, and moved his head fractionally in the direction of the hall. 'Out!'

'I did not make Miss Caroline tired, Papa,' said the child in a small voice. 'Truly not.'

'No, really she did not,' protested Caroline, as Vale bundled his daughter outside, and shut the door with a snap. Caroline came to her feet, letting the rug fall to the ground. She said indignantly, 'I really do think I might be allowed to decide what tires me, and what does not.'

He came over to her then, smiling slightly. 'Certainly. You may tell me if this tires you, Juliet.' And before she could utter more than a startled squeak of protest, he was kissing

216

her mercilessly, hungrily, like a man who has found food after a long starvation. Presently, he raised his head to say softly, 'Well, my little love? Does this tire you?' But he gave her no chance to answer, for he was kissing her again.

'But why did you leave me alone so long?' Caroline demanded later, much later. 'I had begun to think you must have taken me in disgust, my lord.' He did not answer, for he was fully occupied with exploring a new area of silken soft skin which his roving hands had discovered. She trembled on the verge of laughter, and tried to imprison those gentle, burning fingers. 'The doctor said you thought it improper to visit me upstairs.'

'He was quite right, of course,' said Vale, raising his head. He smiled crookedly down at her flushed face and tumbled hair, and said, 'I would have been tempted to do some very improper things to you, as you must know. The sooner I make an honest woman of you, Miss Caroline, so much the better.'

She looked at him, not sure of his meaning, and said, 'Are you asking me to marry you, my lord, or not? You don't need to, you know. I think you might find it dull, being wed to an honest woman – and I don't think I could bear that.'

He said gently, with a serious look which she had never seen: 'I'm asking you to marry me, yes. But I'm not so arrogant as to suppose that I can make you happy. I've made a damnable husband once, and may well do so again.'

She said nothing. She felt no need for words; indeed, she barely heeded what Vale was saying, for she was in a strange and delightful turmoil, amazed at herself, revelling in the new wanton feelings which his love making had brought to life.

But Vale meant to have his say. He continued seriously, 'As for making an honest woman of you, no marriage vows could do that. I thought there were no honest women; but now I'm not so sure.' He added, with a sort of suppressed violence: 'Don't ever lie to me, Caroline. Don't ever . . . '

'No, my lord,' she said obligingly. 'Of course not.'

'And don't keep calling me "my lord!" ' he exclaimed irritably. 'You make me feel like your grandfather!'

He looked so furious, that Caroline started to laugh, which tickled up her tiresome cough, and she started up a paroxysm of coughing and gasping which left her limp and exhausted.

'Sip it slowly,' said Vale, holding her fingers round the glass as she obeyed him. 'And don't try to talk.'

She smiled at him, loving him for his look of concern. She pushed a strand of hair out of her eyes, aware that she must look a fright. He took her hand in his and laid it down on her lap, telling her severely to leave her hair alone.

'That's one of the things I find reassuring,' he told her, presently. 'It was no part of my scheme of things to grow to love you, and I'd been telling myself it was not so. But when I saw you looking like a drowned kitten on the Sweeny's Head rocks, and still had this irresistible urge to take you in my arms, I gave myself up for lost.'

'But I thought you only held me close because we were so cold and wet, and you wanted to hold me for warmth!' To Caroline it did seem a most shocking waste that he had not told her then. Instead he had subjected her to a sort of catechism, asking her question after question about the night people, what Gilbert had said about his dealings with them and the Serpent, making her recall all that Gilbert had told her. 'You kept on and on about that crypt place where they met . . . '

'I had to, my darling,' he said. His expression was sombre as he went on, 'You had given me the clue when you spoke of a whispering voice that came from nowhere. I knew, then, that it could only be Richard – and once I knew that, all the rest began to fall into place.'

She looked at him curiously, and he answered her

218

unspoken question. 'My father must have told Richard about the whispering stair. As the eldest, he should have shown it to me – but Father always liked Richard best, and treated him as though he were going to inherit Mount Sweeny one day. What Richard could not know, of course, was that my grandmother had shown me the stair years before, just months before she died.'

Caroline lay back against her bank of soft cushions, and watched his long, grim face. She could feel the pain and sadness in him, as though it had been her own. He said presently, 'I blame myself. There's no escaping it. So many people would still be alive, if I had seen what was there to see. But I did not want to see. I hated this place after O'Grady was hanged, and even more so after Sybilla was killed. But the clues were all there. Richard has always disliked and resented me. I knew that. But I never dreamed of the depths of his jealousy. He must have been consumed by it, night and day.'

She did not argue, or try to persuade him that this was not true. Rather, she tried to divert his thoughts by asking him why he had pretended to be dead. 'When I saw your ring on Richard's hand, I thought it must be true! Was there really a body found on the rocks?'

He nodded. 'Mannering arranged it. You see, I went straight to Mannering, and he agreed that the only way to catch Richard off his guard, and get proof of his guilt, was to let him think he had won. It worked. He was bound to go to Whitefield to destroy that letter; but of course we had none of us expected him to arrive with you, my darling. I confess, my heart failed me when Slattery came out to tell us that you were there.'

She shivered, and he bent forward to kiss her gently – only to straighten up as the door opened and Jemima came running into the room. She said urgently, 'Papa! There's a litter of kittens in the dairy. May I keep one? May I?'

'A kitten?' said Vale, turning to look at Caroline. 'What do you think, Miss Caroline? Do we want a kitten in the family?

219

You don't think, perhaps, that one ill-conducted step-daughter and her puppy are enough?'

'Step-daughter ... ' Jemima's eyes widened, and she stared from Caroline, who was looking pink and dishevelled, back to her father. 'Oh, Papa! Are you going to marry Miss Caroline?'

'That depends,' he answered gravely. 'Miss Caroline once told me that she had no notion to be married. The question is, what can we do to make her say yes?'

Jemima looked at Caroline, and her thin little face had suddenly grown pink with pleasure and excitement. 'You will say yes, won't you, Miss Caroline?' She added confidingly, 'I think you would like it, being married to Papa. I'm sure you would.'

'Do you think so?' Caroline looked at her gravely. 'He's a Great Catch, you once told me. I daresay I ought not to miss such a chance.'

Jemima turned to Vale and said rather reprovingly, 'You really ought to kiss Miss Caroline, Papa. That might help.'

'To be sure, it might,' murmured the Earl, much struck. 'Very well, Jemima. Go and find your kitten, and I'll see what I can do.'

'Oh? May I truly have one?'

'You may have two, or three or more,' said Vale propelling her towards the door, 'only go away, now, and speak to the dairy maid.'

He shut the door upon his small daughter for the second time that day, and came back to Caroline. He pulled her to her feet, smiling. 'Now, Miss Caroline,' he said quietly, 'before you start coughing and spluttering again, I'm going to take Jemima's advice.'

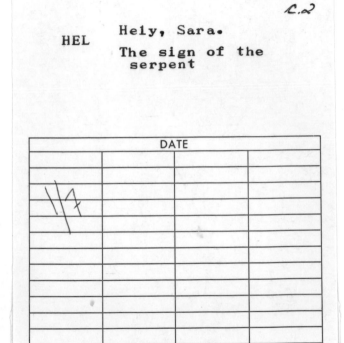

C.2

HEL Hely, Sara.

The sign of the
serpent

DATE			

© THE BAKER & TAYLOR CO.